Speed Demons MC Virginia Chapter

Book Two

Jules Ford

ISBN: 9798289686817

Copyright 2025 by Jules Ford

All rights reserved.

This is a work of fiction. Names, characters, businesses, places, and incidents are either the product of the author's imagination or used in a fictitious manner. Any resemblance to actual living persons, living or dead, or actual events is purely coincidental.

ALL RIGHTS RESERVED

This book contains material protected under International and Federal Copyright Laws and Treaties. Any unauthorized reprint or use of this material is prohibited. No part of this book may be reproduced or transmitted in any form or by any means, electronic or mechanical, including photocopying, recording, or by any informal storage and retrieval system without express written permission from the author/ publisher.

Cover Design by: JoeLee Creative
Cover Model: Drew Truckle
Photographer: Eric David Battershell
Formatting by: Md Foysal Ahmed
Proofreading by: Nicola Thorpe & Jayne Rushton
Editor: Nicola Thorpe

With thanks

Dedication

For all the poet's souls.

Note to Readers

This book contains scenes of violence, death (including spousal), and stalking.

Other Books by Jules

Speed Demons MC ~ Wyoming Chapter

Bowie

Cash

Atlas

Snow

Breaker

Colt

Stone

Dagger

Speed Demons MC Virginia

Hendrix

Iceman

Lucky Shamrock Series

On the Rocks

Shaken not Stirred ~ Coming Soon

Soulless Assassins MC

Tyrant's Revenge (co-author Raven Dark)

Character List

VIRGINIA CHAPTER ~ ARROW POINT

President, Jameson 'Hendrix' Quinn

Vice President, Nate 'Blade' Hollister

Sergeant at Arms, Damian 'Diablo' West

Head Enforcer, Jacob 'Iceman' Irons

Enforcer, Adam 'Pyro' Reyes

Road Captain, Patrick 'Trick' O'Brien

Handler / Tech, Colter 'Colt' Van Der Cleeve

Treasurer, Gael 'Gambit' Ortiz

Doctor/ Medic, Grayson 'Bones' Locke

Wise Man/ Chaplain, William 'Will' Quinn (Hendrix's father)

MEMBERS

'Picasso' (Cass)

'Rockabye'

'Slasher'

'K9'

'Mac'

'Hammer'

'Ghost'

'Fletch'

PROSPECTS

Gopher

CLUB STAFF

Carina ~ House Manager (Daughter ~ Giselle/Gigi)

Ciara ~ Bar Manager

Arizona ~ Club Girl

Heather ~ Club Girl

Fifi ~ Club Girl

Rory ~ Club Girl

Lacey ~ Club Girl

Tia ~ Club Girl

TOWNSFOLK

(Olivier) Cross ~ Owner of Watershed (nightclub) and Arena (underground fight club)

Larry Cross ~ ex-owner of Arena (Cross's uncle)

Roxanne Silver ~ Cross's assistant

Moses ~ Cross's security

Gordy ~ Cross's security

Sheriff Luis Navarro

Deputy Tom Larson

Officer Lana Prince

WYOMING CHAPTER

OFFICERS

President, Xander 'Cash' Stone

Vice President, Kit '(Heartbreaker) Breaker' Stone

Sergeant At Arms, Danny 'Atlas' Woods

Enforcer, Gage 'Bowie' Stone

Road Captain, Tex

Treasurer, Reno

Secretary/ Tech, Arrow

Table of Contents

Prologue i

Chapter One...............................1

Chapter Two 15

Chapter Three...........................30

Chapter Four.............................48

Chapter Five 61

Chapter Six................................73

Chapter Seven 87

Chapter Eight..........................102

Chapter Nine 119

Chapter Ten 133

Chapter Eleven 149

Chapter Twelve.......................162

Chapter Thirteen.....................175

Chapter Fourteen....................189

Chapter Fifteen	204
Chapter Sixteen	218
Chapter Seventeen	235
Chapter Eighteen	241
Chapter Nineteen	247
Chapter Twenty	253
Chapter Twenty-One	262
Chapter Twenty-Two	268
Chapter Twenty-Three	274
Epilogue	283

Prologue

Saint ~ Two Years Ago

The first time I saw him was like a lightning strike. It electrified my chest like a physical force, knocking the wind clean out of me. But then, what did I expect when he was so beautiful that he grabbed me by the throat and squeezed?

Dark blond hair, longer on top and styled into a scruffy mohawk, and icy blue eyes glowing like gems under the stage lights. A square jaw, carved by Michelangelo himself with the obligatory smattering of stubble. His body was large and muscled, with thick thighs and a high ass that I knew would rock a pair of jeans. He held the kind of beauty that haunted a girl, but it wasn't just that; it was the restlessness bubbling under his pretty tan skin that mesmerized me.

On the surface, he held halcyon-like control, but under the black suit, crisp shirt, and earpiece, I could sense his rawness. I knew with one glance that he could wield his power in a way that I'd find both terrifying and magnificent.

Something about him represented security in every sense of the word, and it wasn't because that was his job. Just being around him made me feel safe.

My eyes closed at the thought of those big, muscular arms wrapping me in their warmth, and a shiver shook me from head to toe because I'd never experienced that feeling before.

Not ever.

Blue chips of ice slid my way, and I held my breath as they passed through me before veering back again, and my throat burned as they rested on mine, and everything inside me stilled.

I was a straight-up person who shot from the hip. Playing the mating game didn't interest me. If I felt it, I acted on it, and that night was no exception. Maybe I should've blushed and allowed my gaze to skitter away coquettishly. Perhaps I should've smiled serenely and lowered my gaze to the ground before taking another glance up again to convey my interest.

But that wasn't me.

Instead, my stare held his, challenging him, while one side of my mouth hitched slightly. I wanted to know him, and I didn't care to play coy. He'd passed the first hurdle by grabbing my interest, especially since not many men did these days. Now, I needed to see if he could handle me being my usual confident self.

He looked me up and down, and then my heart took a nosedive as his eyes drifted away.

My lungs expelled the air I'd almost suffocated myself with.

Well damn.

Maybe he just wasn't that into me.

I wasn't everybody's type because I carried extra weight. It never bothered me because why should it? I'd met the models everybody saw in magazines, and nobody could airbrush them in real life. I saw the smoke and mirrors and knew all the right angles to stand in and pose if I wanted the camera to catch my best angle. I was familiar with the extent of editing and photoshopping that went into making famous people perfect. Except perfection to me wasn't about image.

For me, it went deeper, so it was disappointing when a man who I felt an instant connection to dismissed me with one look.

I turned away, so caught up in the empty feeling in my chest that I didn't notice him turn back to me. Therefore, I also didn't see his lips quirk as his stare raked down my body, or his icy eyes glint like a cold winter frost when they rested on my ass as I gave him my back and walked away from him. My mind was already elsewhere, forming words and melodies because he'd made it so I couldn't help myself.

Art was created when I was inspired.

That was my life, my everyday, and the consequence of having a poet's soul. I felt things deep, even fleeting looks with beautiful men who I didn't need to interact with to know they could have been something to me. Those things touched me in ways that made words erupt from my pen like a spitting volcano, its lava burning my soft poet's soul.

Reaching into my pocket, I pulled out my notebook and began scribbling words while simultaneously moving toward my dressing room.

Stage lights, sultry nights, halcyon ice blue.
Crowd chants, and your face haunts. Empty without you.
Lost pride, lost chance, lost love, lost souls.
Beyond my comprehension. Beyond my control.
Crowd chants, but your face haunts. I'm empty without you...

I was so into the music playing inside my head, the cadence of the lyrics, and so completely caught up in the writing process that I didn't sense anything was amiss. The words kept flowing, and I kept scribbling, not looking where I was going and completely unaware of my surroundings.

You mattered, though we had no time,
Invading my bones, though you were never mine.
Lost prize, lost luck, lost bet, lost wants,
Still, the crowd chants louder, and your face still haunts.

Stage lights, sultry nights, but I'm hollow without you...

The blow to my head, when it came, was so unexpected that I just stood there, swaying and shell-shocked. I groaned out loud as throbbing pain began to radiate through the back of my skull, and I cried out as I was shoved hard against a wall. Bile rose through my throat as the touch of cold hands slithered under my top and curled hard around one of my breasts.

That was when my senses rushed back to me like a vacuum whooshing inside my head, and I knew I was in trouble.

I'd never been touched like that before. Handsy stylists had brushed my skin inappropriately once or twice, but a hard look usually made them back off, especially when the band was in the same room.

But this was something else. This was full-blown sexual fucking assault.

With a shout, I tried to shove my attacker away, but he was too strong. Suddenly, I found myself pinned by his body. My eyes darted around, looking for a means of escape, trying to engage my brain and work out how the hell I was gonna get the asshole off me, which was when I felt his erection pressing against my stomach.

I gagged, my eyes darting up, trying to see if I knew the asshole. Maybe if I'd seen the guy around or spoken to him, I could have reasoned with him, but he was pressed against me so closely that I couldn't see above his stubbled chin.

"Get off!" I shrieked, but he just pawed me harder.

My eyes lowered, and I spotted a tattoo on his chest. A holy cross with roses wound around it, their green stems thorny and sharp. That was when I heard a rip, and I knew he'd torn my top. His hands ran over my skin, everywhere he touched, crawling with ants under the surface, and I knew I was in deep trouble.

Iceman

The blonde was gorgeous. So gorgeous in fact, that I had to consciously drag my eyes away from her face and focus my attention back on the crowd.

Dischordium's management had hired me and a few of the brothers to cover their personal security at a festival they were playing in Napa. The sponsors of the gig had supplied their own men, but now Dischordium had recently had a single enter the charts and were riding on such a high that their manager wanted to increase their protection.

After a quick scan of the audience, my stare flicked back toward the hot chick, and my mouth watered.

The blonde had turned her back to me, so I got an eyeful of her ripe, juicy ass. I had to adjust my crotch at the thought of grabbing a handful of that while sliding in and out. If that hot piece walked into the clubhouse, I'd be all over her like a cheap suit, but I was here to do a job, so I had to make like one of Snow White's dwarves and say it's off to work I go.

As I turned back toward the crowd, I caught sight of some dude slipping past one of the security guys and jumping up onto the stage near the wings. I glanced around to see if anyone else had caught it, but there was nobody around except for me. My eyes narrowed when I saw him go after the blonde, furtively looking around as he went.

Alarm bells went off like sirens in my head. The entire sitch felt shifty as fuck, but he didn't notice me checking him out, which meant I'd get the jump on him if I needed to.

I followed, watching closely as he kept his ass to the shadows, which only put me on even higher alert. The asshole was an idiot. He was acting so suspiciously that he may as well have stuck a flashing beacon above his head that spelled out, 'Weirdo stalker.'

It was fucking laughable, but then he was probably a rock groupie stoner who was too herbed up to give his surroundings a second thought. I suspected this because the stench of wacky baccy that wafted from him was eye-watering. I'd also been on his ass for a while and he hadn't made me. He was so caught up in the girl that he'd forgotten to check his six.

The tool was giving more Joey Tribbiani vibes than Joe Goldberg.

Fuck my life.

The blonde, completely unaware she was being followed, made her way deep backstage toward the dressing rooms. She passed a roadie and acknowledged him with a fist bump with her pen and notebook still in hand, before continuing on her journey and going back to her writing. A corridor loomed ahead, and she headed right and fell out of sight. The guy followed closely, and that was when I heard her cry out.

I hauled into the corridor, my temper flaring when I saw the weirdo had the girl pinned against the wall. Her shirt was torn, and she had a dazed look about her that made my blood boil.

"Get off," she shrieked.

His reply was to roughly grab a breast and try to kiss her.

I moved toward him before grabbing him by the scruff of the neck and dragging him away from her. Then, I pulled my fist back and smashed it into his jaw. With a curled lip, I watched as his head snapped to one side with the force of my punch, and he fell to the ground with a loud grunt.

My stare swung to the girl who was watching me, wide-eyed, with her lips parted in shock, and asked, "You okay?"

She pulled her clothes straight and nodded before whispering, "What the hell just happened? Then her shocked stare slid down to the floor where the dude lay, demanding, "And who the hell are you?"

He let out a groan.

"I gotta call someone to have him dealt with," I explained. "Are you okay?"

"Wait," she murmured, her eyes turning to slits. Taking a step back, she let out a cry and gave the dude a hard kick in the ribs. She reached down to retrieve the notebook she'd dropped on the floor, then straightened up again and squared her shoulders. "Now, I feel better," she declared.

Her voice was soft and melodious, and it hit me somewhere deep. She sounded like a song, even when she spoke a normal sentence, and it grabbed my attention. It also hit me in the dick because suddenly, all I could think of was that same soft melodic voice crying out my name while I feasted on her sweet little cun—

"Thank you," she said, her tone earnest.

I grinned down at her. "Just doin' my job, darlin'."

Her cheeks pinked, and she stuck out her hand, "I'm Saint."

"Saint, huh?" I took her hand, lifted it to my mouth, and touched my lips to the back of her hand before breathing, "Jacob."

"Jacob." She whispered my name like she was trying it out in her mouth just to see what it would sound like and fuck me if I didn't like it a whole damned lot. The tip of her tongue came out to touch her lip, and I wondered how such a shy, nervous gesture could make my cock kick harder than Morten Andersen going for a Superbowl-winning PAT.

It wasn't just about that, though. She was fucking beautiful, curvy like a fifties pin-up girl, with a face that could soften the most jaded of men. Her lips were pink and puffy, her hair bleached blonde, and face framing where it was cut just below her jawline. It should have looked harsh, but the peachy softness of her skin and the appealing roundness of her face balanced it all out perfectly.

There was no doubt she bordered on angelic, but what really did it for me were her eyes.

They were big, round, and the bluest blue I'd ever seen, darker than the summer sky but lighter than the ocean. I couldn't describe the color because I'd never seen it before. Her clothes were cool and edgy with a pretty girl twist. Even her name was hot.

Stare never leaving hers, I reached into my pocket and pulled out my phone, only glancing down briefly to click the top name of my call log. After a few rings, my brother Diablo answered with a loud, "Yo!"

"Gotta sitch, brother," I told him. "Back corridor leading to the dressing rooms. Caught a guy going after a girl who works here. I put him on his ass."

Blondie's eyes drifted back to the weirdo on the floor, and her face hardened.

I liked that about her too. Saint wasn't hysterical or losing her head. She was keeping it together in a way that proved she could hack my life. I wouldn't have blamed her for being upset; she had been attacked after all, but she also saw the situation was in hand.

"Be right there," D barked.

"Roger and out," I muttered and disconnected the call.

"Army?" she asked, referencing my military speak.

"Air Force," I corrected. "Fighter pilot. You sure you're okay?" I asked, my eyes locking with hers, suddenly feeling winded by the intensity in them.

She shot me a smile bright enough to blind me. "Yeah. I've had worse."

My chest twisted because I didn't like that. I didn't like the way she was so blasé about being fucking attacked. It wasn't something she should be used to, and certainly not something she should normalize because that shit was as far from normal as you could get.

My gaze caught on her chest, and I frowned at the angry mark there. "Where did he grab you?"

"He just groped my boobs mostly." She shuddered.

Turning, I stooped down, pulled my fist back, and punched the fucker across the side of the head again, ignoring Saint's gasp.

He let out a groan and began to come to just as the sound of boots echoed, and Diablo's voice barked from the ether, "Brother? What the fuck's goin' on?"

"Here." I hauled the pervert up by the collar and slammed his back against the wall just as Diablo rounded the corner, closely followed by our brothers Pyro and Mac.

"What the fuck?" he exclaimed, his eyes narrowing on the guy I had pinned. "This the asshat?"

"Yeah." I tugged the sick fuck away from the wall and threw him in the direction of my brothers. "Fucker needs to be on a goddamned watch list."

Pyro caught the dude by the back of his shirt and shoved him toward Diablo, who took a handful of the fucker's hair before getting in his face and snarling, "You a fuckin' pervert, boy?"

"N-no," he stuttered. "I just wanted to talk to he—"

Diablo pulled his head back and smashed his skull into the fucker's face. Blood sprayed, and I heard a sickening crunch. "I'll cut your fucking fingers off," the SAA growled. "See how well you touch women then."

Saint let out a little squeak, and her eyes veered to me.

The dick may have just assaulted her, but I kinda got how she didn't want to see my boys convey to him why that was a bad idea. She'd been through enough.

"Take that shit outside," I told them, tipping my chin toward her. "And keep it on the down-low."

Diablo jerked a nod before hauling the dude to his feet. He gestured to Mac and Pyro to follow him as he pulled the fucker toward the nearest back exit so they could finish the job.

I gave them chin lifts, raising a hand to swipe my hair back as I watched them go.

"Hey," Saint exclaimed softly, grabbing my hand to examine it. "Your knuckles are all busted. We've established that I'm okay, but are you?"

Her question stopped me in my tracks. Nobody ever asked me if I was okay. Honestly, I was used to it; my knuckles were usually busted, especially after fight night.

I wiggled my fingers to test that they weren't broken and shrugged. "Not unusual. They're usually fucked up in my line of work."

"We need to get them seen to," she told me in a no-nonsense voice.

I laughed. "I'm not going to hospital. Jesus, baby. I'm fuckin' badass."

She rolled her eyes. "Who said anything about the hospital?" Grabbing my shirt, she pulled me down the corridor, then turned toward the dressing rooms, announcing, "Just gotta get my bag," before ducking inside a door.

I took the opportunity to pull out my cell and shoot off a message to our SDSS chat, relaying I was gonna see the chick safely home. After getting a flurry of eggplant, winky face, and thumbs-up emojis back, I tucked my cell away, looking up just as the door opened, and Saint emerged with a big canvas bag slung over one shoulder.

"Ready?" she asked.

I looked down at the ripped jeans, tiny titty top, and Chucks she'd changed into and grinned. "As I'll ever be."

My security job was about to get very fucking interesting. I hadn't felt this kind of pull toward a girl since Allie. The promise of her and everything she could be to me sank deep into my core, leaving me warm. And I knew in my heart she'd be someone special.

"You like Chinese food?" she inquired as we made our way through the hustle and bustle of backstage toward the staff exit.

"Fuckin' love it." I glanced down into clear azure blue eyes, and my heart swelled inside my chest. "Lead the way, blondie."

Chapter One

Iceman

Two Years Later

It wasn't a day for riding.
New Orleans was usually hot and humid, but often, on blistering summer days like today, the heavens wept, but then, they had good reason.

I always found it crazy how I could sweat through one-half of my clothes while, at the same time, a tropical storm soaked the other half. NOLA's climate was a bitch, and I didn't miss it one fucking bit. But there was one thing I did miss, which was why I was here, paying my annual visit.

My wife.

Over my years in the United States Air Force, I missed a lot of Allie's birthdays. Eleven years before, I made God a promise that I'd never miss one again if he gave her back to me. Even though he didn't keep his end of the bargain, I always kept mine, even in death, maybe because of the guilt I'd buried somewhere deep for not being around for so many when she was alive.

Allie loved birthdays, Christmas, Easter, the Fourth of July, Thanksgiving, and Superbowl Sunday. Those days were all about family and being together, and even though we weren't blessed with kids, we had close bonds with our families.

I used to tease her relentlessly, telling her that no beautiful twenty-something woman liked to hang with her (and my) mom all weekend instead of going out and partying in the city with our friends. But she'd just smile sweetly and tell me how spending time with family was a blessing we should never take for granted.

And it turned out she was right.

But then, my Allie was always the smart one.

And gorgeous.

And sweet.

And kind.

And funny, cute, adorable.

And mine, oh so fucking mine that some days I missed her so fucking bad that I felt as if I was slowly dying without her.

I had her for twenty-five years of my life, and she'd been dead for twelve, but I still felt her in everything I did. Allie was the person I could sit in silence with and feel everything. What we had wasn't perfect. Hell, some days, she pissed me off to the point where I wanted to walk away and not go back. But I always stayed because what we had was honest and real, and there was nobody else on earth who was worth fighting for more than my Allie.

Then she left me, permanently.

Over time, the pain of losing her became easier to live with. I threw myself into my work and my new life because what else could I do? My wife was a memory, and some days, it scared me that I struggled to conjure up the only face I never wanted to forget—because if there was ever a woman who deserved to be remembered, it was my Allie.

Rolling off the throttle of my Sportster S, I downshifted and braked until I eventually came to a halt outside the ornate gates of the memorial park. I could've ridden in, but my bike was noisy enough to wake the dead, and it would have been disrespectful.

Iceman

Plus, as much as it crushed me every time I walked inside those gates, the time it took for me to get to Allie gave me a chance to get in the right headspace so I could face my wife.

Dismounting, I took my helmet off and hung it from the bars. Then I untied the balloons I'd fastened to my handlebars. A couple of them tried to make a break for it, but I hauled them back into submission before making my way inside what I could only describe as a park.

Allie loved nature, so trapping her inside a box didn't seem right. She would have wanted to be outside with the trees and birds, so that's what I gave her. I wanted a place where me and her family could come and be at peace, and more than that, I wanted her to be at peace, too.

Following the path that led to her always felt dream-like, and that day was no exception. I took in the flowers laid beside the plaques fixed flat into the ground and, for the millionth time over the years, wondered how somebody so full of life and so vibrant could be taken so suddenly.

She was twenty-seven when she died—eleven days younger than me. Our moms had been best friends since kindergarten, and I couldn't remember a time when I didn't love her. My first memory was of Allie, and there wasn't a doubt in my mind that her last thought would've been of me.

I knew they were there before I saw them because I heard the music and their laughter, so when I rounded the corner and saw them all sitting on fold-out chairs, holding beer bottles and sipping wine from plastic glasses, it wasn't a surprise.

Jean, Allie's mom, noticed me heading their way first. She put one arm in the air and hollered, "Woohoo! The wanderer returns. Come see."

I grinned, shaking my head.

"What the fuck time do you call this!" my dad called out. "We've been here for hours. Where y'at?"

Taking in the empty bottles and his inebriated state, I believed him. "I'm good, Pop. It's a long ride from Virginia."

"I told you to fly in last night," my mom berated, her words slightly slurred from the copious amounts of wine she'd no doubt been consuming. My ma wasn't a wine drinker—or really a drinker at all—but every year when we came here to party, she always cracked a bottle open in Allie's memory 'cause it was my wife's drink of choice.

Leaning down, I gave my mom a kiss on the cheek, then turned and kissed Jean's cheek too. "I told ya, I was working."

"Partying more like," she grumbled as I gave my dad, who'd stood up to greet me, a man hug, then leaned over and gave Allie's father, Malcolm, a handshake.

"I *was* working," I reiterated. "We were covering an amber alert, and they needed me to man the drone."

"Did you find the kid?" Dad asked.

"What do you think?"

Dad gave my shoulder a hard clap. "Good man."

I got down on my haunches and tied the balloons to the roses laying by my wife's name plaque.

"Miss you, baby," I whispered, touching my fingertips to my lips and then the plaque. "Happy birthday."

Allie's voice echoed through my head. *Miss you, too.*

I stood and turned toward my family, nodding as Malcolm gestured to the empty chair beside him.

"How long did it take ya?" he asked.

"About fourteen hours," I replied, picking my way over and taking the seat. "I rode through the night, so I missed all the traffic." My eyes fell back onto the massive bouquet I'd had delivered to my mom's house the day before. "Flowers are pretty. Allie would've loved 'em."

"She would," Jean breathed, her eyes falling on the red roses. "They were always her favorite, and you never forgot. I love how you still don't forget."

Silence fell over the group, no doubt because we were all thinking back to the times we gave Allie flowers, and she acted like somebody had given her the Hope Diamond.

My wife loved the simple things. She was also stubborn and liked me to splash out on birthdays, so a bunch of gas station flowers wouldn't cut it. Once, as a joke, I gave her a rose in a vial. For a while there, I thought I'd be walking around with it shoved up my ass for the rest of my days.

"How's Hendrix?" my dad asked, taking a sip of beer.

I grinned, "Good. Loved up and taking to fatherhood like a duck to water. He's obsessed with JT. Poor kid doesn't get a minute's peace from him."

"Never thought I'd see the day," Malcolm interjected.

My thoughts went to my bud and how he'd pined for his woman over the years they'd been apart. "I did. Knew if he ever got another shot with Anna, he'd make it work. It was rocky there for a while, but he did the job. I'm happy for him. She's a good woman and a great mom. He deserves this."

"You deserve it too," Mom murmured. "Isn't there a girl who's caught your eye? You're still young, Jacob, and Allie wouldn't want you to be alone."

Heat burned through my throat.

The answer was no.

I always thought I was lucky to meet the love of my life so young, but after Allie died, it quickly became a curse. How was I meant to find something that special again? Whoever I met had a lot to live up to, and it wasn't fair to compare any woman to perfection.

In all the time since Allie's death, I'd come across two women who made me feel something. One of them was now married to a brother, Atlas, and had two daughters with him, whereas the other...

A vision of blonde hair flashed behind my eyes, and my heart leaped ten feet high, though, for the life of me, I couldn't understand my ongoing reaction to her. We only ever got to spend one night together, and I hadn't seen her in years.

"No," I muttered. "It's hard to beat perfection."

Dad's hand reached out, clasped my shoulder, and squeezed. "She means well," he said under his breath. "You take the time you need, Son."

"It's been twelve years, Doug," Ma cut in. "Jean and I want grandchildren, and Jacob's not getting any younger,"

"Kathy, will you leave the boy alone?" Dad bit back, his tone exasperated. "He's still in mourning."

"He's hardly a boy," Ma sniffed. "He's knocking on forty's door. Allie would slap him upside the head if she saw how he was wasting his life away."

Jean shrugged. "She's got a point."

Malcom sighed.

Dad's lips pursed.

I grinned. "Hardly wasting my life, Mom. I run with a band of mercenaries, fly planes, shoot evil motherfuckers, and generally help save the day. If I never had another girlfriend again, I'd die a happy man 'cause, for a while at least, I had Allie and even knowing her means I've been luckier than some."

"Do you date?" Jean asked quietly. "Allie would want you to date."

The memory of the train I helped run on Tia forty-eight hours before flashed through my mind. "I see women," I admitted. "But I wouldn't call it dating."

"Those girls at the club don't count." Mom sniffed haughtily.

"What do you know about girls at the club?" I asked.

Her eyes bored into mine. "I've seen *Sons of Anarchy*."

"So have I," Dad muttered. "And I reckon those girls count just fine."

Daggers flew from Mom's eyes at Dad's head.

"Those girls are okay for the short term, Jacob," Jean pointed out. "But they're not the settling down types. How about me and ya mama introduce you to a couple of nice girls?"

My eyes slid toward my wife's grave marker. "This is weird as all hell. It's Allie's birthday. I've ridden nearly a thousand miles to come and raise a glass to my dead wife, and her ma's tryin'a set me up with other chicks."

Malcom sat forward and shrugged. "You know ya mamas, Jake." He pointed his finger at his temple and moved it in a circle. "They're loopy as the day's long."

"And pie-eyed," Dad added, nodding toward the two empty bottles of wine lined up on the grass.

"Oh, hush now, Doug," Ma muttered. "We just want Jacob to be happy."

"I am happy," I assured her. "It's just not the kind of happy *you* want. I love my life, and I love my job because I get to do things most men only dream about. After I lost Allie, I needed something more than the Air Force, and I got it with the club. Can't that be enough?"

The moms glanced at each other.

"Ma," I chastised gently. "You gotta let me work this out my way. I'm not averse to meeting somebody and settling down, but I am averse to forcing it with the wrong person and ending up in a worse position than I am now. If Allie taught me anythin', it's that life's too short to waste by being caught up in something that ain't right."

"I just worry you're waiting for another Allie," Jean stated.

My throat began burning like a motherfucker. "There is no other Allie. What I had with her was ours, and it was everythin'. What I get with the next woman will be ours too, but it'll be different 'cause again, she won't be Allie, and honest to God, Jeanie, whoever she is, I just want her to be her..." My voice trailed off as a cool, guitar rift played over the radio and a clear, sweet, angelic, raspy, sexy-as-all-fuck voice began to sing...

Stage lights, sultry nights, halcyon ice blue.
Crowd chants, and your face haunts. Empty without you.
Lost pride, lost chance, lost love, lost souls.
Beyond my comprehension. Beyond my control.
Crowd chants, but your face haunts. I'm empty without you...

My heart kicked inside my chest.

God, I fucking hated that song so much, but at the same time, I fucking loved it.

Over the last couple of years, it had gotten more airtime on the radio than any other song. Everybody raved about it, and it had made Saint McClure and her band famous.

"Empty" had hit number one all over the world and subsequently launched the band Saint's Rapture into the stratosphere. The song had also won a Grammy, an AMA, and an MTV award, and had launched the corresponding album into the number one spot in multiple countries too. The lyrics were critically acclaimed, and admittedly, there was something special about Saint's Rapture songs that buried deep, so I got it.

Iceman

Saint herself had won writing accolades for the album, and "Empty" in particular, which not only pissed me off but also jaded me a little because how the fuck did that bitch get bestowed all the success when there were so many more deserving people out there?

Though to be fair, she was talented, I had to give her that. All the songs that came after "Empty" were just as good, and they'd turned Saint's Rapture into global superstars. Saint was considered the leader and frontwoman of the band and the main singer-songwriter, and it was her talent that had garnered their success.

Still, I was an out and proud Saint 'bitch' McClure hater. Even saying her name stuck in my throat like a bitter pill that refused to be swallowed down.

Fuck her.

Fuck her.

"Allie would've loved this song." Jean smiled, leaning back in her chair. "It's the kind of song you and Allie would've danced around the kitchen table to."

My mother-in-law was right, but still, I wasn't about to admit it.

"Nah. Allie would've thought it was pretentious crap," I argued. "And the singer's a diva by all accounts, so she would've hated *her* more."

"Saint McClure's a diva?" Mom questioned. "She's always seemed nice on the interviews I've seen with her."

I popped open a bottle of beer, suddenly needing a goddamned drink. "The Dischordium boys know her. They run in the same circles, and one of 'em says she's an entitled bitch." I took a swig and blew out a hard breath. "Fame's probably gone to her head."

"Or she's a strong woman who knows what she wants," Jean cut in. "You know how females get the short end of the stick when it comes to sticking up for themselves in the entertainment industry."

I took another pull. "Blue reckons she's up her own ass."

"Blue probably tried to get in her pants and got knocked back," Mom bandied back.

The thought of that made a curl of heat lick through my chest, but I pushed it down.

It wasn't my business if Blue De Santis tried to fuck Saint McClure. I mean, it wasn't like he didn't fuck everyone else. Still, I didn't think he was that much of an asshole to bad-mouth her for turning his ass down, and it had nothing all to do with me anyway. She'd made that abundantly clear when she screwed me over in days gone past.

"Delphine Babin's divorce just came through," Jean announced, throwing my mom a sly look. "She's on the market now. Maybe you should give her a call and see if she wants to go to dinner while you're here."

I tipped my head back and looked at the sky, cursing under my breath.

"Woman, leave the boy alone," Malcom snapped. "He's told you where he's at, and you're still goin' on at him."

"I was just sayin' is all." Jean raised her glass to her mouth and took a sip. "Allie came to me in a dream and told me Jacob has to find a good woman. She also said she'd give him a sign, and there's no sign bigger than a pretty lady from a decent family who just came back onto the market."

Malcolm rolled his eyes. "Allie comes to you in a dream at least four times a week. She must be fucking exhausted from all the flying through Heaven to get to your ass with all these messages about Jacob. The poor kid spends more time with you now she's dead than when she was alive." He looked at Dad and made big eyes.

Pop grinned, his eyes sliding toward me, and murmured so only I could hear, "I told ya, Son. They mean well."

My eyebrow cocked, and I shook my head exasperatedly.

There was a reason I only visited a couple of times a year, and this was it.

I loved that I had a relationship with Allie's folks where they thought enough of my unworthy ass to look out for me, even if the way they did it bordered on highly inappropriate. The problem was that Jeannie and my mom were like Dobermans with a bone once they got going. Weirdly, though, all the fix-up talk didn't make me uncomfortable. It was funny, and although it was weird, I knew if Allie were here, she would piss her pants laughing at her mom's antics. The way my wife found humor in darkness was another reason I loved her so much, 'cause I was the same way.

It may have seemed strange to some people, but Jean and Mal saw me as the son they never had, and twelve years had gone by since Allie's passing. They didn't want me to be lonely, and they thought they were honoring their daughter by giving me the green light to do what Allie would've wanted me to do and move the fuck on already.

Except, I had moved on, just not in the way they wanted.

I dated, I fucked, I worked; I had a good time with my brothers and generally whooped it up. The way I honored my wife was by living my life to its fullest in all the ways she couldn't. Except I hadn't met the woman I wanted to spend the rest of my days (and nights) with yet.

A memory flashed through the recesses of my mind again of the bluest eyes I'd ever seen, darker than a summer sky but lighter than the oceans.

There'd been nobody who'd piqued my interest since Saint. I'd tried. Recently, I'd gotten to know a girl called Marnie, who turned out to be as much of a bitch as Saint was, though honestly, I kinda had a feeling from the jump that she was a dead end but still forced it anyway. I'd tried to date, but the connections I found never seemed to live up to what came before—first, Allie and then Saint.

As much as I hated to admit it to myself, the cute, curvy singer had me in a chokehold. No other woman since Allie had moved me in a way that made me wish for more.

What a shame the promise of her turned out to be a lie. I thought there was something between us, something pure and honest, except it wasn't honest at all because she turned her back on me without a word of explanation.

"Remember her twenty-fourth birthday?" Jean asked, leaning down for her plastic cup. "You were deployed, and she was furious with you."

"I think she was more furious about that damned singing telegram turning up at her office," Malcom muttered, sipping his beer.

I busted out a laugh. "I thought it was cool as fuck, charming even."

"I did too," Malcom agreed with a grin. "But then what do I know? I married her mother."

One shoulder lifted in a shrug. "Nothing says 'I love you' more than a man in a gorilla suit singing "Crazy in Love."

"I've still got the video," Jean murmured, her eyes taking on a faraway look. "Her face was a picture. I thought she was gonna sink through the floor with embarrassment. She'd only been working at that job for a couple of months, and there's this big hairy gorilla in her face singing Beyonce at the top of his lungs while doing the moves. After she'd calmed down, she called me laughing and said, 'That's what I get for marrying a fighter pilot. A life that revolves around time zones and gorillas.'"

The best kind of laughter filled the air, the kind that could only come from remembering somebody so well loved. My eyes fell on my wife's plaque, and for a second, I imagined she was with us, shaking her head and smiling her beautiful smile as she rolled her eyes.

There weren't words in existence to describe how much I missed Allie or to describe the pain that sliced through me every morning when I woke, and it hit me that she was gone. It was never-ending; I went through the hell of losing my wife on the daily. She was always there in the back of my mind, at least except for one time when I saved another girl from being attacked backstage at a rock gig. That was the only time Allie had ever taken a back seat, and probably why I was so fucking obsessed with Saint McClure when really, she should've faded into obscurity a long-damned time ago.

Girls were easy come, easy go, especially in my lifestyle, but one in particular refused to fade into the background. In a single night, Saint showed me I was still vital, still alive, and that I wasn't as broken as I'd thought.

For one night, she made me feel whole again.

Then, days later, she turned into a ghost, and it was like she'd died too, to the point where, for a while there, I spiraled. The club was just getting off its feet. Our brother, Ace, was still in the picture, and there wasn't much in the way of discipline to pull me back from the brink of self-destruction. I drank, I fought, I fucked, I caroused and generally acted the fool until a few months later when our new VP Blade turned up, sat me down, and told me if I didn't pull my shit together, he'd have to demote me from the enforcer role.

Losing Saint wasn't in the same league as losing Allie. Still, it hurt more than it should have, and it affected me in ways I couldn't explain. I was constantly reminded of our one night and the way she made me feel, but it wasn't in the same way I remembered my wife.

With Saint, the memories crashed over me every time I heard one of her songs playing on the radio or when I opened a magazine, and there she was with her blue eyes gazing out of the pages into mine.

Allie was dead, and Saint was very much alive, but still, it didn't stop me from being haunted by two very real women.

Allie died suddenly and unexpectedly, and I never got to say goodbye. Maybe in order to vanquish the ghost of Saint, I needed to have a conversation and let her know what a bitch move she'd pulled, especially after just days before when I'd saved her ass from some crazed fan.

For two years, I'd stayed quiet and convinced myself I was done with her, and I was, but being here with Allie made me realize that perhaps there was something I needed from Saint 'bitch' McClure.

Just, for once in my life, maybe I could get some goddamned closure.

Chapter Two

Saint

Looking down at my notebook, I watched almost trancelike as the flow of words appeared on the paper I'd been hunched over for the last thirty minutes.

It was always like this for me: when I wrote a song, my insides turned to mush, and they wouldn't straighten out until everything came together. It was like I needed to get the music out of me and onto the paper before I could function right again.

The riff Boomer had composed a few hours before echoed through my brain on a loop of notes and arrangements. There was something about it that hooked me, and suddenly, the words floating through my pen seemed to slot into places that made the track pop.

"Guys," I called out, craning my neck toward where the band was huddled over the mixing desk. "I think I've got the chorus down." Grabbing my guitar, I looped the strap around my neck and began to strum, humming the intro as I went. Then I opened my mouth and sang the lyrics I'd been working on.

I was so engrossed in the song that I hardly noticed Jonny start drumming out a soft backbeat or Sam's bass guitar play some funky chords that added dimension. Boomer's riff accompanied my words until the only thing I could hear was the collective sound echoing through the rehearsal room, enhanced by the built-in acoustics.

My eyes automatically went to Boomer, and a look of understanding passed between us.

I'd met him in a coffee shop the day I got off the bus in LA with a guitar on my back and a thousand bucks in the bank. He gave up his couch for me—much to the annoyance of his girlfriend at the time—and we'd been best friends ever since. We were so in tune with each other that it was scary, though our closeness had always stopped at friendship and had never progressed further.

Boom was like the brother I never had. We were tight. I told him everything, and he did me. There was nobody in this world I trusted as much as I did him. We made beautiful music together, though music was as far as it had ever gone. Would life have been easier if I could have developed romantic feelings for him? Of course. But it wasn't something we could or would ever force.

The door to the recording studio opened, and Talia, our manager, walked inside, nodding to Skip, our producer, who was no doubt doing a take of our rehearsal. Her eyes met mine, and she gave me a small nod, indicating it was time to talk.

I glanced at Boomer, who was looking between me and Talia with interest, before I pulled back from the microphone. "Time to take a break, boys," I called out. "Talia needs to talk with us."

The music died down, and loud chatter resumed as Sam began to bust our drummer, Jonny J's chops about missing a beat, even though Jonny never missed shit.

While the guys were bantering loudly, Boomer sidled up to me and, in a quiet but demanding voice, asked, "What the fuck's goin' on?"

My gaze darted to Boom, and I grinned.

I never could get anything past him.

"She needs to talk to you all about me," I admitted. "I don't want a fuss, but Tally seems to think it's important enough to get you all involved."

My friend's lips thinned. "I can guess," he muttered before turning to the other guys. "Get your asses out there and stop fucking around. It's important. Tally's here to talk about Saint."

"What have you done now?" Jonny drawled, eyeing me curiously.

"Nothing," I replied defensively, punching my hands to my jean-clad hips. "And you've got a nerve even opening your mouth after that reality starlet swore blind that you'd impregnated her. The one time Talia comes for a meeting to discuss something about me, you automatically think the worse, even though I'm the best-behaved one out of all of us."

"I'll give you that," Jonny muttered. "But you gotta admit, being the best-behaved doesn't really mean jack shit in the great scheme of things, seeing as we're usually the worst-behaved ones in the fuckin' room."

My lips twitched. "There is that."

Sam stalked toward me and placed his hands on my shoulders, staring into my eyes. "You okay?"

"Yeah," I breathed. "It's probably nothing. We just need to keep you guys briefed about a few things."

He slid his arm across my shoulders and guided me out of the soundproofed studio. "Best go see what she wants then."

My eyes strayed up to Sam's face, and I caught him studying me thoughtfully.

He looked like your typical Cali blond boy next door, though, in reality, he was as far removed from the boy next door as you could get.

Sam was a nepo baby, though we didn't know that when we hired him to be our bassist. He got the gig through pure talent, even though his dad was a guitar hero from the seventies who now lived on his private estate with his twenty-two-year-old fourth wife.

Incidentally, Sam *was* someone I'd gone there with just once.

A couple of years ago, I'd had a crisis of confidence and decided to drink it out of my system. Sam joined me, and we ended up in bed together. There was a window of time when things were awkward between us because he wanted more than I could give. He was a nice guy, but I didn't want to shit where I ate. Luckily, we'd gotten over our awkwardness and were friends again now.

Talia sat on one of the couches and leaned over the huge coffee table, where she was setting out various glossy photographs.

My heart sank because I'd seen them before, many times. It wasn't that I'd meant to hide shit from the boys. It was more that I didn't take it too seriously. Weird fans came with the territory, as did dirty online trolls and anonymous abuse from cowardly, envious little individuals who were so heartsick with self-hate that they projected it onto us. I was the only female in the band, and although I'd seen other women in the entertainment industry get it worse than I did, I still got trolled relentlessly.

Was it right? No, of course not, but it was part of the job, and I refused to let a faceless coward who only had the balls to spout their boring drivel under a fake name and profile picture affect me.

I didn't concern myself with critical reviews, and I didn't seek out other people's opinions. I just did what

I loved. Whoever wanted to come on board for the ride was welcome; the rest could eat shit for all I cared because, really, what the fuck did I have to feel bad about? My successful career?

Yeah... No.

I'd learned many years before that the only person in life I needed to please was myself. If I didn't give the first shit about what my morally demanding God-fearing father thought about me, then why the hell would I be bothered about what a complete stranger said?

Except one stranger, in particular, was beginning to make Talia nervous, and the thing about our manager was that she had balls of steel. She'd come from humble beginnings to make it to the top of her game in a world ruled by men. There wasn't much that fazed her, so if Tally got nervous, I tended to get nervous too.

Hence the meeting.

Talia looked up at us as we took our seats and sat straight. "Three months ago, Saint started getting letters from a fan." She waved her hand nonchalantly. "I know, I know, pretty run-of-the-mill stuff, which is why nobody questioned it. At first, they were sent to the PMB, and the fan club department dealt with them, but six weeks ago, they began to arrive at Saint's house along with flowers and those weird assed gifts." She nodded down at the photographs she'd laid out on the table.

Boomer glanced at the photographs and did a double-take. "Is that a butt plug?"

Talia stiffed. "That one was delivered to Saint's house four days ago, along with a fan letter explaining in detail exactly how they were going to use it on her."

Boomer's entire body locked, and he bit out, "What the fuck?"

"Yeah," Talia replied, her mouth going tight. "There's a new state-of-the-art security system going into Saint's house as we speak. The problem is that the stretch of beach she lives on isn't private. Also, whoever's sending them has got resources. The diamonds on that butt plug are real."

Boom let out a low whistle, and then his face turned toward me. "You gotta move."

I laughed. "I'm not moving. It took me months to find my beach house. I'm not giving it up for some lunatic who doesn't understand the concept of boundaries."

"It'll just be for a couple of months until we find out who's doing this," he urged. "Rent an apartment or something where there's a doorman and better security."

"It's already been suggested," Talia interjected. "The record company has a couple of places they have for visiting VIPs that Saint could use, so we're going over all the options."

"Stay with me," Boomer offered.

"Or me," Sam suggested with a casual wave of his hand. "Though I don't think you've got anything to worry about. It's probably just some sad, googly-eyed, ugly little motherfucker, who still lives with mother and is angry about their lonely, pathetic life. These weirdo stalkers usually are."

I let out a snort.

"Well, you're not staying with me," Jonny J muttered. "You whine too much."

"I don't whine," I argued, my tone affronted.

"You're like my second mom," he pointed out. "Every time I light a joint, you nag."

"Hello. Newsflash. It's because I care," I said sarcastically. "I don't want you to fall into the sex, drugs, and rock 'n' roll fame trap and lose everything like we've seen so many fucking times before."

"She's gotta point, dude," Sam stated.

I sighed. "Thank you for the kind offers, but I'm not staying with anyone. Talia's got another proposal, one that affects all of us."

Every eye turned expectantly to our manager.

"After the success of the first album and your growing popularity, the record company and I think it's time to hire personal security," she stated.

"Bodyguards?" Jonny cursed under his breath and rolled his eyes.

Sam laughed.

Boomer's lips thinned.

"What did you expect?" Talia went on. "You're an award-winning band with a critically acclaimed album under your belt. The buzz around the new tracks is crazy, and you're adored by millions. It was only a matter of time. Regardless of whether this happened to Saint or not, it's something we would've had to look at eventually anyway. You're followed by paparazzi everywhere you go, and things have gotten dicey for all of you at some point with over-enthused fans."

"Okay, so hire them," Boomer acquiesced. "Just make sure we get the ones from Proximity. Those guys are cool."

"We've already approached them," Talia confirmed. "They can do it, but they're booked up for the next three months. How do you feel about hiring the boys from Covershield while we wait for Proximity to start their contract?"

"Those dudes are uptight," Jonny pointed out. "Plus, one of 'em tried to get up close and personal with Saint last time we used 'em. It took all three of us to get him outta her house, and even then, Sam ended up with a black eye."

Tally held her hands up defensively. "I know, I know."

"He belonged on a fucking psych ward," Boomer continued. "They obviously don't vet their guys that well. I say we use Noah Hart's dudes. The time we used 'em, one of their boys saved Saint from that handsy fan at the Festival of Rock."

"SDSS?" Tally's eyes slid to me, and she murmured, "They're pretty new to the game."

I could've kissed her for trying to make excuses to put me at ease, but there was no need. Years had passed, and I was over what Jacob did. Personal feelings didn't come into it anyway. I wanted my boys to be comfortable with the guys we used because having twenty-four-hour security was a big deal, and we had to gel with them purely because they'd be around us all the time. And anyway, what were the chances of Jacob being part of the team they sent? Their club was big and even took on government jobs. Jacob was an officer. I doubted they could spare him for three months to run around after a rock band.

I sat back and sighed resignedly.

God, I hated this. It was almost embarrassing. All this fuss about something that wasn't even likely to happen. Whoever was sending the weird stuff to me had stayed in the shadows for months, and like most cowards, they wouldn't come out to hold their head above the parapet because that would mean they'd have to own up to their bullshit.

"I vote we go for SDSS," Sam announced.

"Ditto," Boomer agreed.

"Anyone's better than those uptight Covershield assholes," Jonny murmured.

I filled my lungs with air, trying to center my nerves before declaring, "I'll go with the majority. We're only having to do this because of me, so I want you guys to feel as comfortable as possible."

Nothing was likely to happen; I mean, we were hardly the Beatles circa nineteen-sixty-five, but the gifts were getting weird. I'd almost had a fucking aneurysm when I opened my front door to be confronted with a huge bouquet of flowers alongside a diamond-encrusted butt plug.

"Still. I'm sure there's nothing to stress about, right?" I said brightly in an attempt to buy my own line. "It's probably just a harmless freak with too much free time on their hands."

Boomer eyed the photographs and grunted.

"I wouldn't mind takin' that butt plug off your hands." Sam grinned, waggling his eyebrows.

Everybody groaned.

"What?" he demanded. "Got Jolie Fontaine coming for dinner later."

Boomer's head reared back. "The supermodel?"

"Yeah, the supermodel," Sam replied sarcastically. "You know any other women called Jolie Fontaine?"

"Alright, smartass," Boomer retorted. "It's just weird that you walk into rehearsals and announce you're having dinner with one of the most desirable and beautiful women in the world as if it's nothing. When the fuck did you meet her?"

"She was walking her dog on the beach earlier. I came outta the surf with my board and ran into her. I recognized her, she recognized me, and boom, next thing I know, she's accepting my offer of dinner at my place."

"And you think she'll let you use a diamond-encrusted butt plug on her on the first date?" Jonny drawled.

"Not banking on it," Sam admitted. "But it'd be good to be prepared just in case."

"I think you're livin' in goddamned Narnia," Boomer muttered. "You better go looking for an old wardrobe, dude, 'cause you've got as much chance of ass fucking Jolie Fontaine on the first date as you have of meeting a talking lion."

"Speak for yourself, asshole," Sam responded, leaning forward until his elbows hit his knees. "She's seen my abs. There's no stopping me." He straightened and lifted his Metallica tee, showing off his washboard abs. "Once the ladies get sight of all this, they can't help themselves."

"Spoken like a true narcissist," Jonny muttered, his lips twitching. "Your dad probably bought them for ya like he did everything else."

Sam raised a hand to his mouth and coughed out the words, "Broke ass."

Boomer looked at me and rolled his eyes.

I smiled back at him and shrugged.

The boys' banter was usually the highlight of my day. I'd never had any of this growing up. The house I grew up in wasn't filled with family jokes and laughter. My dad was a pastor and my mom his assistant, and they laid down the law, especially when it came to my friends.

I was only allowed to go to school, church, and home. There was no dating or movies, or hanging out at the diner. There was only bible study, prayer, and services. It was no wonder I escaped the day I turned eighteen, and apart from a few phone calls home to my mom, I had nothing to do with the church or my dad.

It wasn't that I hated him; I didn't. My dad never treated me badly or beat me. He was just overstrict. He disowned me the first time he saw me singing with the band on TV. It seemed having a rock singer for a daughter didn't fit in with his religious aesthetic.

Talia swiped her cell phone from the table and began to scroll through it. When she found her target, she clicked and put it to her ear. After a few seconds, she said, "Noah? It's Talia Fields. I'm trying to hire personal security for Saint's Rapture. Do you think SDSS would be interested? The contract will be for a few months until Proximity Security frees up some guys." She nodded. "Cool. Can you ping that over to me?" Another pause, then, "We're just being cautious.

Iceman

Saint's got a fan who's getting a bit too close for comfort, and we want to cover our bases." She glanced at me and rolled her eyes. "Yeah. One minute, I'll put her on." She handed the cell to me and gave me big eyes.

Taking the cell, I held it to my ear. "Hey, stranger."

"You okay, babe?" Noah asked gently.

I smiled at the concern in his tone.

Noah Hart used to be a biker. Maybe he still was. Who knew? He was also the frontman of a band called Dischordium, who'd recently broken out onto the scene. Their first album had done really well, and like us, they were working on their second. Me and Boomer had seen them play at a bar over in Wyoming years before and had asked them to support us on a ten-gig tour we were putting together. They started gathering a following, and the rest was history.

"I'm good, thanks, honey," I murmured. "Like Tally said, it's just an over-zealous fan sending shit to my house. But it's made us realize we need to step up security."

"Honestly, babe. Surprised it took you this long to get it," he rumbled. "You're talented, and you're fine as hell. It was only a matter of time."

"It's come from left field. I stay out the spotlight unless I'm out with Hunter, and even then, it's usually industry shit, so it's security controlled."

"You still with that guy?" he asked.

"On and off," I admitted, "You know how it is."

Noah laughed. "Yeah. I do." He paused before declaring. "Tell Tally to hold off calling Hendrix. I'll do it now and get him to call her. I'll ask him for a special favor. I'll get you sorted, Saint. Don't worry."

My heart melted at Noah's kindness. "You're a good friend."

"Only payin' it forward, sweetheart. You guys have done a lot for us. Feels good that I can help you out for a change. Tell Talia I'll speak to Drix now and to look out for his call. In the meantime, you watch your back and call me if you need me, okay?"

"'Kay," I breathed. "Thanks again, Noah."

The line clicked, and I handed the cell back to Talia. "Noah said to hang fire. He'll call Hendrix and ask him to contact you."

Her head tipped to one side, "Thanks, babe. He always did have a soft spot for you."

"For all of us," I corrected. "We got Dischordium the supporting gig, remember?"

A slight smirk curved her lips. "Oh, my sweet summer child. Noah Hart wants to fuck you into next Wednesday. Make no mistake about it."

"We're just friends," I argued.

Boomer let out a snort. "You are, but he still wants to fuck you into next Wednesday."

"Bullshit," I snapped.

My friend turned to the other two guys. "It's like she doesn't look in the mirror. She's got sass, great tits and ass, a tiny waist, curvy legs, fantastic hair, and eyes so blue that they remind me of a beautiful white walker, and she still can't believe men want to fuck her."

"I know, right?" Jonny concurred. "She bagged the biggest action-hero star on the fucking planet, and she can't see how."

I waved a nonchalant hand. "You know my relationship with Hunter isn't serious."

"He still fucks you though, right?"

My eyes lowered.

If only they knew.

"Stop embarrassing her," Talia scolded. "Us girls aren't like you silly boys who boast about their conquests. We've got more class." She checked her watch. "Right, you've got an hour's break, then back to work. I've ordered pizza and salad. I've arranged for someone to replenish the fridge with beer, too. I know

I always say you shouldn't drink on the job, but I think it's been a weird day, and you all need to unwind."

"We write better full of beer anyway," Jonny muttered, getting to his feet.

"You also trash hotel rooms," Talia bit back.

"Nah." Jonny grinned. "That's the cocaine and tequila."

"Jesus help me," Tally murmured. "It's like wrangling toddlers."

Boomer and Sam got to their feet and followed Jonny out of the recording studio. "Thanks, Tal," Boom called back.

"What for?" she asked.

He craned his neck, looking back at us. "For looking out for our girl." He sent her a little wink. "You're the best."

Talia's face pinked up. "Go eat," she ordered.

He gave her a loose salute and disappeared through the door.

My gaze followed him. "They're assholes," I murmured to Talia. "But they're our assholes. I know the boys are hard work, but they mean well. I always feel as if they've got my best interests at heart."

"I know." She leaned forward and lowered her voice to a whisper. "You haven't told them about Hunter?"

"What am I supposed to say? Oh, by the way, you know that action-hero boyfriend of mine? Well, he's actually gay and in love with his manager. His career's at its peak, and he doesn't want it getting out in case it hurts his macho image, so I agreed to be his beard to raise the band's profile." My eyes bugged out at her. "They'll think I'm a sell-out."

"That's not why you did it?" she argued gently. "You agreed to it for Hunter."

I shrugged. "It's still a showmance."

"One that you're doing for the right reasons," Talia pointed out. "Stop being hard on yourself."

"Maybe it's time me and Hunter broke up," I stated.

"Do what you want," she told me. "Just make sure you give me plenty of notice so I can get the publicists ahead of it."

My mouth twisted. "It's time to do that now; I don't want Hunter involved in all this stalker business. It's too dangerous."

Her chin dipped, and her eyes held mine. "Or maybe you want to be officially single for when you get your new bodyguard."

My stomach tightened at the idea of seeing Jacob again.

We'd only spent one night together, but to my mind, it had gone down in history as one of the best nights of my life. I really thought we had something special, but he turned out to be just like all the other assholes, and that knowledge had always cut me deep.

For a long time, he was my muse. The entire first album was about Jake, and the lyrics of the song I wrote when I first laid eyes on him had won me countless awards. That night, something about him had inspired my soul, but then it all crashed and burned, and he turned into just another disappointment in a long line of disappointments.

But hey, they always said the best songs come from a place of pain, and the Grammy above my fireplace proved they were right, so how could I be mad about it? Everything happened for a reason, and maybe I had to meet Jake to bring those songs out of me, even if he did turn out to be a cheating asshole.

"I don't want to be single for my new bodyguard," I denied. "I'm happy with my life the way it is. Uncomplicated and simple."

"Also boring, uninspired, and colorless," she added.

"I'm good," I assured her.

"I know, Saint, but you're also stagnating. You need some excitement in your life." As Tally spoke, her cell rang in her hand. She glanced at the screen, tapped it, then held the phone to her ear. "Talia Fields." She paused while the person on the other line introduced themselves, then smiled. "Hendrix! Good to hear from you. Thanks for calling so soon." Her eyes came to me, and her smile widened to a grin before she declared, "I've got a proposition for you."

Chapter Three

Iceman

My fist tightened around Arizona's hair, and she moaned around my cock.

The vibrations slid through me down to my balls, and I pushed an inch deeper down her throat, my eyes rolling in my head at the sensation of her tight throat muscles closing around me. Lifting my head, I looked down at Arizona's blonde hair bobbing, her lips suctioned to me as she slowly sucked me down deep.

Jesus fuck.

Heather, the new girl, let out a frustrated little mewl. "What's wrong?" she whispered. "Why did you stop?"

I turned back to her glistening pussy. "Nothing's wrong, babe. Just enjoying the view." Lowering my head, I slid my mouth over her slick, juicy clit and sucked it, my cock kicking as her hips bucked against my face.

"Fuck, you're good at that," Heather groaned.

My reply was to slide a finger deep inside, adding another when she groaned her approval. Spurred on, my mouth moved against her urgently, gently nipping and sucking on the sensitive skin of her cunt. The walls of her pussy contracted around my fingers so forcefully that my balls tightened at the thought of what they would do to my dick.

Raising my head again, I barked, "Wrap," then rolled onto my back, my hands gripping Heather's thighs and pulling her with me until she straddled my face.

Within seconds, I felt Arizona throw a leg over me and grab my dick to position it before slowly sliding down until she was seated with me deep inside her.

I began to eat Heather again. Moaning my pleasure as Arizona's tight little cunt squeezed my cock as she rode me hard, her cries and whimpers filling the room as my hips thrust up to meet hers.

Arizona's pussy pulsed around my cock.

Jesus, she was primed. I'd eaten her out before Heather, but stopped just before she came and made them switch positions. Now, I had one bitch coming on my face while the other came on my cock and fuck me if it wasn't one of the hottest things I'd ever experienced.

My balls tightened and began to draw up. Counting from ten backward, I willed myself not to come, needing the girls to get there first. I'd only gotten back from NOLA a few hours before, and I needed sleep, so the thought of a drawn-out sexathon didn't fill me with glee.

This was what I needed to help me sleep. I was exhausted already from being awake for days and riding through the night. This would relax me to the point of oblivion when I finally got some shut-eye.

The second the girls climbed off, I jackknifed up, grabbed Heather, and shoved her onto her back.

Her eyes went wide as I hitched up one leg, wrapping it around my ass. Then I grabbed my cock, guided it to her opening, and drove in hard.

She let out a squeal.

I stilled my hips, my cock buried deep, and rasped, "Fuck, you're tight."

"And you're big," she whispered, letting out a moan as I pulled out to the tip before driving inside her again.

"Arizona," I muttered. "Get your sexy ass up here."

Ari moved up the bed, bent over, and began to make out with Heather. Their quiet moans filled the air, and I watched them go at each other, nipping and sucking on each other's soft lips.

Hitching Heather's leg higher, I buried my cock to the root and began to fuck her into the mattress, my eyes glued to the girls as they continued kissing each other.

It didn't take long. Within a minute of grinding my cock into Heather, I felt the build.

"Jesus," I muttered, bucking my hips harder, the nerves in my lower back tingling until I felt it coming.

Arizona turned her head until her eyes met mine. "Fuck her hard," she whispered. "Wreck that pussy."

That was all the encouragement I needed. Letting out a low groan, my hips bucked, and my cum erupted. I lost all rhythm, my ass and hips jerking uncontrollably while I filled the condom covering my dick.

Seconds later, I opened my eyes, eased my cock from Heather's cunt, released her leg, and watched as she groaned and rolled to her side, continuing to make out with Heather.

A small smile crossed my face. "Sorry, ladies, but if you wanna carry on the party, you'll have to do it somewhere else. I'm bushed."

Arizona pulled back again. "Don't you want round two? You usually go all night."

I rolled off the bed and grabbed my jeans. "Been up for days, babe. Need some sleep."

She pouted. "I'll go get Trick instead."

Pulling my jeans up, I slid them over my ass. "Fill your boots, Ari. Just do it somewhere else, alright. Shouldn't need to tell you twice." I nodded toward my bathroom door. "Gonna go take a shower while you girls go take a hike."

"No need to be an asshole about it," Arizona snapped.

I scraped a hand down my face. This was the last thing I needed. I just wanted them to clear out while I grabbed a few hours of sleep. I felt bruised and battered from visiting Allie and seeing the parents. Maybe I should've held off banging club whores for a few days until I got myself together, but I needed a release, and I needed to sleep without dreaming. All I could see when I closed my eyes was my dead wife's face. Exhausting myself was the only way to vanquish her ghost from inside my fucked-up head.

I walked into the bathroom and switched the shower on, listening to the sounds of the girls getting dressed and leaving. As soon as the door shut behind them, I breathed a sigh of relief and stepped inside the cubicle, lifting my face into the spray of hot water raining down, making me clean again.

Screwing other women seemed to banish Allie for a little while, at least. Except now I had another ghost to contend with because somehow, Saint McClure had gotten inside my head too, though honestly, she'd been there since our night together. Between her and Allie, I didn't stand a goddamned chance. Peace was something I yearned for, but always seemed to be just out of reach.

Steam filled the shower, and I closed my eyes, trying to breathe through the flood of emotions threatening to overwhelm me.

The last few days had been draining. Losing Allie never got easier, especially around this time of year. It felt like I had a well of memories and feelings inside that usually stayed buried. Then, Allie's birthday would come around, and those feelings would rise so suddenly and quickly that they overflowed.

Grabbing my body wash, I lathered up, shampooed my hair, and rinsed the soap away before stepping out of the shower and drying off. I brushed my teeth on autopilot before stumbling back to my bedroom, pulling the blinds, and falling into bed as naked as the day I was born.

Closing my eyes, I tried to clear my mind, knowing full well that Allie's pale blue eyes would flash through my mind to torment me, but instead, all I could see was Saint's glowing blue orbs.

I shifted on the bed, needing to sleep but also filled with so much restlessness that I knew I was fighting a losing battle. Suddenly, I wished I hadn't sent the girls away. At least while I was with them, I wasn't thinking about *her*.

It was almost a relief when my cell pinged, the sound alerting me that Hendrix had called Church. I sat up and shifted my ass to the edge of the bed, holding my head in my hands while I tried to get my thoughts in order.

Allie's sweet voice whispered through my head. *No rest for the wicked, baby.*

The corner of my mouth twitched because she wasn't fucking wrong.

Grabbing my phone, I read the group message.

BLADE: Church in ten

Then, with a sigh, I stood, went to my drawers, grabbed a fresh pair of jeans and a tee, and put them on. Shrugging on my cut, I made for the door and hauled ass down the stairs, hitting reception in record time.

As I headed down the corridor toward Church, a clipped British-accented voice called, "How was NOLA?"

My steps faltered, and I craned my neck to see Gambit walking up behind me. "Hey!" I greeted. "It was as good as these things can be."

A hand hit my shoulder, his dark eyes studying my face. "You look tired."

"I'm fuckin' exhausted," I admitted. "Maybe havin' a threesome with Ari and the new girl the second I got back was a step too far even for me."

"Ahh," he said knowingly. "The lovely Heather. She's somethin' else, right? Her tits are banging."

My lips tipped up at Gambit's Brit speak, and we resumed our journey down the corridor. "Did I miss much while I was gone?"

"Not really. Prez is all caught up in JT, so we haven't seen much of him. They're still moving into his aunt and uncle's place, so they've been down there with the kid mostly, planning what they wanna do with the place—"

"Wait," I interrupted. "Anna still wants to move into the house where she was held captive by a lunatic ex-club whore and fuck buddy of her ol' man?"

Gambit barked a laugh. "She's got balls, right?"

"Damned straight." I shook my head. "Any word on Ace or Daisy?"

"Nah. Colt did a trace on the vehicle we saw driving away from the river. It was registered to Aces Security. He wasn't hiding his involvement or the fact he went to get Daisy outta there. Her body hasn't been found, so we assume she's still alive."

"We need to give Anna shooting lessons to make sure next time she gets the heart," I muttered.

Gambit nodded as we approached the door for Church. "Too right." He keyed in a sequence of numbers and then stood still until the retinal scanner did its job. Then the locks disengaged, and he pushed on the door, breezily saying, "Morning, all. Lovely day for it," as he strutted inside.

I followed and was met with grunts from Blade and Diablo. Then, the most vile, rancid smell I'd ever had the misfortune to encounter hit me.

"What the fuck is that stench?" Gambit demanded, holding his hand up to cover his nose and mouth.

The door swung closed behind me, and I balked.

"JT took a shit," Blade muttered, swiping a hand across his face, "Swear to God, it was so strong it made my eyes water."

My stare fell on our Prez, who had the baby on his back, laying across his lap while he expertly changed the kid's diaper. "What the fuck are you feeding him?"

"Breast milk, you halfwit," Hendrix clipped, snapping the poppers closed on JT's romper. "What the fuck do you think we're feedin' him? Steak and fucking foie gras?"

I balked again.

"It's not normal," Diablo grunted.

"How the fuck do you dare talk about normal?" Hendrix demanded, his face turning an angry shade of purple. "A baby taking a shit is normal. What's *not* normal is a grown-ass man cutting off body parts and keeping them in jars on a shelf *while illuminating them with different colored fucking Christmas lights.*" His voice rose to a bellow. "I dunno how you have the brass balls to sit there criticizing my son's ass when your room stinks of goddamned *roadkill!*"

Gambit sank down in his place at the round table, chuckling to himself while I took my seat next to Diablo.

The door swung open again, and Trick appeared, followed by Pyro and Will.

Trick's face turned green. "What the fuck is that smell?"

Hendrix sighed.

"What?" the road captain demanded. "I'm very sensitive to aromas."

"So why the fuck do you stink like rancid old pussy most of the goddamned time," Hendrix shot back.

"'Cause I fuck a lot of it." His stare slid to me. "Talking of which, is it true you turned down a second go with Arizona and Heather doin' girl-on-girl? Did your dick break or somethin'?"

Every eye turned to me, and Diablo's narrowed. "None'a those bitches have done girl-on-girl for me." He sniffed.

"That's because they're too busy shitting their panties in case you get a hankering to cut off one of their fucking toes or something," Blade snapped.

Diablo turned to Veep. "Have they done girl-on-girl for you?"

Blade rolled his lips together. "A gentleman never tells, but yeah."

D's stare swept around the table, taking in the men shifting in their seats while they looked everywhere but at him. "Jesus fuck," he rasped. "First Gambit gets multiple mass cock sucks, then they do girl-on-girl for the rest of you shitheads. Why the fuck don't they come up with hot shit like that for me?"

Will waved a nonchalant hand. "Not just you, brother."

"You don't fuck the whores," the SAA said accusingly. "Plus, you're like, a hundred and goddamned three. They're probably scared they'll kill you off."

Will grinned. "True. Though, come to think of it, Arizona and Tia did offer me a lil' show for my birthday last year. Turned 'em down though. You're right; I'm too old for that shit, and with havin' a dodgy ticker and all..." He patted his heart comfortingly. "Let's just say they probably *would* kill me off." Will went over to Hendrix, rubbing his hands together. "JT wants to come to Gramps."

"Fuck off," Drix snapped.

"You've had him all day," Will argued.

"He's my kid," Hendrix reminded him.

Will grabbed his cell from his inside pocket and stabbed at the screen. The sound of ringing filled the room, followed by Anna's voice saying, "Hey, Will."

"Sweetheart," Will crooned. "Have a word with your ol' man, will ya. He's hogging the baby."

Hendrix's head reared back. "Did you really just call *my* woman and tattle on me?"

Anna laughed softly. "Jamie. Give him the baby."

"Fuck no," Prez muttered. "He's all 'let me hold JT' when I've just changed the kid's diaper. When the kid shits his diaper, the old fucker's nowhere to be seen."

"The perks of bein' a grandparent instead of a parent," Will grumbled. "It's your job to change shitty diapers, not mine. I did all that with you, and you had the shittiest ass I've ever encountered. When you came outta your ma, you were an ugly little thing. Your head was distorted into a cone shape because it was abnormally big, and your mom had a job squeezing you out. The nurses had to use those suction cup things and suck you out. What with your shitty ass and your weird cone head. I thought your ma had been abducted and impregnated by aliens. I used to say, Sweetheart, are you sure you don't remember getting beamed up to the Starship Enterprise? 'Cause our boy sure does resemble a fuckin' Vulcan." His voice dropped, and he muttered, "I was a hairsbreadth away from naming you goddamned Spock."

Diablo roared, choking out, "Fuckin' cone head."

I chuckled.

Blade's lips twitched.

Anna giggled down the phone.

Hendrix looked at the ceiling and sighed out his frustration. "Can we get on with fuckin' Church?"

Will said his goodbyes to Anna and ended the call. "Gimme the baby," he ordered, "Or I'll tell 'em about the time you thought your ma was haunting you, and you pissed the bed."

"A lotta kids have trouble controlling their waterworks," Blade interjected,

Will smirked. "When they're seventeen?"

The men snickered.

"For fuck's sake, take the baby," Hendrix bit out.

Will grinned and made a grabby-hands gesture. "Give him here." He moved toward Drix and leaned down, transferring JT into his arms. "There's my little fella," he crooned, pulling the baby into his chest and moving toward his seat.

JT let out a little mewl before snuggling into his gramps and falling back to sleep.

Hendrix picked up the gavel and smashed it into the sound block, startling JT out of his sleep. The baby opened his mouth and let out a piercing cry, angry at being disturbed.

I couldn't help myself. I sat forward and began to bust a gut.

Will slowly stood, rocking JT from side to side, trying to soothe him. "What the fuck did you do that for, you idiot?" he whisper-shouted.

Hendrix looked up at the heavens and sighed.

"Shouldn't he be with his mom?" Pyro asked.

Hendrix's eyes narrowed on my buddy. "You'll get kicked outta Church before my boy does. Anna's busy making inquiries about the empty salon in town, so I'm on daddy duty."

"You can't babysit. You've gotta club to run," Pyro shot back.

Hendrix's face blanked. "Come again?"

Pyro looked confused. "What?"

"Do I look like a fuckin' babysitter?" Hendrix asked.

Pyro shook his head. "That's my point. We need to get down to business. You can't do that while you're babysitting."

"I'm not babysitting," Hendrix spat. "I'm being a parent. It's as much my responsibility to care for my boy as it is my ol' lady's. Hence, I don't babysit my own son; I care for him like any father should care for their kid."

"Well said," Will muttered. "Maybe you're not a lost cause after all."

"You, shut the fuck up," Drix ordered. "I've banged the gavel, which means Church is in session. As of now, I'm in charge, not you."

Will shrugged and took his seat again. "Well, just be in charge a bit quieter. Don't wake the baby."

Prez raised a hand to his temple and rubbed. "Can we get back to business now?"

A chorus of whispered ayes went up.

"Right," Drix murmured. "First on the agenda. Adrian Lis is coming to visit. He'll get in about six tonight. He's gonna spend a couple of hours with Anna and James, then head up to DC."

"As simple as that?" Diablo asked.

Hedrix shrugged. "I dunno why it has to be complicated. He wants to meet his nephew. Anna's cool with it. Job done."

"He's one of the most dangerous men on the east coast," D pointed out.

"So am I," Hendrix answered. "Up to now, he's played ball. If he stops playing ball, we'll deal. Until then, I'll go along with what Anna wants."

"At least let me take extra precautions while he's here," Diablo requested. "Wanna make sure your woman and kid are safe."

Hendrix's face softened. "Can't argue with that, brother."

"Extra guards on the gate. Men dotted around the place. We'll all be armed, and you'll stay with Anna at all times. We can do all that discretely, seein' as Lis doesn't know how we usually operate. As far as he's concerned, it's a normal day at the office."

"Sounds good," Drix agreed. "Ice, Gambit, and Picasso, hang around while he's here. Blade and Pyro, you hang in the background. D, take Fletch and Mac for the gate."

We all murmured our agreement.

"Okay, next on the agenda. We've had a job come in. It's a three-month gig. Personal protection for a rock band."

My ears pricked up, and I sat a little straighter.

Six of us were licensed for close personal protection. Me, Picasso, Gambit, Trick, Ghost, and Fletcher. I was the highest-ranking officer out of all those boys, so I usually took the lead on bodyguard jobs. However, usually, Prez came to me before he announced anything to the brothers so we could plan the job. On this occasion, he hadn't, and it rang alarm bells.

"Who's the band?" Diablo asked. "Dischordium again? Or one'a them boy bands who have all the girls screaming, you know, like the Backstreet Boys?"

"Backstreet Boys?" Trick questioned. "Jesus, man. How old are you?"

"What?" Diablo said defensively. "They were good." He began to sway from side to side and clicked his fingers rhythmically. Then suddenly, he pointed at Trick and started to croak out the chorus to "As Long as You Love Me" very badly.

Trick's lip curled, and he snapped, "Get the fuck outta here with that bullshit."

Gambit chuckled, shaking his head. "Our boy bands were way better than those wannabes. Take That were the dog's bollocks."

"Nah," Trick disputed. "Boyzone was where it was at."

Hendrix looked between them, his eyes getting bigger, then he glanced at Blade. "Have you got a clue what the fuck they're talkin' about?"

"They lost me at Backroad Boys," Blade said dryly.

"It's Back*street* Boys," Trick corrected.

Our VP waved an uncaring hand. "What the fuck ever. I'm not a teenage girl like you princesses. The names of boy bands don't concern me. What concerns me is the job at hand and the fact your prez is tryin' to tell us about one, but he can't"—his voice raised to a yell—"because you bunch of little pussies are so busy wetting your day-of-the-week panties over the Backroad Boys *that you won't let him fucking talk!*"

Silence fell over the room, and Blade turned to Prez. "The floor's yours, boss."

Hendrix's lips twitched. "Much obliged." He picked up the iPad on the table and tapped on it, pausing when the massive surround screens on the walls came to life with images, and the wail of guitars filled the room.

My stare locked on an image of Saint McClure, and every muscle froze as I studied the face that haunted me.

As much as the bitch seemed to be everywhere, I always refused to take notice. When her song came on the radio, I either switched it off or turned my mind to something else. When images of her and her band came on TV, I switched the channel, and if I turned the page of a magazine to see her there, I flipped it again as fast as I could.

What I didn't do was look. Not ever, because studying Saint's beautiful face or her pure, blue eyes would be like admitting she existed for me, something she ceased to do the instant she ghosted my ass... mostly.

But being forced to study her now, it became clear how different she looked.

Her blonde hair had been dyed black and was gleaming under the lights. I had to admit, it looked good. She'd lost weight; the curves I loved so much were still there, but pared down. Saint was still gorgeous, albeit more polished and rock star-looking, but her eyes seemed weary, as if she was tired of the world and everything it had to offer.

My heart went out to her because after seeing the life behind her eyes on the night we spent together, it hit me how dead they'd become. As much as I shouldn't have cared, I couldn't stop myself from wondering why I felt a pang of concern.

Seeing Saint's face so big on the screens had transported me somewhere else, so when Hendrix spoke, I jumped, slightly startled as his voice brought me back into the room.

"Saint McClure, lead singer and frontwoman of the band Saint's Rapture, hit the big time about a year ago with their song, "Empty." All's been going well until recently, when she started getting letters and gifts that stood out to the team who sorted the band's fan mail. They kept on keeping on until a few weeks ago when the letters and gifts started getting delivered to Saint's house"—he paused, his eyes sliding to me—"by hand."

Bile rose through my throat.

"Their management has reached out to see if we can assist with the band's personal protection," he continued. "They're starting a contract with another company based in LA, but the firm can't start the contract for a few months. That's where we come in."

His eyes swept around the room but avoided me. "Trick, you're up alongside Ghost. Between the two of you, you've got the boys."

Hendrix's stare finally met mine, and I braced for what was to come. Sitting up straighter, I squared my shoulders, waiting for my name to be called, but instead, Prez announced. "Gambit. You're on twenty-four-seven watch with Saint."

My body jerked.

"You fly out to LA tomorrow, and you'll be there a while, so pack cases, not bags. You need to take suits with you as well as jeans. If you need your wardrobes replenished, you can do it in LA and put it on expenses. The band's in rehearsals, putting the finishing touches into writing their new album. As soon as that's done, they're heading to New York to record it, and you'll be goin' with 'em."

Staring at my prez, I felt my lip curl.

What the fuck was he playing at?

"I'll brief you all later, but for now, you can start packing. I'll see you all in my office at 16:00 hours for a meeting. Remember, this job is professional. You may be looking after a rock band, but that doesn't mean you can party like one. Got it?"

Murmurs of agreement went up.

Hendrix picked up the gavel and banged it into the sound block. "We'll discuss plans later. Want you to go get your shit packed and do what you need to do before you leave. Iceman, you stay behind."

My jaw clenched, and I jerked a nod, ignoring the curious looks the other guys threw my way as they exited Church.

It must've seemed weird to them. I was the officer in charge of close personal protection, and I wasn't going with them to protect Saint's Rapture. Not only was it odd, but it was also unheard of, seeing as I was always the first one up when it came to CPP.

The instant the door clicked shut, I looked at Hendrix pointedly.

"You're too close," he declared.

"You're wrong," I argued. "It was one night, and I wasn't her CPP. Didn't even know who she was then. If I'd known she was in the band, I never would've gone there."

"I'm trying to save you from the hassle," Hendrix explained.

"Of doin' my job?" My mouth twisted. "Thanks for that." I leaned toward him, leaving him in no doubt about the seriousness behind my next words. "I liked her—a lot. Saint was the first woman I'd liked a lot since Allie. She ghosted me, and it wounded my pride, but it was a long time ago. If I'd known back then that confiding in my best friend would one day work against me, I would've thought twice, just like I'll think twice next time." I got up from my seat and made for the door.

"Jake," Hendrix called out.

I stopped and craned my neck to stare at him.

"I'm trying to stop you from gettin' hurt again," he explained gently.

"No, Prez," I bandied back. "You're trying to control a narrative that doesn't exist. I'm nearly forty years old. Don't need you or anyone to look out for me when it comes to women. It tells me you don't trust me as a man or as a brother, and after the way I've stuck by you through thick and thin, that hurts me more than Saint McClure ever did. We could put what happened behind us, or I could get even more pissy with her. Who the fuck knows? But either way, it wouldn't stop me from bein' respectful or from doing my job, Jimmy, and you fuckin' know it. Never done anything to make you think you can't trust me, brother, but after this, I can't say the same for you."

He stood and moved toward me, and his hand shot to my shoulder. "Sit down, Ice."

I glowered at him.

He sighed his frustration. "Jake. Please. Sit down."

My jaw tightened to steel, and I returned to the table before flopping back down in my chair.

"I'm sorry, brother. Thought I was helping you out," he muttered, taking his seat again.

"No, you didn't," I argued. "If that was the case, you'd have called me in for a meet and given me a heads-up."

"You've been away," he pointed out.

"Oh, I'm sorry. Did all our cell phones get cut off without me knowin'?"

"You were visiting Allie," he said gently. "Didn't think it was right to call you about another woman on your wife's birthday."

"My *dead* wife's birthday," I reminded him. "She's been gone twelve years, Jim. I'm not gonna break 'cause you call me on Allie's birthday and mention Saint McClure."

He smiled wryly. "Yeah. I see now I did you dirty. If you wanna take on the job, then do it. We can take Trick off the team and send you instead." His stare held mine. "How was NOLA? You okay?"

"It was fine. Good to see our folks." I decided to throw him a bone. "The moms are tryin'a fix me up."

"Jesus," Drix breathed.

"Believe me," I drawled. "Jesus was no help."

He nodded thoughtfully. "How you feelin' with everything?"

"Exhausted, unsettled, antsy, and ready for a job." I grinned. "Some time in LA could be just what I need." I gave him a tight-lipped smile. "I won't be an asshole to her, Jimmy. But it'll also be good to get some answers. Maybe this is just what I need so that after I finish the job, I can look forward instead of looking back. The moms are right. If I want kids and a family, I need to get my ass moving."

The years hadn't dulled Saint's appeal, which was probably why I didn't let myself dwell on her. Though deep down in my soul, I always knew this day would come.

Finally, it was time to get some answers and, more importantly, some goddamned closure.

Chapter Four

Saint

"How the hell did they get so close?" I whispered, looking down at the glossy black-and-white photographs that Talia had laid out on my patio table.

"That's what I asked just before I fired the dude from Covershield's ass," my manager said with a cock of her perfectly shaped eyebrow. "I swear to fucking God, Saint, trusting somebody to just do their fucking job is like pulling teeth. I needed them to look after you for three days until the boys from SDSS flew in, but nooooo, those dicks were more interested in watchin' TV than looking out for you." She took a sip of her cooler, her gaze sliding out to watch the waves rolling in from the Pacific Ocean. "Luckily, the SDSS boys' flight should have landed by now."

Ignoring the uneasy feeling in my stomach, I allowed my eyes to drift across the beach. The ocean didn't just inspire, but it settled me too, which was good because I'd been coming out of my skin since the minute I'd heard that Jacob would be part of the security detail hired to look after us.

Talia's voice pulled me away from my thoughts. "You okay, babe?"

I nodded, forcing a smile. "Yeah... Just a little freaked out."

She scanned the pictures and muttered, "Understatement. This shit's disturbing even for me, and I'm not even the poor bitch getting papped when I'm in a state of undress."

A cold shiver ran through me at the thought of somebody violating me in that way and in the privacy of my own bedroom. I'd literally run out of the bathroom to grab a robe, and he'd caught me topless with a long-lens camera. "If these get into the press, my dad will have a fucking stroke. It's not just about my privacy being invaded; it's about how vulnerable being photographed without my knowledge or consent makes me feel. I can't stop my mind racing with worst-case scenarios, like salacious tabloid headlines and the paparazzi swarming like vultures."

Talia's hand covered mine comfortingly. "I won't let that happen, babe. I've got the publicity team on it. You're covered."

I smiled, and then my head turned slightly as I caught the sound of footsteps echoing from my house, along with voices and laughter. "The boys are here," I murmured, craning my neck to look toward the back door, where Jonny J appeared, followed by Boomer and Sam.

Immediately, Jonny peeled off his tee and shucked off his jeans, his hands whipping down to cover his junk as he ran for my pool. He divebombed in with a loud *whoop* before surfacing and shaking the water from his black hair.

"We're supposed to be having a meeting," Talia yelled, her tone filled with the type of annoyance a mother would show her wayward toddler.

"I'm here, aren't I?" Jonny shouted.

"And he's sober," Boomer muttered, pulling out the chair beside me and dropping into it. "Count your lucky stars."

"You should get in, Saint," Jonny urged. "The water's fine."

"I'm not wearing a bathing suit," I told him.

He grinned. "What about you, Talia?"

She cocked an eyebrow at him disdainfully. "You just wanna see my tits."

"You've seen mine," he laughed. "And can friends really call themselves friends if they haven't seen each other's tits?"

Tally rolled her eyes. "Behave, Jonny. The bodyguards will be here soon. Let's at least *try* to make a good first impression."

Jonny swam to the side of the pool and hoisted himself out. Water sluiced off his glistening muscles, and he didn't bother covering his junk with his hand that time. Instead, he strutted to a pool lounger and grabbed a towel that was neatly folded on it. He dried his hair off, then wrapped it around his Adonis-belted waist before stooping to grab his clothes from the ground where he'd left them.

"Getting dressed," he called over before disappearing inside the house.

Boomer stood from his chair. "Need a piss," he declared, following after Jonny.

Sam glanced at the images, still spread out on the table. "You better put these away before security gets here."

"They want to see everything," Tally explained. "Saint's problem is the reason we've called them in. Granted, you would've needed personal protection soon regardless, but it's escalated because of what's happening."

Sam touched my hand. "I really think if they wanted to hurt you, they would've done it by now. My dad gets this shit all the time, has done for years, and he hasn't been attacked yet. Sometimes, fans just get carried away. I've seen it all my life."

Talia tapped the topless image of me with her finger. "That's a violation."

Sam's gaze came to me, and he smiled. "I'm sorry it frightened you, babe. But it comes with the territory. We don't belong to ourselves anymore. We belong to everybody else."

"Why does it have to be like that?" I asked. "We give them enough of our souls with our music. Can't we keep something for ourselves, too? I don't want a stranger spying on me through windows and taking naked pictures of me without my consent. That's for me, not them."

"You're right," he acquiesced. "I hate the thought of you going through this. You know I'm here if you need me, and the offer to stay at my place still stands. The house is massive, and we've got one of the best security systems in the world. Nobody will get to you there."

"Thank you, Sam," I murmured, meaning it down to my heart. "I'm good for now, but if things get worse, I'll keep your offer in mind." I beamed a smile at him, suddenly grateful that we were able to get over our blip. Back when we slept together, I was a mess. I'd just discovered Jacob had lied to me, and I didn't know what to do with all the emotions I felt, so I tried to drown them in tequila.

It was a big mistake and not one I had any intention of repeating. It wasn't that I didn't like Sam, I loved him, but we made music together, and that shit never went well. The true love of my life was Stevie Nicks, and if there was one thing Stevie had taught me, it was not to shit where I ate, especially when you were in a rock band.

Thinking of my night with Sam made me remember the reason it happened, and my belly gave a little leap.

Over the last few days, I'd been stressing about seeing Jacob again, though I didn't know why. He probably didn't even remember me.

I was embarrassed by what happened because it shouldn't have hurt so much when I discovered his duplicity. It was one night, and I'd told myself I'd forget him over time. But something about Jacob Irons had buried deep inside, and however hard I tried, I couldn't shake him off.

Talia's cell buzzed again, and she plucked it from the table and checked her messages.

"They're here," she announced.

Stomach churning, I went to stand, but she shook her head at me. "I'll go. I'm weirded out that somebody could be waiting with a long-lens camera, ready to pap you again." She stood and headed toward the kitchen, her confident stride belying her tension.

Sam's reassuring hand squeeze didn't do much to calm me down, but I sat straight, filled my lungs, and plastered a smile across my face anyway. Fuck the stalker fan and fuck Jacob. I'd drink my own piss before I let either of them see how much they'd gotten under my skin.

Chatter came from the kitchen, and I turned to see Boomer and Jonny walking out of the patio doors.

"Good timing," I called over. "SDSS boys are here." As the words left my mouth, I caught more movement from the kitchen, and Talia appeared, flanked by four tall, handsome men in dark suits wearing sunglasses.

My heart did a backflip.

Jacob stood out to me straight away. He looked every inch like a professional bodyguard. Tall and built, his designer suit accentuated his broad shoulders and slim waist. His hair was shorter, and he'd lost the mohawk, but he still possessed the same edge as before. Confidence oozed from him, and the rawness from the night we met seemed to reach out and grab me by the throat.

His gaze swept my back patio and garden, assessing every corner like a lion eyeing its territory. Then, his piercing gaze met mine, and for a moment, time seemed to stand still.

My nails dug into my palms under the table, trying to hide the sudden surge of emotion that seeing him again stoked inside me.

The memories of our night together flashed through my mind—his protectiveness and the way he effortlessly diffused the threat of the crazy fan who attacked me settled deep inside, and suddenly, for the first time in weeks, my nerves settled.

I stood to greet the guys while clearing my throat, my smile fixed and strained. "Hey!"

Jacob approached me, stretched out his hand, and rumbled, "Good to see you again, Saint."

He grasped my fingers, and my belly shook at his touch. Squeezing my hand, he immediately dropped it, leaving me cold, before moving to one side to shake hands with Boomer and the rest of the band while allowing his team to greet me.

I sat back down, watching the SDSS guys take seats around the table. My gaze involuntarily drifted towards Jacob's and was met with a familiar twinkle of mischief.

Time hadn't changed him much. He looked more slick than before, but that could've been the suit. A faint grin tugged the corners of his mouth, and he stared at me head-on in silent challenge.

My pulse kicked up a notch.

"Thanks for coming," Talia drawled, her gaze going from one man to the next. "We're grateful you're here on such short notice."

"Wish it was under better circumstances," Jacob murmured, and my stomach fluttered at the deep, rich rumble in his tone. "Can you fill us in?" As he said the words, his stare dipped to the table where the photographs were still strewn, and his body jerked.

Reaching down, he picked up the topless image of me, and his jaw clenched.

Suddenly, I wished the ground would swallow me up.

"How long's it been since you got the first one?" Jacob demanded, looking up to meet my eyes.

I opened my mouth to speak, but my voice faltered.

"The one you're holding is the latest piece of weird in a long line of weirdness," Talia spoke for me. "The gifts began to arrive about a week ago. The weird fan mail goes back months, as far as we know. It could've been longer, but that was when the department that deals with fan mail for the band noticed a pattern."

Jacob's stare slid toward his colleague, who'd introduced himself as Gambit. "He's escalating."

"You think it's a guy?" I asked.

He picked up the image of the butt plug. "This speaks volumes to me, but I've got a brother with connections who can look into these further and profile the sender."

"Like *Criminal Minds*?" Boomer asked.

Jacob examined the other photographs. "Seeing as he's an FBI agent, then yeah."

Sam grinned. "Your brother. Is he as smart as Spencer Reid?"

Jake's eyes snapped up, and he lifted an eyebrow at him. "Nope. My bro's smarter."

"Right on," Sam murmured, visibly impressed.

Jacob reached into his inside pocket and pulled out his phone. After clicking it, he held it to his ear, his blue eyes fixed on mine. He greeted somebody by the name of Colt, then said, "Gonna get some photographs overnight couriered to you. Need a full examination of them and a profile put together."

A wave of calm washed over me, and I closed my eyes.

This was exactly what I needed. Amongst all the anxiety and uncertainty, I couldn't help feeling grateful for Jacob's no-nonsense attitude and air of capability. Despite our complicated past, he was here when I needed him, and okay, he was getting paid for his trouble, but the peace of mind it brought me was priceless.

Jacob was displaying the same protectiveness as the night we met, and it filled me with a sense of comfort that I hadn't felt in weeks. I couldn't have been more appreciative of how his confidence instilled the same assurance in me.

My shoulders relaxed, and for the first time in a long time, a genuine smile crossed my face.

"Thanks, brother. Appreciate you. I'll keep you posted," he muttered before saying his goodbyes and ending the call. Slipping his phone back in his jacket, he leaned across the table to address me. "You don't leave my sight," he stated. "If I go anywhere, Gambit takes over until I get back. He's ex-SAS, British Special Forces, and his instincts are on par with mine. No midnight walks on the beach and no silly games where you decide you don't need protection and try to slip away. This is serious, Saint. Whoever's doin' this to you is getting more desperate for you to notice them. You need to accept that until we catch this guy, you've got a new shadow."

"She'll be good," Talia assured him.

"Need to hear it from you, Saint," he insisted, his icy blue stare still locked with mine.

"Of course," I agreed. "I'm not stupid. It's starting to hit me just how serious the situation is."

As much as I wanted to wave everything off and put it down to an over-enthusiastic fan, I was beginning to see just how dangerous things were becoming. Those topless photographs had made me feel so goddamned vulnerable that it was no longer something I could brush off.

"No unnecessary risks," he ordered.

"Agreed." I gave him a resounding nod and repeated, "No unnecessary risks."

He nodded thoughtfully before turning to his men. "Gambit, you're with Boomer. Ghost with Sam, and Trick with Jonny. We'll keep vigilant around Talia, too. The first thing we need to do is sweep the house, check for anything that shouldn't be here, then walk the perimeter and discuss how we can increase security." He turned back toward the table and tapped the topless image of me angrily while lifting his stare to me. "This is unacceptable, and it won't happen on my watch, but it means you have to play it smart. You can sit out here in the daytime but not at night, and never alone."

"Saint had a new security system fitted a few days ago," Tally relayed.

"We'll need to go over it," Jacob advised her. "I also want the details of the company that fitted it so we can vet them. From now on, wherever Saint and the band go, my guys dig into the people they're meeting in advance. Colt can do a deep dive in minutes, so it shouldn't inconvenience you too much."

Talia grinned. "I'm starting to see just how shitty at security Covershield really is."

Jacob shrugged. "We're ex-military, so we don't cut corners. You may think we're over-cautious at times, but Saint's stalker is getting more confident and more desperate. That confidence may give us an advantage eventually, but in the meantime, I don't want to take any chances."

"It wasn't a criticism," she assured him. "I'm glad you're taking Saint's safety more seriously than Covershield did. Whatever you need from me or the label is yours."

"We'll start with the band's itinerary," Gambit interjected. "We can ping it over to Colt, get him to check everything out, and Trick can plan the routes." His head turned to one of his men. "Right, brother?"

Trick jerked a nod.

"No last-minute bookings," Jacob instructed. "We know stuff can crop up, and we'll work with it, but we need to plan ten steps ahead. That's impossible if you're throwing spanners into the works."

Tally dipped her chin. "Got it."

"Any questions?" Jacob asked.

Silence.

He got to his feet. "We'll sweep the perimeter, look for any gaps in security. Then we'll all settle in with each other. Sound okay?"

We all murmured our agreements, watching as the SDSS guys stood from the table and headed down toward the beach.

My stare followed Jacob's high, muscular ass as he walked away, and my mouth went dry.

"Put your tongue back in, babe," Tally whispered from beside me.

"What?" I muttered, feeling my cheeks pink at being so blatantly caught checking out a member of the opposite sex. I was all about respect and consent, but something about that man messed with my control.

"What's with you and Jacob Irons?" Boomer asked.

Every gaze turned to me, and my warm cheeks began to burn red. I widened my eyes innocently. "Dunno what you mean."

One side of his mouth tilted up. "Did you fuck the bodyguard?"

I raised one brow and glared. "And that's your business, how?"

He raised his hands. "Just asking. If you have, I was gonna suggest we swap bodyguards. Don't want you to feel uncomfortable if there's history there, and if my memory serves me, he was the same guy who helped you out with that lunatic fan at the Festival of Rock a couple of years ago, right?"

My stomach twisted at the thought of losing Jacob as my security. "Yeah, and that's why I don't want to swap bodyguards. I feel safe around him. I didn't know how much I needed that until it was taken away."

My friend leaned to the side and slid his arm around me. "I didn't realize how much all this stalker business had affected you. Why didn't you say something?"

"I didn't know myself, Boom. I thought I was handling it okay until the gifts began to show up. Then those topless images." I swallowed down the sudden surge of emotions. "I'd fucking die if they got into the hands of the tabloids. My dad..." My voice trailed off because the guys and Talia knew about my family dynamic and how screwed up it was.

"It won't come to that," Jonny said reassuringly, nodding toward the spot where Jacob and the other guys were discussing the boundaries of my property. "These guys obviously know what they're doing. I don't think your stalker stands a chance against them. Also, Jake never took his eyes off you. I think if any fucker tried anything, he'd slice their throat."

My heart skipped a beat, but I blanked my face, trying to play it cool even though I felt like punching the air in glee. "Jacob's just doing his job. Don't read too much into it."

Jonny glanced at Boomer, who barked a laugh. "This is gonna be interesting."

I twisted my neck to stare haughtily at my friend. "You've been binge-watching rom-coms again, haven't you?"

"Riiiight," he drawled, his gaze going over my shoulder toward the men. "He couldn't tear his fucking eyes away from you. Don't care what you say; that dude's invested. I'm still trying to work out if he wants to strangle you or fuck you, but either way, you've got him by the balls."

"Know how he feels with the whole strangle fuck thing," Jonny muttered, his stare drifting to Talia. "I feel like that about somebody we know."

"Oh, for fuck's sake, Jonny," Talia snapped. "Stop being so goddamned dramatic. I've told you. I don't take shits on my own doorstep. It's too messy, and I hate having to clean up. Go find yourself some airhead reality star who'll bleed you dry for everything you've got before sucking the life out of you." She paused, holding a finger in the air and looking thoughtful. "Oh, wait... didn't you just impregnate one?"

"Told ya," he drawled. "It's not mine."

"This time," she bandied back pointedly. "You won't be so lucky if you carry on giving Don Juan a run for his money."

"Don who?" he asked, his eyebrows drawing together.

"God help me," Tally said with a sigh. "It's like running a damned kindergarten. Thank God for Saint, or I would've walked years ago."

I grinned because that was such a lie.

Tally loved us, but I suspected she loved Jonny J the most. Not that she'd ever admit it, though I couldn't blame her for that. Relationships within bands never worked out well, and when everything imploded, you were stuck with an ex whose guts you either still loved with all your heart or hated with all your soul. And to top it all off, you had to face them every damned day.

Yikes.

My eyes drifted to where Jacob stood chatting with his men, and I wondered if it was the same for bodyguards.

As much as I yearned to believe Jonny and Boomer about Jacob having feelings for me, I knew it was a lost cause.

Even if Jake was single now, he still hurt me last time, and that wasn't something I could forgive easily. It was going to be hard to stay aloof and even harder not to smile into his eyes like a lovestruck fool.

But he was here to do a job, and I was going to let him because I might not have trusted him romantically, but he'd only ever shown me care when it came to keeping me physically safe. Right now, he was exactly the man I needed around me.

If anybody could keep the monsters at bay, it was Jacob Irons.

But I couldn't help wondering who would keep my heart at bay from *him*.

Chapter Five

Iceman

"All the producers and sound engineers have come up clean, brother," Colt relayed down the phone. "Checked the interns, the receptionist. Hell, I even did a deep dive on the cleaning ladies. All good."

I stared out of the glass bi-fold doors into Saint's backyard, where she was sitting on a sun lounger, scribbling on a notepad. "That helps. They're mainly in the rehearsal studio this week. They've got an industry party tomorrow night, but it's a closed-door event for Dischordium's new release. Carbine keeps his shit tight, and he knows what's goin' on with Saint, so he's no doubt already alerted his band's security."

"That fucker will probably carry and conceal himself," Colt muttered. "He thinks the world of Saint."

My eyebrows pulled together. "Huh?"

"Yeah," Colt confirmed. "You think he'd have gone to all this trouble for her if he didn't? Noah raves about her. Says Saint, along with Maeve O'Shea, are the coolest chicks he's ever met."

"Blue De Santis can't stand her," I pointed out.

Colt snorted. "Blue De Santis probably tried to get into Saint's pants and got told to fuck off. He's a whiny little fucker, has been since the band hit the big time. The fucker's ego's through the roof these days."

"That's what he said about Saint," I murmured, almost to myself.

"I'd take everything Blue says with a grain of salt," Colt advised. "I'd hardly call him the fount of knowledge when it comes to treating women well."

One shoulder lifted in a shrug. "True."

Saint's brow furrowed in concentration, a lock of hair fell over one eye, and I smiled as she tucked it behind her ear, engrossed in her writing. "Can you check out the record execs next? Her stalker knows where she lives, but it's not easy information to get. Saint keeps her life on the down-low. She doesn't go to the opening of an envelope or court publicity. I can't shake the feeling there's more to this."

"I'm already working on it," he confirmed. "Not found anything solid yet. I'll keep digging, and I've sent the images to the profilers. They've already started to build a background, and they'll step that up as soon as the originals get delivered."

The second I saw the topless shots of Saint, a knot formed in my stomach that hadn't unraveled yet. The attention was unhealthy and sinister, and although she was putting on a brave face, I could see how much it had shaken her up.

"How's things there?" Colt asked.

"Worked in shittier places," I relayed. "Saint's house is on the beach. I'm surrounded by bikini-clad babes, rock bands, music, and showbiz parties. It ain't bad."

"It's fake as fuck," he corrected.

"Yeah," I breathed. "It is. Still, I'm here to do a job, and I'll do it to the best of my abilities. Just wish we'd been called in before all this. I can't help feeling that management left it a little late to call in reinforcements. We could have been ahead of all this."

"You think Talia Fields is behind it?" Colt asked.

"I'm not ruling anyone out. I don't get the gut feeling Talia's to blame, but who knows? This industry is crazy."

"Those gifts are sexual, so it's either a gay woman or a male. It's definitely somebody who fantasizes about Saint."

"That rules Talia out then," I mused. "She's straight."

"She could swing both ways," Colt said. "Look, I'm playing devil's advocate here. My gut tells me it's a guy. I don't think you've anything to worry about with Talia Fields, though I agree it's weird she waited so long to get Saint some help."

"In her defense, they must get a lot of this. It's a different world, brother. I know you grew up rich as Midas, but fame is a whole other ball game. Talia told me that initially, the letters and gifts were nothing out of the ordinary. Certainly not weird enough to call in specialists. As soon as shit got worrisome, she made moves to protect the band."

I pushed off the door frame, my eyes still fixated on Saint as her eyes dropped to her notepad, and she jotted something down. "Thanks for checking, Colt. Keep me posted."

"Goes without sayin', brother. Later," he replied before ending the call.

I slipped my phone back into my suit jacket, my eyes still glued to the woman whose face had haunted me for two years.

Seeing Saint again affected me in ways I couldn't explain. Just functioning like a normal person around her took every piece of self-control I had.

Jesus Christ, I wanted to kiss her, ached for it, but I had to ignore the urge and keep her at arm's length.

Over time, I'd tried to convince myself that I'd exaggerated the connection I felt for her, that maybe

I'd inflated its significance to fill the void Allie left, but seeing Saint again and feeling the pull between us shattered the lie.

She was spectacular.

The smart thing would have been to swap places with Gambit, or better still, get on the first flight home and send somebody else in my place, but after seeing those photographs and understanding the seriousness of the situation, there was no way I was leaving Saint McClure, at least not until I'd caught the fucker tormenting her.

The air between us felt charged, as if there was a storm brewing, and I was about to get caught up in its force. It was becoming clear that I wouldn't be able to ignore her pull. Maybe I should just tell her once and for all how her disappearing from my life had shredded me.

Or maybe I needed to keep my big ol' mouth shut and just let things play out in the way they were meant to. Saint was going through a lot, and the last thing she wanted was an old flame piling on the pressure.

My job was to make her life easier, not to make her feel even more uncomfortable. I was the help, and she was my boss, my ward, and a client. She was the woman I was being paid to protect. Therefore, I needed to keep my mind on the goddamned job.

Except I couldn't keep denying her pull.

The truth was, I hadn't just missed her. She'd been missing from me. And I didn't quite know what to do with that.

Saint glanced up from her notepad, and our eyes locked.

Something flashed behind her expression, and then her face blanked of all emotion as she mentally pulled herself together. Her appearance may have changed, but she still wore her heart on her sleeve, and it was a comfort that despite all her success, she hadn't lost that quality.

The urge to kiss her reared up again, but instead of going outside, grabbing her by the throat, and angling her face into a position to take my tongue, I broke our stare, went to her refrigerator, and pulled out a pitcher of juice with fruit floating in it. After pouring two glasses, I carried them outside, approached the sun lounger, and handed her one.

The familiar scent of her perfume—hints of jasmine and vanilla—wrapped around my senses. A memory flashed through my mind of tasting Saint's skin while I moved inside her, and my cock stirred.

She must've picked up on my dirty thoughts because her cheeks pinked up prettily. She tucked a lock of hair behind her ear, a nervous habit I remembered from our life-changing—at least for me—night together.

"You wearin' sunscreen?" I asked, sounding like a fucking idiot.

She grinned and gazed up at me with azure eyes. "Yeah, but thanks for caring."

I let out a snort and walked over to the shaded table on the patio where we'd sat earlier and flopped down in a chair, making sure to manspread to fuck so Saint could get a good look at my junk.

Her eyes went there immediately, and I bit back a smirk.

Not so fucking immune after all.

"Whatcha doin'?" I asked.

"Writing."

"Whatcha writing?"

"A song."

I cocked an eyebrow. "Just like that? You're writing a song?"

"Well, contrary to popular belief, they don't write themselves, Jacob," she sassed. "And contrary to the asshole naysayers, nobody writes them for me."

I leaned forward, elbows to knees, drink hanging from my fingers. "Talk to me like that again, and I'll put you over my knee."

She burst out laughing. "You'd have to catch me first."

"I'll lock you in my lair," I threatened, a smile tugging at the corners of my mouth.

She hitched a pretty, dark eyebrow. "Or maybe I'll lock you in mine."

A chuckle escaped my throat, and I took a sip of my drink. "I wouldn't know the first thing about writing a song. It must be pretty complicated."

She lifted one shoulder in a shrug. "It's as complicated as you make it. I find clearing my head and letting my emotions do the talking is the best way to get the words out. It's like any other job; you have good days and bad days. Sometimes, everything flows and seems to come together all by itself. Other days, you have to work at it." She smiled. "Maybe I'll give you a lesson sometime."

I leaned back in my chair, crossing my legs at the ankle. "I'd need more than a few lessons to match your talent."

Her smile faded, and she murmured, "Flattery will get you everywhere, Jacob."

A warm feeling spread through me at the sound of my name on her lips.

I'd always loved the way Saint spoke. Even when she wasn't singing, her voice was beautiful, and sometimes, her words were so poetic that it made my heart beat faster. Two years had passed since we'd had a moment like this, but it felt like yesterday.

"So," I began, trying to keep the mood light despite the weight of loss I felt at being without her for so goddamned long. "What's the song about?"

"Love," she murmured. "Loss, yearning, and wishing things could've been different."

"Thought you'd write about your stalker," I muttered, trying to tamp down the uneasy feelings that the meaning behind her words evoked. "Isn't that what songwriters do? Take inspiration from their lives?"

Her azure blue eyes bored into mine. "None of my wounds came from adversaries, Jake. They all came from the people who said they loved me."

I cleared my throat, trying to contain the flood of emotions threatening to drown me. "Poet's soul," I murmured to myself.

Saint looked at me quizzically.

"That's what you told me the night we met," I reminded her. "You've got a poet's soul."

"You remember that?" she breathed.

"Yeah," I admitted. "I remember everything."

"Then why..." Her words trailed off as if the question suddenly became too hard to ask.

"Why what?" I prompted.

Her deep sigh was audible, and I watched, fascinated, as once again she blanked her expression. "Nothing." She stood from the sun lounger. "Are you hungry?"

I checked my watch, realizing I hadn't eaten for hours. It was nine P.M. in DC but only six P.M. here. "Starving."

She gestured toward the kitchen. "I'll show you where everything is. I have a housekeeper who comes in three times a week, so she'll keep on top of your laundry and take your dry cleaning to be done with mine. I also have a chef bring meals in, so there's a freezer full of high-protein dinners and lunches you can help yourself to. If there's anything in particular you want, write it down, and I'll ask Catalina to pick it up."

Draining my drink, I stood and followed Saint into her huge, white kitchen. I took in the sleek lines and clean appliances, noting how it still felt homely even though it probably cost more than most people earned in a year.

Saint walked to an integrated tall freezer and opened the door wide. "You've got mainly chicken and salmon meals. But if you dig deep in the pantry, you'll find some pasta somewhere."

I walked toward her and picked up a few of the containers, frowning at how light they weighed. "Probably need six of these and a plate of potatoes to fill me up, babe," I muttered.

"I'll ask Cat to grab some on her way here in the morning. Do you want steak too?"

"Yeah, and bacon, sausage links, pancakes, fresh bread, not the packet shit, proper bread from a bakery, and real dairy butter." I went to her fridge and checked inside to see mostly fruit, veggies, and drinks. "Eggs, milk—the real stuff, not diet shit—and caramel creamer."

"I'd better add coffee to the list in that case," she muttered.

My eyes widened. "You don't have coffee? You love coffee."

"Yeah, with cream and sugar," she bandied back. "That's why I don't drink it anymore."

My head reared back. "Please don't tell me you're on a diet."

"My entire life is one big diet," she stated. "Luckily the Ozempic stops me from being hungry."

I felt a muscle twitch in my jaw. "What the fuck you on that stuff for? You're not fat."

"No, I'm not," she agreed. "Because I take Ozempic. You're in Hollywood now, Jake. It's the staple diet in these parts."

My jaw dropped at how blasé she was about it. Weight-loss medication had its place for sure, but she didn't need it. I tried to wrap my head around the fact that somebody so beautiful and so perfect could be made to feel like she needed to take such extreme measures.

Fuck Hollywood and its unattainable standards.

I shook my head, not wanting to accept her explanation. "You're perfect now, but I also thought you were perfect with more curves. You shouldn't have to change yourself to make other people happy."

Saint let out a brittle laugh. "Thanks. I actually agree with you. I never concerned myself with a number on the scales, and when I walk away from all this, the first thing I'll do is eat a cheeseburger. But trust me, Jake. If you lived here long enough and moved in my circles, you'd understand why people resort to extreme measures. I have a lot of people relying on me to maintain a certain image. Then there's social media, the showbiz magazines, and the trolls who comment on every extra pound. It's bullshit, but it's also part of the job."

A sudden surge of protectiveness rose up along with the fierce need to shield her from the vultures who preyed on women's insecurities.

My jaw clenched so hard that I thought I'd crack a tooth.

I'd never been a fan of skinny women, and honestly, most of the men I knew didn't give a fuck about it either. In fact, the majority of my buddies loved curves, tits, and ass. There was nothing better than cuddling up to something soft and sweet at the end of the day, so the thought of somebody as beautiful and talented as Saint allowing assholes to dictate what she ate made my blood heat in my veins.

It was fake bullshit.

I needed to change the subject before I got an ass hair to hunt down the doctor who'd prescribed weight-loss meds to a perfectly healthy woman who clearly didn't fucking need them.

"What time do you wanna go to rehearsal tomorrow?" I asked.

Saint picked a meal from the freezer and walked over to the microwave. "About ten, if that's okay? The boys usually roll in about lunchtime, but I like to arrive early to get in the zone. I also need to speak to our producer about an arrangement that's bugging me." She popped the container in the microwave and pressed some buttons to start it.

"That's cool," I assured her. "Is there anywhere I can work out?"

"I have a small gym upstairs. Just weights, a treadmill, bicycle. A punching bag and rowing machine, but it should do the job. Also got a sauna out back. If you want a more professional setup, there's a gym about a mile away. I used to go there, but when the album blew up, people started to take my picture without me knowing and sold them to the tabloids, so that put an end to that." She shrugged. "Shame really. I always loved going."

"Got a boxing gym close by?" I asked.

"No idea. Maybe if you go further into the city, you'll find something."

"I'll Google it," I declared, watching her stop the microwave to give her food a stir and pop it back in again to finish heating. "Come with me. I'll make sure nobody bothers you. It's what I'm here for."

She stilled before slowly turning her head toward me and whispering, "Thanks. I'd like that."

Fuck.

She spoke like I'd offered her the world.

"It's just a gym trip, babe," I told her gruffly. "Not Disneyland."

She turned and leaned her back against the counter. "I don't get to do normal stuff anymore. I miss the gym, grocery shopping, walking on the beach, coffee shops, and honkytonk bars." Her eyes took on a faraway look. "More than anything, I miss having a dog."

Without a thought, I reached out and rested my hand on her shoulder. "Why can't you have a dog?"

She smiled sadly. "I travel too much, and I can't leave the house to walk it. I'm in rehearsals or the studio, and on tour, or doing publicity. It's hard to devote the time to anything else."

"Bit dramatic," I muttered.

She laughed. "Maybe. But walk in my shoes for a few days, and you'll see."

"If you want it, make it work," I told her. "Stop making excuses. No reason you can't take a dog with you to the studio and places. You're a fuckin' rock star. You can do what you want."

A slow smile spread across her face. "True. But can you imagine the headlines? Diva Saint McClure makes outlandish demands about her dog."

"Meh." I shrugged. "You'd be a legend amongst other dog owners, and it's way more interesting than the headlines calling you a diva for making your assistant pick out all the red M&Ms."

She let out another soft laugh. "Thanks, Jacob. You're good at putting things into perspective. Sometimes, I get caught up in it all too much, and I need somebody to bring me back down to Earth. The gifts and photographs haven't helped." Her eyes drifted to mine, and my heart clenched at the emptiness in them. "I'm starting to wonder if it's all worth it."

"Aren't you happy?" I asked.

She frowned. "I haven't been truly happy since..." Her voice trailed off, her eyes still locked with mine, and for the third time that day, I watched her shoulders straighten as she mentally pulled herself together. "Anyway. You don't want to hear me whine. There's nothing worse than some spoiled, rich rock star who has it all complaining about her amazing life."

The pressures she faced didn't sit right with me. The entertainment industry had toxic expectations, and Saint seemed to be struggling with them. Still, she showed grace and humility, even self-deprecation, so the girl I met two years before was still in there.

Still, the world-weary look behind her eyes made me yearn to reach out, take her hand, pull her close, and soothe the tension away. I wanted more than anything to be that for her, but after ghosting me, it was clear she didn't.

That was why I watched her take her ridiculously minuscule portion of bland chicken and vegetables from the microwave and dump it on a plate. It was also why I kept my hands glued to my sides as she grabbed a fork and then turned her back on me as she walked into another room to eat.

And lastly, it was why I sighed and pulled my cell back out to look at the DoorDash app so I could order some real fucking food, all the while thinking how much I fucking hated this town.

All that glittered certainly wasn't goddamned gold.

Chapter Six

Saint

"I love that bridge," Skip declared. "It's fuckin' Taylor worthy."

"I'll take that as a compliment," I murmured with a smile. "Love TS or hate her; everyone knows she's the queen of the bridge."

"After releasing that, you will be, too," my producer muttered, holding a headphone against his right ear. "That melody is fire. What the fuck's got into you today?"

My eyes drifted toward the window, where I could see Jacob sitting in the green room, typing on a laptop.

I knew exactly what had inspired me. Jake had been my muse since the night I met him. There was no rhyme or reason to it, but then there didn't have to be. Emotions and feelings had no rhyme or reason anyway.

"Who knows?" I shrugged.

"That arrangement's been bugging me for days," Skip went on. "Something about it wasn't right, but I couldn't work out what was annoying me. That change of key in the middle is genius. It really adds the layer we were missing."

"Sometimes it's the simplest things," I agreed. "It came to me last night, so I tried it out on my mixing desk at home, and bam, suddenly it just came together."

"I think that song's finished now," he told me.

Slowly, I nodded. "Yeah. I'm happy with it, too."

Jacob looked up, and our eyes locked. His smile took me by surprise, and without thinking about it, I beamed a smile back.

I'd been watching him on and off ever since we'd arrived at rehearsals a few hours earlier.

The sight of him there, focused and lost in whatever he was doing, stirred something inside me.

Jacob had struck a chord that kept resonating and refused to be ignored. It felt like we'd never been apart. The familiarity of his presence still settled me. Jacob was a paradox—tall, strong, and alpha as hell, but still almost childlike, mischievous, and unpredictable.

It was his mix of strength and vulnerability that drew me in from the moment we met, along with the rawness just underneath the surface that threatened to burst free when I least expected it.

Thrilling.

Enthralling.

Consuming.

An enigma that hijacked every thought and feeling.

Reaching for my pen, I opened my notepad to a clean, blank page and began to write. My mind was already elsewhere, formulating words and melodies simply because I couldn't help myself.

Art was created when I was inspired.

My poet's soul reared its head, and I became lost in the words buzzing around my brain like bees desperate to get out.

I poured my heart out, not even noticing when, one by one, the rest of the band arrived or even when Talia stuck her head around the door to say hi. By the time I was ready to tear my focus away from the song I was writing, the afternoon sun had moved across the sky, and my stomach rumbled from hunger.

The door to the sound room opened, and I glanced up to see Jacob move inside, holding a takeout juice drink and a big plastic bowl of salad.

"Eat," he ordered.

I took the food from him, asking, "What's the time?"

"Coming up to three. Your boys have been jamming out in the rehearsal room. They told me to leave you to write, or else you'd turn into a Banshee."

I chuckled. "The only time I get snappy is when somebody interrupts my writing process. When I'm in the zone, I like to stay there, or else I lose my train of thought."

"You're being okay with me now," Jacob pointed out.

"I just finished," I explained, opening the top of the clear plastic container and grabbing the plastic fork that came with it. "This looks good. Thanks."

"Have you eaten anything today?" he asked.

My heart fluttered at his concern. "Only the big pile of eggs you made me this morning."

He grinned. "Anyone would think I was one of those weird feeders."

"Aren't you?" I challenged, eyeing the salad pointedly.

"If I were, that salad would be tacos," he muttered, nodding toward my lunch. "Not shrimp and goddamned chicken rabbit food."

"I love shrimp and chicken," I muttered, forking a heap of food into my mouth.

"So do I when it's from a Chinese restaurant."

I chewed my food and swallowed. "I love Chinese food, too."

He flashed me his sexy grin again, "We went to a Chinese place after the festival, remember?"

"Yeah," I breathed before turning his words from the day before back on him. "I remember everything."

Jacob's gaze flickered as it held mine, and for a moment, I was transported back to the time we spent together.

A flicker of resentment ignited inside me.

We were both there that night, and I knew he felt the same things I felt. It hurt knowing how easily he'd carried on with his life when, without my music, I think I would've fallen apart.

Jacob cleared his throat, his face taking on a guarded look as he stepped back.

"Enjoy your lunch," he said, his entire aura suddenly distant. Then I watched him turn around and leave, his easy demeanor replaced by a tension I couldn't explain.

It was like he'd closed the curtains on his emotions, and I was on the outside trying to see in, only to be shut out.

I stabbed at my food, trying to shake off the unexpected ache in my belly from the surge of emotions. Maybe I needed to purge my feelings into a song and just move the fuck on already.

I felt my throat start to tingle.

God only knew why I kept trying to flog the dead horse that was Jacob Irons. It may have felt right, and our connection may have been stronger than I'd ever experienced before, but sometimes, what felt true and honest, in reality, was very wrong.

And after two years, it was time to start accepting it.

I spied Boomer's approach through the glass window. He opened the door, poking his head around it. "Are we gonna rehearse the new arrangement? Skip's gone over everything with us, and we've got it down. We just need your eight-string and some vocals."

Boomer's easy energy lightened the heaviness in the room, and I forced a smile, pushing away all thoughts of Jacob. "On my way." Then, grabbing my salad, drink, and notepad, I followed my friend to the rehearsal room.

"How do you like the changes?" I asked, walking over to Sam to give him a one-armed hug, then fist-bumping Jonny, who was already sitting at his drum kit.

Just being amongst my bandmates lifted my spirits, and suddenly, I felt lighter. This was what I needed to focus on. Whenever I stood up with my boys, my troubles melted away until all that was left was the music.

When we started the band, we swore we wouldn't sell out and that everything we did would be about the music. Back then, we were naïve, sweet summer children who looked at the world through rose-tinted glasses. Over time, I learned that along with success came expectations, and I found most of the pressures fell on me.

This business was harder for women. We had to work twice as hard as the men to achieve the same accolades, and even then, we were judged harsher, criticized more, and had to endure so much overt misogyny that some days, I just wanted to walk away.

Because of that, I tended to pick my battles wisely. I lost weight in order to help the record company cash in on my image. I listened to the stylist who was forced on me, and I smiled sweetly in interviews whenever the journalists asked the boys about the music while asking me about my love life.

It was worth all of that because if I did as I was told, I found that creatively, the record company left me alone. But then, it was in their interests, seeing as I made them millions of dollars.

I knew if I worked hard and played their game, one day I could dictate my terms, and it would be the record company who'd have to fall into line with my wishes. I could eventually set up my own label and have full control of everything, but until then, I had to keep on keeping on and smile my way through all the bullshit.

Jonny counted us in on three, and I felt a semblance of peace wash over me.

Boomer began to play the opening riff to the song I'd rearranged earlier, and the resonating beat kicked in.

I closed my eyes and began to strum the accompanying chords while Sam slapped out the bassline. Then, I stepped up close to the microphone, opened my mouth, and began to sing.

"Lovin' that new bridge, Saint," Jonny said approvingly from the couch opposite. "That key change really elevates it." His hand dived into a bag of Goldfish crackers, and he tossed a handful in his mouth.

"Thanks. I don't know why I missed it before, it seems so obvious now we've changed it."

Boomer nudged me from my side. "I've told you before. Stop doing that."

I laughed. "I accepted the compliment."

"You did, then you followed it up with a jibe at yourself about missing the key change. Remember when you taught me that songwriting's a process, and sometimes it takes time for every component to fall into place?"

"Okay," I acquiesced good-naturedly. "You've made your point."

"Good," he muttered.

"Are we all going to the Dischordium party tonight?" Sam asked. "I've asked Jolie to come with me. It'd be good if you all met her."

I grimaced slightly.

The party would be cool, but I was exhausted. Songwriting always took it out of me emotionally, and with Jacob and the rest of the security team hanging around the studio all day, I'd had to concentrate more to keep my focus.

A couple of times, Jake had walked past the window, and I'd forgotten the words or bummed a note, which wasn't like me at all.

All I wanted to do was go home and curl up in front of the TV, but I'd made a commitment to show my support, and after everything Noah had done for me and the band recently, I didn't want to let him down.

"I'll go, see their set, then leave. I want to get some sleep tonight because I want to spend tomorrow working out the arrangement for the new song I wrote earlier."

"Thought we were having a rest day tomorrow?" Jonny cut in. "Was gonna party tonight. It's been a while since I've gotten wasted."

Boomer barked a laugh. "It's been three days, dude."

"That's what I said," Jonny muttered indignantly. "A while."

Sam chuckled. "Just keep the drunken lurching to a minimum." His eyes met mine. "Are you coming into the studio tomorrow?"

I shook my head. "Not much point. I'll do it at my home studio. It'll work for what I need."

"Want me to come over?" Boomer asked.

"I can come too," Sam offered. "I could bring Jolie."

My heart warmed because I knew they were trying to support me and take my mind off all the negative stalker bullshit. "Thanks, but you should make the most of your day off. I won't be working for long, and it's not like we get much time to ourselves these days."

"Sooo," Jonny murmured delicately, throwing a cracker at Sam. "You gonna tell us about this girl of yours?"

Sam dodged the cheesy Goldfish, picked it up, and threw it back at Jonny's head. "What can I say. She's beautiful, sweet, and smart."

Jonny grinned, waggling his eyebrows. "Sure she is. You're with her for her intelligence, right?"

"I wouldn't date her if she had nothing to say for herself." He grinned. "But I'd still fuck her. She's hot."

I shot the boys a glare. "Can we not talk about women like they're sex objects? I thought I'd enlightened you assholes about that years ago."

Boomer nudged me. "To be fair, Saint, she opens and closes Victoria's Secret shows, and she's got good tits. I'm more than a little curious about her."

"So, meet her and ask her about her life," I bit out. "You don't have to do what these guys do and talk about her like a fuck toy. Women are here to do more than service your dicks, and to downplay her for just being a model with good tits is disrespectful. She's probably got more brains than all three of you pricks put together, seeing as those tits you love so much are earning her a damned fortune. Maybe think of that before you degrade her to a fuck toy." Through my anger, I didn't notice the door opening behind me.

Jonny rolled his eyes. "Chill out, babe. You on the rag or somethin'?"

"Jonnyyy," Boomer murmured, drawing the name out with warning in his tone.

"No, I'm not, shithead," I snapped. "Are you? I mean, you are acting like a little bitch."

"That's a fuckin' joke, comin' from the biggest bitch of them all," Jonny shot back. "You think you're so much better than everyone else, but you're just another wannabe riding the coattails. In an alternate universe, you'd be a groupie, sweetheart. In this one, you just got lucky."

"Shut your fuckin' mouth, Jonny," Boomer warned, eyeing something over my shoulder.

"Who made you the fuckin' boss? You're getting as whiny as that cunt," Jonny spat out, nodding toward me.

I went to launch myself at the asshole when suddenly, I was pushed out of the way. My head whipped around to see Jacob stalking across the room, and in a flash, he had Jonny hauled up against the wall.

"Who the fuck are you calling a cunt?" Jacob rasped, his face in Jonny's with his hand gripping his throat.

Jonny J's eyes bugged from the pressure of Jacob's hand.

The other security guys all moved toward the two men, closing in.

"Let him go, Ice," Gambit ordered.

Jake's growl came from deep in his chest.

"I think he should strangle the fucker," Sam said dryly, lounging across the couch nonchalantly, clearly enjoying the drama that was unfolding.

"Not helping, brother," Boomer muttered.

Without missing a beat, Jacob's grip tightened on Jonny's throat, his icy blue eyes blazing with fury, and he rasped low and menacing, "Say it again, fucknut. I dare ya."

Jonny struggled against Jacob's hold, gasping for air as the other security guys hovered. Trick, Jonny's bodyguard, moved in closer, his expression taut. "Put him down, Ice. You don't know where he's been."

But Jacob wasn't having a bar of it. His jaw clenched, and his muscles bunched as if he were about to do a lot more than choke the air out of Jonny.

Sam barked a laugh. "This is the most fun I've had all week."

Boomer shot Sam a look of disbelief before turning back to Jacob. "Come on, man. Let him go. Jonny's not normally this much of an asshole. He's coming down from a high and taking it out on the wrong person."

Jacob's glower never left Jonny J. "Say sorry," he snarled.

Jonny fought for air.

"Maybe loosen your grip a little, Iceman," Trick suggested with a hint of laughter in his tone. "He can't grovel while you're choking him to death."

I watched, fascinated, as Jacob's hand relaxed, and he begrudgingly dropped his arm.

Jonny sucked in air and doubled over, coughing uncontrollably.

A loud *harrumph* came from the door, and Talia's voice demanded, "What the fuck's going on?"

"Nothing," Sam called out breezily. "Security's about to murder Jonny, is all."

I looked around to see Talia stomp toward the men. She popped her hip, folded her arms across her chest, and snapped, "What the fuck did you do now?"

Jonny J, still bent double, stretched a hand out and pointed at Jacob. "I want him fired," he rasped.

"Oh, stop being a big baby," Tally retorted, rolling her eyes. "You were lucky Jacob got to you before Saint did. She'd have kicked your balls so far up your stomach that they'd be tickling your tonsils right about now. What did you do this time?" She looked around the room and demanded, "Well?"

"He called me a cunt," I told her, lips twitching.

Talia rolled her eyes. "That's rich coming from the biggest cunt in the room." Her glare slid back to Jonny, and she cocked an eyebrow. "Do I need to book you into rehab?"

His lips thinned frustratedly, and he shook his head curtly.

"Any more shit from you, and I'll ship you out to the Arizona desert so quickly you'll think you've been transported by tractor beam," Tally warned. "If you're struggling with booze and pills, speak up. I can't help you unless you talk to me."

"I'm good," Jonny muttered. "Just need an early night.

"Well, that's tough," she argued. "You've got the Dischordium party tonight. I suggest you all go home, grab a couple of hours' rest, then turn up for the cameras refreshed and rejuvenated."

Jacob stood there, his expression unreadable as he folded his muscled arms across his bulky chest. The short sleeves of his shirt tightened around his tattooed biceps that popped out as he tensed his arms.

My belly wobbled.

I could sense he was fighting to get himself back under control. His mouth was an angry line, and a muscle ticked in his jaw with suppressed rage.

It was moments like these when I was reminded of the raw power that lay dormant underneath Jacob's friendly demeanor. He had a way about him that put everybody around him at ease, but another side of him simmered under the surface. It was the side that made me feel as if he'd burn the world down before he ever let anything hurt me.

The same side that made me feel safe.

"That's enough drama for one day, boys," Talia declared, her firm tone holding a hint of exasperation. "Let's focus on the real threat at hand instead of bickering amongst ourselves."

Jonny straightened to his full height, and his hand went to his neck, still red with the force of Jacob's hold. "I mean it, Talia. I want him out."

Our manager's stare slashed toward him. "And I mean it when I tell *you* that if you continue to abuse the woman in this band the way you just did, I'll replace you quicker than the time it takes you to shoot your cum into a groupie with a golden snatch. Then I'll sue your scrawny, spoiled, entitled, booze-ridden ass for every penny you haven't already wasted by snorting it up your good-for-nothing nose. Since when did it become acceptable for you to call the woman who writes the songs that keep you in booze and drugs a cunt? Since when did it become okay for you to speak to *anybody* in this band with that much disrespect? You can banter all day long, Jonny; it's all good with me. But when you take it to a place where security has to pin you against a wall by the throat, you start becoming a fucking liability. I hired Iceman to protect Saint. He did his job. End of. Get it? Got it? Good. Now, do yourself a favor, and move the fuck on because I'm starting to lose patience."

The room fell completely silent except for Sam, who barked out another laugh.

Jonny's eyes narrowed on our manager, and then he pushed off the wall and stormed out the door, slamming it behind him.

Tally looked to the heavens, letting out an audible sigh.

Jacob's eyes turned on me, still blazing from his altercation with Jonny, and he rasped, "You okay?"

I beamed. "Yep!"

The angry flush faded from his neck, and I watched his shoulders slump as he physically relaxed. "I get it if you want me off the job," he declared. "But none of us are the type of men who'll stand by and watch any asshole speak to women in that way when they've done nothing to deserve it."

"Agreed," Trick muttered in his hybrid American-Irish accent. "If Ice goes, we all do."

"Nobody's going anywhere," Talia announced. "Jonny's got to get his booze and drug problem under control. It was only a matter of time before something like this happened. He's been getting out of hand to the point where me and Boomer have to organize damage control every time we let him loose. Jonny has to either wake the fuck up or get the fuck to rehab. If being pinned against a wall by a burly fucker with shovels for hands doesn't give him the wake-up call he needs, I don't know what will." She huffed out a breath. "Though if you attack him again, make sure you don't break his fingers. He needs to be able to hold his drumsticks."

Boomer chuckled. "You're all heart, Tally."

Her eyes twinkled with humor. "You know me, Boom. Full of sweetness and light." She clapped her hands together twice. "Come on. Let's get the fuck outta here. I've got to go get myself beautified for tonight's star-studded party. After Jonny's performance, I've decided I don't want to work anymore, so I need to find myself a sugar daddy. Better still, if he's too old to want any sugar." She gave us big eyes. "I need to look extra pretty if I'm gonna reel that decrepit fucker in."

The boys all began to laugh, except for Trick, who stared at Talia with open admiration.

"Come on, assholes," she yelled. "Let's get moving. Time's a ticking."

Jacob walked up beside me. "You ready?"

I nodded, smiling, still warmed by the way he had my back. "Yeah. Just need to get my purse. It's in the sound room."

"I'll grab it," he offered, giving his team chin lifts as they shouted out their goodbyes.

The second everyone had left, Talia sidled up to me. "Dunno what's going on with Iceman, babe, but he's acting like a man on a mission. I think we chose correctly when we picked SDSS to look after you all. For a hot minute there, I thought he was going to rip Jonny's head off."

"I know," I murmured, biting my lip thoughtfully.

"It gave me cunt flutters," she added, staring in the direction Jacob had disappeared to.

"I know," I repeated, turning to her and making an 'eek' face.

"You're gonna have to jump on that D soon, babe," she warned. 'Cause if you don't, I will."

I sighed wistfully. "He's married, remember?"

Talia actually looked crestfallen. "I forgot about that."

"Lucky you," I drawled. "It's all I've thought about for the last two years."

Her eyes sparkled with mischief. "At least tonight you can make the fucker jealous."

My eyebrows pulled together. "How am I going to do that?"

"Spoke to Hunter just before I arrived here," she announced. "He's going to the party with you. I explained how Jacob 'Iceman' Irons fucked you over. He's on board to make some memories with his beautiful singer-songwriter girlfriend and in full view of her bodyguard, too." Her lips twisted in amusement. "I've arranged to get some outfits sent over to your place in an hour, so you better hurry home."

Slowly, I closed my eyes, and my heart sank. "Tally," I wailed softly. "What did you do?"

"You can thank me later, sweet Saint," she crowed. "Because by the end of tonight, Jacob Irons will know exactly what he's missing, and he won't be able to stand it." An evil grin spread across her face. "Hunter's going to make sure of that."

Chapter Seven

Iceman

Somewhere between getting pissy with Saint for making me want her so fucking much that my wayward dick kept hardening whenever she threw a smile my way and pinning Jonny 'fuckwit' Jansen up against the wall by the throat, I'd decided that me and the sexy little rock star needed to have a talk.

My aim was to do that on the way home from the studios, but Colt had other ideas when he called me to discuss the profile the FBI had put together on Saint's stalker.

Colt was right; it was a straight male, aged between thirty and forty, and he had money. He was successful, confident, entitled, and thought the world owed him something.

Basically, the majority of the male population of Hollywood.

By the time Colt hung up, we were already at Saint's beach house, and she'd wandered upstairs to get ready. While she was out of the way, I checked the alarms and cameras and made sure the motion sensors were all working as they should be. Then I took in a delivery of a fuck ton of dresses for her before hustling to my room to grab a shower.

I stepped under the hot spray, the water cascading over my tense muscles and washing away the day's frustration. The second I heard Jonny J call Saint a cunt, I saw red. I didn't remember how I got to him. All I recalled was how the devil himself couldn't have held me back.

I was nowhere near over Saint, but that wasn't exactly a shocker. If I were honest with myself, I was aware of my lingering feelings even before yesterday when I stepped foot in her house and saw her again for the first time in two years.

Her vibrancy and energy had stayed with me over the time we were apart. I knew exactly how Jonny J must have felt an hour before with my hand wrapped around his neck, because Saint had me in the exact same chokehold, though mine was emotional.

I struggled to think straight whenever she was around me, but the irony was that I also struggled to think straight when she wasn't.

As the steam filled the bathroom, I couldn't shake the image of her face from my mind. Her azure blue eyes and pretty pillowy lips, her clear, olive skin, and the intelligence behind her eyes. But more than anything, her vulnerable heart and her poet's soul affected me in ways that sent me off-kilter.

I got hard just thinking of her face.

I'd been looking for Saint in other women, and for two years, I'd never found anything that came close. Sex was meaningless and empty, but necessary for me to get through the night without waking up in a cold sweat. But even then, I needed it to be extreme to get hard because if I couldn't have intimacy, I could only deal with kink.

My dick hardened to steel, and my hand slipped down to grip the base with my fingers.

It didn't take long for my thoughts to regress to the night I spent with Saint two years before. Memories played like a movie in my head, and I let out a low groan while fisting my cock.

Saint's little mewls and sexy noises floated through my mind, along with her musical voice begging me to slide deeper and telling me how good I felt when I moved inside her.

My grip tightened, and I twisted my hand a little as I beat my fist up and down, my thigh muscles rippling with the force of my body's reaction to my dirty thoughts.

I'd never let myself remember before because it hurt too much. But now the floodgates were open, I let it all come back to me. The taste of Saint's skin, her quivering pussy, how good the tight slickness of her cunt felt when it gripped my cock, and how I saw stars when she milked the cum from me.

My free hand pressed against the glass shower cubicle, and I bowed my head, gritting my teeth as I felt my balls draw up and my dick swell. "Fuck!" I groaned as my hips bucked into my hand while cum erupted from my cock like a hot geyser.

Everything pulsed—my dick, balls, even my thighs from the force of my orgasm.

Ropes of cum coated my fingers along with the glass walls of the shower cubicle, and I gripped the base harder, squeezing and tugging while I milked out every drop.

With a low moan, I tipped my head back and let the spray of the water clean my body. Finally, I released my dick, grabbed my shower gel, and wiped the remnants of my mess away, making sure it all disappeared down the drain.

I hadn't come that hard or fast for a long-damned time, but at least I knew I'd be able to get through the night without dragging Saint somewhere dark and quiet so I could lift her skirt, bend her against a wall, and show her all the good she'd walked away from.

We needed an honest conversation and a come-to-Jesus moment.

We also needed a day in bed so we could reconnect.

But before that happened, we needed to sit down and hash out what her fucking problem was and why she ghosted my ass when it was obvious we felt something deep for each other.

And whether she liked it or not, it was gonna happen tonight.

Staring in the mirror, I gave myself a final once-over before grabbing my watch and fastening it to my wrist. My suit was sharp, but then that was how Tom Ford made them, and one thing Hendrix didn't want us to cut back on was looking well-turned-out and professional.

For years, I'd lived in uniforms, first in the US Air Force, then in my motorcycle club, but unlike most other bikers, I liked putting a suit on occasionally. Maybe it was why I enjoyed working in close personal protection. I liked the social aspect of it.

Tonight's uniform was a black shirt—no tie—and a black suit. Our clothing changed depending on the time of day, what we were doing, and the event we were attending. Like today, we were hanging out in the recording studio, so it was more casual attire in black pants and tees. Now, it was a party for a rock band, so ties and waistcoats would've been over the top. However, we still had to look the part and represent SDSS professionally.

Slipping my cell into my inside pocket and my Ruger LC9 into my body holster, I turned for the door. Saint had spoiled me with the accommodation. My room was huge with a super-king bed and a sixty-inch flat-screen TV with surround sound. I also had my own private, luxurious en suite bathroom, which was just as well considering the dirty little mess I'd made of it earlier.

I entered the hallway and casually jogged down the stairs into the reception area of Saint's house. The place was large, light, and airy, with big rooms, huge, low-slung, soft couches, white walls, and high ceilings. The kitchen and family rooms that led onto the beach at the back had wall-to-wall windows made the most of the ocean views, but also presented a security nightmare.

After we talked about 'us', Saint and I needed to discuss moving her out of the house for a while. She told me earlier that rehearsals were almost done, and they had the new songs down, so the band wanted to take a week off before they went to New York to record the album.

I wanted to whisk her away somewhere, a road trip maybe. We'd lost a lot of time and needed to make the effort to get to know each other without any distractions. Saint's life was so goddamned complicated, and just for a few days, I wanted to show her that it didn't have to be, and after our conversation in her kitchen the day before about the pressures of her job, I just wanted her to take time to relax, recharge her batteries.

And eat.

There was a car service picking us up to take us to the venue that Talia had arranged, so when the doorbell rang, I stalked straight toward it.

"Car's here," I yelled up the stairs as I moved across the entrance hall.

"Be right down," she yelled back.

Undoing the bolts, I swung the door open to reveal who I thought was the driver.

Instead, I froze, my eyes fixating on a familiar, bearded face, dazzling white teeth flashing as he grinned from ear to ear. Except the feeling of familiarity wasn't from somebody I'd met before or even knew. It was from a guy I'd watched fly spaceships, shoot at aliens, battle the forces of evil, and save the Earth from destruction more than a few times.

Hunter Page. Action hero. Heartthrob. Adored by men and women worldwide.

And Saint's rumored boyfriend.

What the fuck?

A low growl escaped my throat.

I was just about to order him to get the fuck out of there and never darken my woman's door again when Saint's voice squealed, "You're here!"

Hunter Page's dark, brooding gaze settled somewhere over my shoulder, and his mouth curved into a wide grin. His stare scanned down, then back up again. "Fuck me, baby. You look like a wet dream."

Slowly, I craned my neck, and my entire body jerked.

Saint glided down the stairs toward us and fuck me if the sight of her didn't make me almost swallow my tongue.

She wore a slip of a silvery pink sequin dress that hit her thighs just below the cheeks of her ass. The top of it was a halterneck, and the neckline draped loosely to show an expanse of smooth, glowing, firm cleavage. The top part of her long, black hair was slicked back from her face and pinned up to give it height, while the bottom half cascaded down her back. Her eye makeup was dark, smoky, and sexy. My woman's mouth was pale pink and so damned juicy-looking that I couldn't stop the dirty images of sliding my cock between those glossed-up lips from stabbing through my mind.

It hit me then how much I hated Hunter Page with every drop of blood that flowed through my veins, but the asshat was correct about one thing.

Saint *did indeed* look like a wet dream.

Fuck me.

Fuck me.

Heat crawled up my neck, and I cracked it from side to side, my eyes never leaving the sex-kitten who strutted toward us on sky-high silver sandals with straps that crisscrossed up her ankle.

My mouth filled with saliva as Saint's eyes met mine and held.

"You okay, hon?" she asked with a breezy innocence.

I grunted in reply, willing my dick to deflate instead of trying to punch a hole through the inseam of my Tom Ford pants.

One side of Saint's mouth tipped up into a lopsided grin, and her gaze skated away, warming as it fell on the Neanderthal standing behind me. "Hunter," she breathed, moving into his waiting arms before leaning up and kissing his cheek softly. "When did you get back?"

"This morning," he murmured, his mouth going slack as he took in her face, hair, and dress approvingly. "Never seen you looking sexier, babe. I need to take more overseas roles if this is what I'm treated to when I come home."

"Overseas?" she chided. "You've been in Canada."

I almost snorted my disgust.

Obviously, you didn't need brains to be a movie star these days. Hunter may have been an action hero, but in the words of Gambit, Hunter Page was thick as pig shit.

God only knew what the fuck Saint saw in him.

"Been in Thailand, too, remember," he chided back, his eyes coming back to me and dancing with humor. "My girl gets so into her music and songwriting that she forgets where I am most of the time."

I folded my arms across my chest and let out another grunt.

He snaked a hairy-assed arm across Saint's shoulders while holding the other one out toward me. "Good to meet ya. I'm Hunter."

"Ice," I replied, taking his fingers and giving them a firm squeeze.

He squeezed back sharply. "Thanks for looking after my girl."

A cocky grin slid across my face, and I squeezed harder, making him wince before I dropped his hand. "Saint's a dream to look after. Enjoyed every second so far. Shame you're away working so often, and someone else has to do your job, but then, at least I'm military trained, whereas you just act the part."

"Oh, I dunno," he rumbled. "I fought MMA for five years. I think I could handle a bit of CPP. I'm actually bigger than my bodyguards. It's a running joke between my fanbase. My security's more likely to get shit when we're out than I am, but the studios insist." He shrugged. "You know how it is when you make millions of dollars per movie—Oh, that's right. You don't."

My eyes narrowed on his.

His eyes narrowed right on back.

"I do okay," I assured him.

"Yeah," he agreed. "I'm sure you do." His stare softened, and he glanced down at Saint. "Come on, babe. The sooner we get there, the sooner we can leave. I know how much you hate these parties."

Saint glanced up at him before her stare drifted to me. "Are you two okay?"

"Course," he told her with a casual wave of a hand.

"Perfect," I reiterated, squaring my shoulders to make myself appear as big as I could next to the behemoth motherfucker who had Saint on his arm, then added, "I'm a *huge* fan."

"Great!" Saint said brightly.

Hunter Page's beard twitched.

I grunted again and started for the door, muttering, "Let's go." I pulled it open and held it, ushering Saint through, then as Hunter approached, I 'accidentally' let it go.

Page darted forward and caught it with his hand, his eyebrow hitching questioningly. "Hand slip?" he asked coolly.

I almost retorted, *not as badly as earlier when I beat one out to memories of your girlfriend*, but instead, I muttered, "Somethin' like that," before taking Saint's arm and helping her into the waiting limo. I gave the driver (who I'd already vetted) a chin lift as she hustled her ass inside and moved onto the back seat.

I bent down and slid in beside her just as the other door opened, and Hunter poked his head through. "Budge up," he ordered. "Need to get my ass in, and I'm a lot bigger than Iceman."

"Fatter, more like," I mumbled under my breath, letting out a loud 'oof' when Saint's elbow dug sharply into my ribs.

"What's gotten into you?" she whispered angrily.

I sniffed, turning my head to look out the window. "Dunno what you mean. I'm perfectly fine."

"Jesus," she murmured, her pink, glossy lips plumping into a cute little pout.

Shifting in my seat, I covered my burgeoning cock with my jacket just as Hunter leaned forward to tell the driver the name of the club we were headed to.

When he leaned back again, his hand went to Saint's smooth, tanned thigh, and he looked down at her and smiled.

My ribs tightened, and suddenly, I struggled to breathe. My eyes glued to Page's hand, and I waited for the big, hairy fucker to slide it higher just so I could stop the car, drag him out, and beat the shit out of him.

Lucky for him, the car jolted, and his hand fell from my woman's leg.

I sat back in the seat, trying to breathe through the heat rising inside my chest, but instead, I felt as if my fucking brains were about to explode.

My jaw clenched, and I prayed to God I still had Kennedy Stone's number programmed into my phone because unless the big man himself threw me a miracle, I had a feeling my ass would be sitting in jail by the end of the night. If Hunter Page touched my woman one more time, I'd likely be up on goddamned murder charge.

Trick gave me a nudge and nodded toward the DJ booth. "Who'd have thought that Hunter Page, of all people, could DJ as well as save the Earth from an alien force sent to wipe out all of mankind?" He stared across the packed dancefloor at the man in question, who held earphones against the side of his head while his fingers rested on the record he was in the process of turning.

The bassline of an old Calvin Harris and Rihanna dance song thumped through the speakers, and the crowd began to go wild.

The music seemed to make the room throb with heated energy that was synchronized to the crowd's movements. As I scanned the room for threats, my gaze landed on Saint, her figure shimmering in pink under the flashing lights.

Most of the people here were fans of Dischordium and were primed, ready, and waiting for their rock god idols to take the stage to perform a few singles from their new album. It was an industry party, but Dischordium and a few local radio stations had been running competitions for some fans to win VIP tickets to the event.

It was a good idea. The publicity it courted bordered on rabid, and of course, the event had become the hottest ticket in town. Everybody who was anybody clambered for tickets, and I'd already recognized a sultry blonde pop starlet wandering around in a barely-there dress, hanging onto the arm of her young actor boyfriend. Other bands, probably friends of Noah and the boys, were here too, along with DJ Raven, who was the official compere, though it seemed she'd given up her booth to Hunter Page while she got a drink and mingled.

"He's a hairy fucker, right?" I asked.

Gambit's lips hitched slightly. "His mother didn't give birth to him; she knitted him."

"He reminds me of a fat Hairy Styles," I muttered, my face a glower.

Trick joined in the banter. "His pronouns are he/hair."

Ghost chuckled. "He's got the crowd goin', though. Look at 'em all, throwing their hands up in the hair."

Trick busted a gut.

I snickered, my smile fading as I caught sight of a sparkly pink figure rocking it out on the dance floor with Talia, who wore a red, strapless dress that left even less to the imagination than Saint's did.

"Can't believe she's seeing that goon," I muttered for the thirty-seventh time that night.

Gambit shrugged. "I always thought he was gay."

"Hunter Page? Gay?" Trick blustered. "Get the fuck outta here with that bullshit. He saves the goddamned world three times a year."

"You can still be gay and save the world, asshole," Gambit shot back. "Anyway, it's not a big deal. I just always got a bear vibe from him."

"Really?" Trick asked, cocking his head as he studied my nemesis.

"Yeah, but it's not like I'm an authority on it," Gambit muttered, scanning the crowd.

My eyes flickered over to the area where Saint was dancing, and my mouth went dry.

She was sure giving me a run for my money.

I nearly had a damned conniption when I opened the door to Hunter Page. It wasn't like he was some wannabe asshole who was way out of her league; he was actual competition.

She'd been back in my life for just over twenty-four hours, and already my head was full of her, and my heart was in pieces because if she had a boyfriend and they were solid, I didn't stand a fucking chance. Page may have been a hairy fucker, but he was still a good-looking dude. Women all around the world lusted after him, so what chance did I fucking have?

Still, I couldn't give up. I'd found something worth having, and I knew how rare and precious that was. How could I walk away from the one woman who filled me up? How could I turn my back on my second chance?

Fighting for her was a given. I'd fight to the fucking death if I had to, except I had to go up against an adversary who was worthy of Saint. Hunter Page was a millionaire heartthrob for fuck's sake, so I'd have to get creative if I wanted the best man (namely me) to win.

A movement caught my eye, and the hair on the back of my neck stood up. Some young teenybopper dude sauntered onto the dance floor with his entourage, who immediately began pushing people out of the way.

I launched off the wall that had served as my vantage point and immediately began to move toward Saint and Talia, who were still fucking around on the edge of the floor. The good news was, they'd been joined by Sam and Jolie Fontaine, so at least the girls had a dude with them.

Iceman

The thick bassline of the song pumped through the speakers. Bodies moved in time to the resounding beat, and the air became fraught with anticipation. Hunter was doing well to keep the crowd engaged, but they weren't here to see him. Everybody was waiting for the band, and I could feel they were getting impatient.

I watched Saint dance with a carefree abandon that drew the eye of every man in the room, and it was affecting me to the point of distraction. My cock had been semi-hard since she walked down the stairs at her house. I didn't know whether I wanted to take my jacket off and hide her away from the world or bend her over the nearest table, lift her sparkly little skirt over her high, round ass, and show everybody, including Hunter Page, exactly who she belonged to.

Instead, I did neither because I was Saint McClure's goddamned bodyguard, and giving the entire club a peep show would be frowned upon. My job was to stay in the background and observe, so that's what I did, all while keeping an eye not only on Saint but also on the crowd enveloping her.

A buzz went around the room as the stage lights cut out completely.

The club sat in darkness, except for the beams of light shining over the crowd, highlighting the men now standing on stage with their instruments at the ready.

Noah leaned toward his microphone and, in a low voice, said, "Hey. We wish you all a good evening and wanna welcome everyone to our new record launch."

Shouts and catcalls filled the air as the crowd bellowed their excitement.

"Lemme introduce you to the band," he continued. "Meet Styx, Blue, Griff, and Jax, I'm Noah, but you know us better as... Dischordium."

The echo of the drummer beating his sticks together three times clicked through the room before a thumping beat began to resonate. Then, Blue's fingers began to fly up and down the fret of his guitar as he played us a sweet riff. The bass player, Jax, began to slap a rhythm over his strings, and Noah's rich, raspy voice began to sing.

The crowd went wild. Bellows and shouts filled the ether, along with the pulsing energy, and the entire room began to move in time to the music.

The thudding bassline was so heavy I could feel it reverberating through my chest, and my foot began to tap. The crackle of electricity in the air sent a warm shiver down my spine, and the deep, rich tone of Noah's voice filled the room as he belted out how he wanted to rock some chick's world.

Throughout this, my eyes never left Saint.

The way she moved with raw energy had me captivated. Her presence was magnetic, drawing eyes and hard-ons alike. As the crowd cheered along with Dischordium, I found myself caught in a whirlwind of emotions because seeing Saint so happy and carefree made me realize she was a ray of light who chased away the shadows just by being in my life.

Over the next hour, Noah and the boys whipped the crowd up into a frenzy. Their new album was more uptempo than the last. It was a blend of heavy rock and funk, and their fans lapped up every note played and every word sung like they were witnessing the second coming of Christ.

After they'd finished playing their brand-new single that was about to hit number one on the Billboard charts, Noah held up a hand to address the crowd.

"We've got a real treat for you tonight, folks," he began. "Gotta special guest in the audience. Someone who's supported us since the days we played for three people in backroad honkytonks in Wyoming."

The crowd roared.

"Me and the boys would love it if she came up on stage and sang with us," he continued. He threw out a hand, and a single spotlight landed directly on Saint. "We're lucky to have Saint McClure here, but she may need a little encouragement."

Saint froze.

Cheers and yells filled the air, and a low chant began to cut through the ether.

"Saint. Saint. Saint. Saint. Saint."

My back straightened because this was a new development.

The night had been uneventful, but I'd had no trouble staying close and accessible in case she needed me. Saint going on stage to perform posed a problem, though it was something I could easily work around.

The chants became louder and more frenzied until, eventually, Saint handed her drink to Talia and began to move toward the stage.

I moved, too, slipping through the crowd until I walked at her back.

Her neck craned, and her eyes landed on me, softening with relief at my presence.

My heart warmed. I loved being that for her, loved being someone who brought her peace, because she was that for me too, even though tonight Saint was driving me crazy in that dress. My balls were so fucking blue with need for her that they felt like they'd explode.

Very soon, Saint McClure was gonna know exactly who she belonged to, and it wasn't Hunter 'hairy-assed' Page.

Chapter Eight

Saint

I should have been used to walking up on stage with just a moment's notice after all the years I'd been performing.

I'd paid my dues in backroad bars and venues where the soles of my shoes stuck to the floorboards. I'd gotten changed in dirty restrooms, offices, broom cupboards, and even an alley once, but nothing could have prepared me for performing in front of Jacob for the first time.

Braden, Dischordium's manager, ushered me into the wings and up the stairs leading to the stage. Jacob stayed at my back the entire time like an ever-watchful shadow.

It was crazy how his presence could be both comforting and unnerving, like I had a guardian angel at my back who could rip out your throat if needed. But then Jacob had been a walking, talking contradiction since the moment I met him.

Noah appeared in the wings to meet me. "Thanks for doin' this, Saint," he said earnestly. "I know I put you on the spot, but I wanted to mix things up, and you can't buy this kinda publicity."

"I get it," I assured him, and I did because I'd done way more outrageous things for my band—namely, my showmance with Hunter. I understood how important this night and the new album were to Dischordium.

Noah gave Jacob a chin lift. "I'll keep an eye out for her up there. Any funny business and I'll get her out of there. Don't worry."

"You could've called me earlier and let me know what you were thinking," Jacob berated. "I'm not here to shit in your cereal, Carbine, but my priority is Saint."

"Didn't know I was gonna suggest it until I saw her shaking her sweet ass in that dress." Noah grinned.

A dark look swept over Jacob's face. "Are you for fuckin' real?"

Noah raised his hands. "Sorry, brother. Just funnin' with ya."

"Yo!" A shout came from the stage where Griff was gesturing for us to get out there. *"Are we doing this?"*

Noah took my hand. "Come on before Griff shits his shorts." He tugged me out on stage behind him, and the crowd erupted in cheers.

The bright lights blinded me for a moment before my eyes adjusted to them.

Somebody shoved a guitar in my hand, and Blue moved away from his microphone, allowing Noah to pick it up and set it down next to his for me.

He stepped toward his mic and murmured, "Look who I found."

The crowd roared.

Blue approached us, his signature smirk in place as his eyes raked down me and up again to my face, and asked, "What are we playing?"

"What about "Escapism" by Raye? It sounded cool when we jammed out to it together at Jax's party." Noah suggested.

"Got it; gonna improvise, though, make it heavier," Blue stated. "Same as before? Saint takes the lead, and you come in on the harmonies, Carb."

"Sure thing," Noah agreed.

I glanced at both the boys and nodded.

Blue stepped away, went over to the other two boys, glanced at me, and jerked a nod while he relayed the information to them.

After twirling his drumstick in the air, Styx, the drummer, counted us in, and the boys began to play.

I leaned into the microphone, sucked in a breath, and closed my eyes to center myself, allowing myself to get swept away with the notes as I fell into the current of the music. Then, keeping my lungs full of air, I counted down the beats, opened my mouth, and began to sing.

The music wrapped me in a cocoon until nothing else mattered but the meaning behind the words.

I sang for the girl who was shredded by heartbreak and tried to find solace in drink, drugs, and sex, much like I did when I cut Jacob off after discovering he was married.

Blue meant it when he said he was going to play it heavier, but by doing so, he also made it rougher and dirtier. My voice took on a raspy, hard quality, living the story just like I'd lived it two years before when Jacob broke something inside me that I'd never been able to patch back together.

Music made me feel alive. The familiar rush of adrenaline, along with the high I got from performing for a live audience, coursed through me, leaving me intoxicated.

My eyes opened, and I turned to admire Blue's playing, but in doing so, my gaze caught stage left and locked with Jacob's, and my heart stuttered when I saw the rawness blazing from his icy blue eyes.

The intensity of his gaze thrilled me, and everything melted away. In that moment, we were the only two people in the room. I sang every word for him, unable to stop my voice from dripping with the pain he caused, the disappointment wracking me, and the ache I still felt every damned day.

I leaned into the emotions tugging at my heart because that was what I did best. I took the ugliness of pain and turned it into something beautiful, especially when I was on stage. It was my domain, and nobody, including Jacob, could deny it was where I belonged and where I thrived.

Jacob's expression softened slightly, a flicker of understanding passing over his face before he masked it with his usual blankness. Except his face may have been void, but his icy eyes smoldered, never leaving mine as I sang the last words of the song, waiting for the music to fade out.

Just for a split second, silence hung in the air, and then the crowd went wild.

Screams and cheers filled the room, almost lifting the roof. Feet stamped and hands clapped while the audience bellowed their approval.

I broke my gaze with Jacob and looked at the crowd, inhaling a sharp breath when I felt the waves of energy crashing toward me.

Noah put his mouth up close to the microphone and murmured, "You want one more?" Only to be met with screams of affirmation.

A song drifted into my head; one we'd played acoustically backstage at the festival where I'd met Jacob. I leaned toward Noah and whispered the title, watching his eyes light up, and he grinned.

He moved toward Blue and the others, telling them the song, and then I heard a *tap, tap, tap* as the drumsticks crashed together.

Blue's guitar wailed through the room, and a loud roar rose up as the riff introducing Paramore's "All I Wanted" glided from the speakers.

My belly filled with euphoria from the warm tone of the instrument, and I closed my eyes again, allowing the music to wrap around me.

I couldn't help smiling at the way the audience responded to the change in tempo. The song was a favorite of mine, and sexy, low-key energy crackled as the entire room fell silent to listen. My heartbeat regulated in time to the thud of Styx's drums, and I began to get carried away by the words and haunting melody.

It wasn't an easy song to sing, but I loved it so much that I'd perfected it over time. As the music built to a crescendo, my voice rose alongside it, feeling the longing and desire for a lost love threading through the words as they fell from my lips.

Again, my eyes slid to Jacob.

He stood, mesmerized, his body taut, his face stunned. A glimmer of emotion shone in his eyes, and I could tell he was as moved by the beauty of the lyrics as I was.

I sang with everything I had, pouring my conflicting feelings into each verse, hoping that somehow, he'd read between the lines and hear everything I was trying to tell him.

All too soon, the song ended, and I squeezed my eyes shut as the last wail of Blue's guitar faded away.

The crowd's reaction was electric. The deafening cheers, foot-stamping, and clapping sent goosebumps down my arms, or was it the intensity I felt from Jacob's gaze that affected me in such a profound way?

I stole one last look at the wings, and my heart fluttered when I saw what was so plainly written across Jacob's face.

Pure, unadulterated need.

My breath caught in my throat, and my body pulsed with the raw sexuality emanating from him in waves. His usual cold blue eyes weren't icy anymore. Instead, they were pools of molten steel staring at me as if he was about to gobble me all up.

I tore my gaze away, heart pounding in my chest. The room seemed topsy-turvy, or maybe that was just my emotion-filled brain reacting to Jacob's raw need. On autopilot, I smiled and murmured my thanks to the band while also acknowledging the crowd, except I couldn't take any of it in.

All I could feel was Jacob.

My feet moved, carrying me toward the wings and toward *him*.

I needed air, space to breathe, and to get my head straight. If Jacob so much as touched me, I suspected I'd go up in flames. My skin was flushed, and my temperature was set to boiling, like I was on fire from the inside out.

My gaze was pulled to his by an invisible force, and my pussy clenched at the wolfishness of his expression. Over the last couple of days, I'd seen it fleetingly but didn't recognize what it meant until now.

As I approached him, my pulse pounded through my body. Jacob never took his eyes off me: a bomb could have gone off and blown the place to smithereens, and I doubted either one of us would have noticed; we were both so entranced under each other's spell.

He reached a hand out toward me, his nostrils flaring as I placed my fingers in his, and the tiny hairs on my arms stood on end at the contact.

"You were incredible," he rasped, pulling me into his hard body.

"You inspire me," I whispered, my lips parting as I gazed up at him.

"Do you know Hunter's number?" he asked.

My eyebrows pulled together. "No, but it's in my phone."

His gaze stayed glued to mine as he pulled a cell phone from his inside pocket, and his eyes fell to the screen. Holding it to his ear, he waited briefly and muttered, "Colt? I need you to ping me Hunter Page's number."

Whoever Colt was must have agreed because Jacob replied, "Thanks, brother," before cutting the call. Within seconds, his phone pinged, and he clicked again and held it out to me. "It's ringing."

"What's ringing?" I asked confusedly.

"*His* phone." Jacob's jaw ticked angrily. "End it."

"End what—" My eyes widened as the meaning behind his words hit me, and I spluttered, "Jacob—"

"End it, Saint," he repeated, his tone like ice. "Or I will, and believe me, baby, you won't like the way I do it."

Right then, the call clicked in, and Hunter's voice said, "Hello?"

"It's me," I blurted out, my eyes lowering.

Jacob's finger touched my chin and lifted it so my gaze met his again. "Eyes on me," he ordered.

I obeyed.

"Why aren't you on *your* phone?" Hunter asked.

"Look, honey," I breathed. "I don't think we should see each other anymore."

After a brief pause, he chuckled. "I get it, Saint. Your man had a come-to-Jesus moment when I turned up at your place, and he didn't seem like the kind of guy who'd sit back and watch you make nice with another dude. It's all good. Hope it works out for you. Just make sure he's divorced before you fuck him. If you don't, I know you'll hate yourself in the morning."

I felt my spirit go into freefall, and my ass hit the Earth with a big ol' bump.

"Fuck!" I whispered.

"See ya later, babe," Hunter sang, "Don't do anything I wouldn't." And with that parting shot, he hung up.

My gaze lifted to meet Jacob's, and I blabbered, "It was a showmance."

His head reared back. "Huh?"

"It wasn't real," I admitted. "Hunter and I are friends, but our entire relationship was set up by our management for publicity."

His eyes narrowed. "Is he gay?"

"Well..." My voice trailed off.

"That motherfucker," he muttered under his breath,

"He's not a motherfucker," I argued indignantly.

Jacob looked confused for a second, then he grinned. "Not Page, I meant Gambit."

"Why's Gambit a motherfucker?" I asked, tone confused.

Jacob's hand squeezed my waist, and his forehead lowered, resting on mine. "He touched your thigh."

My face scrunched up. "Gambit touched my thigh?"

"Not Gambit. I meant Page," he corrected.

My face scrunched up tighter. "You've lost me."

His mouth curved sexily. "In the car, Page touched your thigh."

"Oh," I breathed, taking in his heated stare. "Did he?"

"I didn't like it, Saint," he bit out. "Next time someone touches you like that, I'll cut their fuckin' fingers off."

I let out a snort. "Right."

His eyes bored into mine. "Saint. Next time a man who isn't me touches you like that, I'll cut their goddamned fingers off. Do you fuckin' get me?"

I shivered at the vow in his tone, and then Hunter's words floated through my head. *Just make sure he's divorced before you fuck him.*

"What about when a woman who isn't me touches you?" I demanded.

He lifted his forehead. "They won't."

"Really?" I snapped. "Not even your wife?"

His skin paled, and that raw look I saw while I was singing crossed his face again, except this time, it didn't convey need or desire, just heart-shredding pain.

My heart jolted. "Jacob," I whispered, my hand lifting to touch his face. "What is it?"

His jaw tightened, and he pulled away from my touch. "I'm not married," he said flatly.

I reached out again, but he jerked away from me, his eyes shuttering closed like a door slamming. "Don't," he growled, the muscle in his jaw working overtime.

"What's going on?" I asked.

"Who told you I was married?" he demanded.

"Nobody. I—" I sighed, trying to pull my thoughts together and calm my nerves, which by then were making my hands tremble. "It was when we met. You left the next day and gave me your number and the number for your club."

"And?" he prompted.

"I called you, but you didn't answer," I explained. "I waited a couple of days, but you didn't get back to me, so I called your club like you told me to. That was when some guy told me it was your wife's birthday and that you'd gone to visit her."

His forehead furrowed. "Did you get his name?"

"Yeah," I told him. "Ace."

Jacob flinched as if I'd struck him.

"What is it?" I demanded. "What the hell's going on? Was he lying?"

He scraped a hand down his face, suddenly looking as if he hadn't slept for a week. "No. He wasn't lying, but he was stirring the shit pot with a huge fuckin' spoon." Jake took a step back from me. "I *was* married, Saint, but my wife passed away twelve years ago."

The back of my throat heated, and suddenly, my knees felt unsteady, as if the ground had shifted beneath my feet, throwing me off balance. All this time, I'd had no idea about Jake's past or his pain and loss.

"I don't know what to say," I murmured.

"Nobody ever knows what to say," he retorted. "But then, what can you say? I was a widower before I was thirty."

"Jacob," I whispered, my fingers going to his arm, trying to offer him comfort.

He shook me off, and his lip curled in disgust at my touch. "I'll ask Ghost to take you home and stay with you tonight. I need some space." He raked his fingers through his hair, his eyes reflecting his sorrow.

He was pulling away from me again. Instead of taking me somewhere quiet where we could talk everything through, he was building those damned walls back up one brick at a time and creating distance between us.

And I was fucking *sick of it*.

"I didn't know, Jacob," I bit out. "All I was told was that you'd gone to visit your wife, and I just assumed—"

"The worst?" he challenged.

"Yeah, the worst," I cried, wrenching myself away from him. "Just like you assumed the worst about Hunter."

"It's a well-known fact that you two are a couple," he pointed out.

"We've never announced that. In fact, we've only ever said we were good friends. It's the tabloids who ran with it and built it up. Did we let them? Yes, because it suited us at the time, but never once did I announce he was my boyfriend. But in contrast, I was told by one of your club members, one of your *brothers*, that you'd gone to see your wife. Why would I not believe you were married?"

His eyes blazed into mine. "You should've asked me!" He jerked his thumb toward his chest.

"And you should've asked *me*," I threw back. "You're such a fucking baby. You're quick to blame me for everything, Jacob, but you're not innocent in all this, either. You never told me about your wife, so how was I supposed to know you'd lost her?"

He leaned down until we were nose to nose. "I didn't lose her, Saint," he snarled. "She died. She had a heart condition nobody knew about, and one day, it just stopped beating. Do you know how fucking soul-destroying that shit is? Knowing the one thing you loved most about a person is the same thing that put them in the fucking ground?"

My heart wrenched.

Jake's pain, his grief, was still so raw, like it had happened only yesterday. His eyes were clouded with memories of love and loss, and I felt a surge of empathy wash over me as the weight of his revelation manifested like a wedge between us.

Two years ago, this beautiful, broken man bound me to him in ways I was still trying to understand. With just a look, he tethered my soul to his, and I'd never been able to cut myself loose. It took one night for Jacob Irons to become the love of my life, but I knew I'd never be the love of his because that spot had already been taken.

And in an instant, I understood the gravity of his grief because I felt it, too.

His eyes searched mine, finally narrowing when he found what he was looking for, and he rumbled, "It's not what you think, Saint. I'm not saying I'm over it because it's not something a man ever gets past, but I've accepted it. I came to terms with what happened to Allie a long-damned time ago."

I felt the burn in the back of my throat, and I croaked, "What if I can't compete?"

His hand cupped my cheek, and my eyes closed so I could savor the contact of his skin on mine. "You don't need to compete," he rasped. "She's her, and you're you. You're different women with different needs and wants. Allie was special to me, but you are too, Saint. You were special the second I laid eyes on you."

My eyes fluttered open, and I whispered, "Same."

His face lowered, and he nuzzled my cheek. "I haven't been able to take my eyes off you all fuckin' night. Then you went up on that stage and blew my mind even more. I've never felt so lucky to know somebody or to bear witness to the magic you create. Do you know how fucking insanely amazing you are, Saint McClure? Do you know how much I respect and admire you?"

My breath caught in my throat.

"I'm a washed-up ex-pilot with a shitty attitude and a chip on my shoulder the size of fuckin' Kansas. You're so far outta my league that I'd have to aim for the stars just to reach you. And you say *you* can't compete." His breath fluttered against my skin with his chuckle. "Get the fuck outta here with that bullshit, woman."

His lips trailed down the side of my neck, and I shivered from top to toe as his tongue flicked out and traced a line. Then, he lifted his head, and his lips met mine, and we came together with such force that I cried out into his mouth.

For the last two years, I'd lain in bed every night burning for Jacob, not even contemplating that he felt the same way. His confession had left me reeling, and my heart pounded as I struggled to process the tidal wave of emotions crashing over me.

I loved how he bared his soul; loved how this strong, capable, alpha man's man could convey words that weaved around my heart and wrapped it up warm and cozy. I loved the safety he offered and the way he saw deeper than anyone else ever had.

I also loved the way his kisses made my thighs clench and my nipples harden. I loved how he could make my pussy wet with just a blazing glance from his icy yet molten eyes, and I especially loved the way he was kissing me right now like he was starving for me.

He terrified and exhilarated me all at the same time. Nobody else could bring my body to life with just one touch. No other man had ever made me feel like I was toppling from a cliff edge, but it was okay to fall because he'd be there to catch me.

The same spark from two years before suddenly ignited in my heart, and I knew if I didn't have him, I'd die.

I wrenched my lips away from his and leveled him with a look. "I want you."

One side of his mouth hitched, and he smirked his sexy smile. His hand caught mine, and he tugged me further backstage toward the dressing rooms, muttering, "Let's fuckin' go."

His grip was firm, his strides determined as he pulled me behind him like an errant child.

I stumbled trying to match his pace, my heart pounding as hard as Styx's drum, and I giggled euphorically at the curious glances of the roadies and stagehands who were standing around chatting in groups.

We rounded a corner, and he pulled a key from his pocket and opened a door to one of the dressing rooms. Immediately, he tugged me inside and pushed my back against a wall, his body pressing into mine. Soft lips found my neck, trailing kisses down toward my breasts. "You sure about this?" he growled, his tone low and scratchy.

I groaned, my eyes rolling into the back of my head when I felt his cock hard and ready against my belly, and I whispered, "Fuck yes."

Jacob's mouth crashed onto mine, the force of his kiss making my mouth open so he could spear my tongue with his. He lapped and lathed and sucked and nibbled until my brain exploded with tiny shocks of electricity. Our teeth clashed as we fought for control, and I felt my lips swell from the force of his incredibly hot kiss.

Strong hands cupped the cheeks of my ass and slid the hem of my dress up to my waist. Then, a ripping noise sounded as he tore my G-string apart before letting it drop to the floor.

I squealed as I was hauled into the air, Jacob's fingers still gripping my ass, and my back slid up the wall as he lifted me until his mouth was level with my pussy.

"Legs over my shoulders," he rasped.

I obeyed, bringing one knee up, then the other, and hooking them over his broad shoulders just like he commanded.

"This fuckin' pussy," he growled against my inner thigh. "Dreamed about it. Jacked off to it, fucking jonesed for it every day for two goddamned years. Don't ever ghost me again. Don't ever keep you away from me 'cause next time, Saint, I'll hunt you down."

My hands went to his hair, and I scraped my fingers through it, his words sending a thrill through my belly, which already clenched with the need for Jake to put his mouth on me.

He stared up at me, the gleam in his dark eyes making me swallow hard. Then his lips curved into a grin, he leaned forward, and he devoured me.

I whimpered at the sensation of his entire mouth enveloping my pussy, and he licked, nibbled, sucked, and fucked me with his tongue until I was a moaning mess. My knees shook, my thighs quivered, and I felt my nipples pebble as he ate like a starving man.

My back squirmed against the wall, and my hands clasped his head. "Fuck yeah," I babbled. "Don't stop, Jacob. You feel so fucking good."

He grunted, the vibrations of it making my inner walls clench, and then somehow, he held my ass up with one hand while he slid a finger deep inside and simultaneously lathed his tongue against my clit.

"Fuuuuck," I wailed, my pussy pulsing in his mouth. "Jesus, Jacob. I'm gonna come."

"Yeah, you fuckin' are," he growled before diving back in.

I clutched his head, urging him on, my words of encouragement low and dirty as I begged him to suck my pussy hard. He fucked his tongue inside me, then moved to my clit while he slid two fingers back inside, good and deep.

His gaze lifted to meet mine, and he licked my clit from bottom to top, like I was an ice cream, and my pussy clenched so hard I thought I was gonna pass out.

That was when I heard voices at the door.

My head twisted toward it, and I let out a gasp as it slowly opened, and Noah Hart stepped over the threshold.

His eyes caught on us immediately, and he froze, quietly exclaiming, "Jesus."

Jacob's head turned toward him, and he snarled, "Fuck off! I'm eating!"

Noah let out a strangled laugh and held his hand up defensively, muttering, "Sorry, brother," before stepping back and closing the door softly behind him.

I stared down at Jacob in shock, and he stared right back at me with a smirk on his face.

His mouth glistened from my juices, and my stomach quivered with pure unadulterated heat as he leaned forward again and licked my clit slowly, his eyes never leaving mine.

"Oh my fucking God," I murmured as my pussy walls contracted, and I started to come.

"Fuck yeah," he rasped before sucking my clit between his lips and growling his pleasure into my cunt.

I went off like a firework, trying not to scream as my orgasm ripped through me. "Fuck yeah, fuck yeah," I chanted, my pussy bucking against Jacob's face as my climax reached its peak.

"So fuckin' hot," he murmured, pecking little closed-mouth kisses all over my inner thighs and across my mound. "You're a fucking goddess."

Coming back to Earth, I let out a groan, my eyes half-mast as I gazed down into Jacob's handsome face.

"You're good at that," I breathed.

He busted out a laugh and slowly lowered me, my back sliding down the wall, before he gently placed me back on my feet.

My knees shook, and my thighs still quivered from the force of my climax. I'd come so hard that it felt as if my legs had been turned into Jell-O.

"You okay?" he asked, his lips twitching.

"I think so." I let out a happy little sigh, and for the first time since Jacob pulled me inside the dressing room, I glanced around at our surroundings. I spied a futon in the corner and jerked my thumb toward it. "You wanna bend me over that weird couch?"

"Maybe we should go," he suggested. "We've already been walked in on by Carbine. I knew he couldn't see what I saw, but if anyone did catch a glimpse, I'd rip their eyes outta their heads."

My face flushed at that particular memory, then my eyes rounded. "But what about you?"

"I'll wait until we're in bed so I can spread you out, take my time, and fuck you in ways you've only dreamed about. Warning ya, though, Saint. It's gonna be a fuckin' long night."

I beamed up at him. "It's okay. I've got the day off tomorrow."

He kissed my lips softly, leaving a slight trace of me on them. "Gonna be inside you all day tomorrow, too."

My heart swelled, and I found myself reaching for Jacob's hand, intertwining my fingers with his. "Is this really happening? Is this real?"

His hand squeezed mine while an arm slid over my shoulder, and he pulled me close. "We'll talk it out soon, baby, but just for tonight, can we enjoy each other? We've got a lot of lost time to make up for."

I nuzzled into his neck and whispered, "Okay."

We had plenty of time to sort out what happened in the past. Now I had all the information, I understood what made Jacob tick and why he reacted the way he did.

This was just the beginning; I had everything I ever wanted holding me in his arms. Life had a funny way of turning itself around, and now I had Jacob back, I couldn't damned well wait to get on with it.

Chapter Nine

Iceman

Saint McClure looked delightfully disheveled, definitely weak at the knees, and it was all my damned fault.

Even though I hadn't given her any dick—yet—she looked thoroughly fucked, but then I'd felt the force of her orgasm when I made her come in my mouth, so that wasn't a shocker.

Now, I just had to get her home, so I could fuck her the way I really wanted to: hard and fast, then slow and deep. My condoms were inside my nightstand, and there was no way I'd go in bareback until I'd organized some tests.

I always used wraps with every woman I'd fucked during the last twelve years, but fuck them I had, so if there was even a sliver of a chance I'd pass something onto my girl, I wouldn't go in bare. Saint would be mine in every way, and it would happen soon, but we both needed to get tested first.

I had to protect my girl, even from me if necessary.

She looked around the room, seemingly lost, before her bright blue eyes came to me, and she asked, "So, what now?"

"Now we go home, and I spank your ass for telling me lies about Hunter Page," I informed her, sliding both my arms over her shoulders and nuzzling her nose with mine.

Her eyes glinted with humor, and she breathed, "Ooh, Daddy."

I threw my head back and laughed.

Fuck me. This girl.

She grinned up at me with a little bit of sass and a lot of sweet, and the combination made me wonder if I was making the best decision of my life in falling for her or the most stupid. But then that was Saint; she was an unsolvable puzzle of a woman who made me question my sanity in the best possible ways. Though I liked a woman who could keep me on my toes, so there was that.

I grabbed her finger, brought it to my lips, and bit down gently. "You're a brat, Saint McClure, but you're my brat."

She leaned up and kissed me softly, breathing against my lips, "And you, Jacob Irons, are a whole lot of big, bad trouble."

As I stepped back, I spied a scrap of lace on the floor. Bending to retrieve it, I realized I was holding the panties I'd ripped off Saint earlier.

My cock was already semi-hard, but the knowledge that my girl wasn't wearing any underwear sent me into overdrive, and I groaned, "Jesus fuck."

Her giggle was like music filling the room. "Come on, trouble. I'd better get you home before you make a mess in that nice suit. Jizzing on Tom Ford is sacrilege."

My eyes raked down her and up again. She looked sexy as fuck, with her hair mussed up, her dress askew, and her lips swollen and bruised from my brutal kisses. I loved it, but I didn't love the idea of other people seeing her that way and knowing what we'd been doing.

"Tell that to his ol' man." I slipped the panties into my jacket pocket before shrugging it off. "Put this on," I ordered, sliding it over her shoulders.

Saint looked down, then up at me, scrunching her nose. "It's longer than my dress."

I chuckled. "Tell me about it. You've been driving me insane all fuckin' night in that sexy-assed scrap of material." Grabbing her hand, I grinned and tugged her toward the door, "Come on, brat. Let's get you home before you cause any more trouble."

"Shit," she cursed. "My purse is still in the bar."

I led her out into the hallway and back out toward the club, sliding my arm across her shoulders and pulling her into my side. My hand went to my pocket, and I pulled my cell out before clicking on Gambit's name.

"Yo!" he barked down the phone, the music in the club thumping in the background. "Where are you at?"

"Taking Saint home," I informed him. "She left her purse at the table. Can you grab it and meet us out front?"

Gambit grunted his acknowledgment before hanging up. I pocketed my phone, leading Saint around the stage area toward the back of the club, where we could exit into the foyer, all while scanning the crowd through the flashing lights. It was still early for some, not even midnight, and I knew the Dischordium boys were having an after-party because we'd been invited. Though as much as it would've been cool to go, the private after-party Saint and I were about to have appealed to me way more.

We hit the foyer, and I kept my arm around Saint, shielding her from the wall of windows at the entrance of the club where the paparazzi lay in wait.

"Ice," a voice called.

I whipped around to see Gambit walking toward us empty-handed.

"It's not there," he told me, his jaw setting in a harsh line. "It's gone."

"Fuck," Saint murmured. "My keys, phone, and a credit card were in there."

"It's either been taken by mistake, or somebody swiped it," Gambit added. "With everything going on, I can't help suspect someone's playing stupid fuckin' games."

Saint's eyes slashed toward me, and she clutched my arm tightly. "I should've been more careful. I thought it would be okay in the VIP area. There's security everywhere. I just went up to dance, then the next thing I knew, Noah called me on stage."

I shot Gambit a sharp look, my mind already running through possible scenarios. "Hundreds of people had access to the area."

He nodded his agreement. "Yeah. I can check the security footage, but it'll be like looking for a needle in a haystack, and unless the cameras were in the spot where it happened at the right time, they wouldn't have picked up on anything."

My arm tightened around Saint's shoulders. "I've got keys to your house, so we can get in, but I think it'll be a good idea to grab some stuff and go to a hotel. I'll arrange to get your locks changed tomorrow and reset your security system."

Saint nodded, biting her lip nervously.

"We'll figure it out," I assured her. "I won't let anyone get to you."

Her shoulders relaxed slightly, and she smiled. "I know you won't. I just feel stupid for being so careless."

"You didn't ask to get your purse taken, Saint," Gambit pointed out gently. "It's not your fault."

"He's right, baby," I concurred. "It could be somebody took it by mistake, or it may just be a chancer out to make a quick buck. We'll go back to the house, cancel your credit card, and pack a bag. We can do the rest of the shit tomorrow."

"Okay," she agreed.

"Saint!" a voice called out.

I turned to see Talia come bustling out into the foyer.

"Where the fuck were you?" she demanded. "I waited, then I went backstage to look for you and saw Noah, who sent me back out, saying you'd gone to dance. I've been looking goddamned everywhere."

"Sorry," Saint murmured, her cheeks flushing prettily. "I must've missed you."

Talia's eyes took in Saint's appearance before sweeping to me. She cocked an eyebrow. "I see how it is. Jesus, it's like a bad nineties movie about the beautiful singer and the bodyguard." Her lips twisted. "Whitney and Kevin, eat your heart out."

Saint's smile was saccharine sweet. "By the way. I ended things with Hunter. You better get behind that."

"Ugh," Tally exclaimed. "And there was me thinking I'd get an easy day tomorrow." Her eyes came to me accusingly. "And what about your wife?"

A strangled noise escaped Gambit's throat, and he let out a cough.

"Tally," Saint murmured. "It's none of your business."

"You're my business," Talia stated emphatically. "And if you're seeing a married man, it's not just the breakup with Hunter I need to get behind, is it?"

I heaved out a breath. "My wife's dead, Talia. She passed away twelve years ago."

"Well fuck," Talia exclaimed. "Now I feel like a cunt."

"If it walks like a duck," Saint snapped. "Why can't you just keep your mouth shut? Maybe Jacob didn't want to broadcast his private information. Jesus, Talia."

A slow smile spread over Tally's face. "Well, check you out, going all Tammy Wynette on me and standing by your man. I didn't fucking know, did I?" Her gaze slid to mine, and she shot me a sympathetic smile. "Sorry."

I shrugged. "No harm, no foul."

"What are you all standing out here for, anyway?" she asked, swiftly changing the subject.

"My bag's missing," Saint informed her. "It's got my keys, phone, and credit card in it."

Talia sighed audibly. "Oh, great. Let's hope stalker weirdo wasn't here and nabbed it. The last thing I need is my star act getting kidnapped in her sleep, although I doubt my star act will be sleeping alone, huh, Saint?" Her lips stretched into a suggestive grin. "Jacob Costner will keep you safe when he lifts you into his strong, beefy arms and carries you to safety, just like in the movies."

"Oh, Jesus," Saint murmured. "Excuse my manager's dramatics."

"I'm heading out," Talia announced, pulling her phone from her purse and checking her messages. "Sam and Jolie already left, and Jonny disappeared somewhere ages ago, too. Boomer's waiting for Gambit, and he's going to the after-party. I'll cancel your credit card and get a new one ordered, and I'll get a new cell phone delivered first thing in the morning. The security company will need to change your locks, too. Are you going home now?"

Scanning the foyer, I noticed people were starting to leave. "Yeah. I was going to take Saint to a hotel tonight and sort the lock issue out in the morning."

"I'll do it now," she argued. "Go home and hang fire."

I checked my watch. "It's just gone midnight."

Talia's eyebrows furrowed. "And?"

"How will you get a locksmith out tonight?" I asked.

"I can get the President of the United fucking States out if I want to, Jacob." Her mouth stretched into a cocky smile. "Don't you know who I am?"

I glanced at Gambit, who was looking down at his boots, grinning. "I've no doubt you can work miracles, but let's not disturb the POTUS over Saint's locks. I'm sure he's got better things to worry about."

Talia nodded and began typing on her phone. "I'll make some calls. You just look after Saint." Her eyes never left her screen as she began to move toward the exit, calling out, "Later, bitches."

"She's a trip," Gambit muttered, his eyes following Talia out of the door.

I tapped a message out to our driver to call him around. "She's a fucking ballbuster, but I can't say I hate it when she uses her powers to look after my girl here."

"Thanks," Saint murmured sweetly. "But I could look after myself."

"You pay her a percentage so that you don't need to, baby," I pointed out, pocketing my phone. "Let her earn her cake." I dipped my chin to catch my girl's eyes. "You ready to jet?"

"Yeah," she breathed, pulling the lapels of my jacket closer around her, flashing me a grateful smile. "It's been a long day."

I gave Gambit a fist bump before placing my hand on the small of Saint's back and guiding her through the thinning crowd.

As we approached the door, she glanced up at me and murmured, "Brace."

The second we stepped outside, blinding flashes went off, and the crowd of photographers began yelling.

"Saint. Where's Hunter?"

"Is it true you sang with the band tonight?"

"How's the new album coming along, Saint?"

Saint instinctively moved closer to me, seeking refuge from the chaos around us. I could feel the tension in her shoulders by the way they stiffened as I hustled her toward the waiting car that had just pulled up. She remained composed, her gaze fixed ahead, and a polite smile plastered across her face as she ignored their bellowing and intrusive questions.

Leaning forward, I went to grab the door handle, glancing back at Saint to make sure she was okay, and that was when I saw him.

A photographer was behind my girl, on his knees, trying to take a picture up her skirt.

White-hot rage flashed behind my eyes, and I didn't think; I just reacted. My hand shot out, and I snagged the photographer's shirt, dragged him to his feet, and slammed his back against the car. His camera went flying, and I caught it mid-air.

My hand went to his throat, and I collared him with it. "You a fuckin' pervert?" I snarled, getting in his face. "You a fucking peeper?" I dragged him from the car and threw him to the ground, watching as he stumbled and went down face-first. I shoved Saint behind my back to protect her from the photographers, who were going crazy as their bulbs flashed, and the shouts became deafening.

Saint grabbed my arm, and she urged, "Jacob. Let's go."

Clasping my girl's shoulder, I crowded her between my body and the car, pulling the door open before growling, "Get in, but do it carefully."

Her eyes were wide with fear, and she nodded, her bottom lip trembling as she perched her ass on the back seat and swung her legs inside while making sure to keep them closed.

I slid in after her, leaning across to swing the door shut behind me, giving us instant relief from the flashes of the cameras and the loud shouts from the paps.

Saint pressed herself back against the leather seat, her chest rising and falling with panicked breaths and her eyes wide with disbelief. "What the fuck?" she whispered, her voice shaky. "I haven't got any underwear on."

My hand went to her neck, where I could see her pulse fluttering, and I stroked my thumb across it, trying to soothe her. "They're fuckin' vultures," I ground out. "That sick fuck was almost laid out trying to fucking upskirt you."

Her hand rested on mine, which still stroked across her throat. "I know," she replied quietly. "Thank you. If he'd have gotten a shot of me bare..." Her voice trailed off, and she closed her eyes. "They sell them to porn sites, Jacob."

Something primal in me rose up, and I pulled Saint closer, trying to comfort her. "I'll call Kennedy," I assured her. "She'll sue his ass into next year."

"Who's Kennedy?" she asked.

I stroked Saint's hair back from her face. "She's an ol' lady at my old chapter in Wyoming. Ned's also a lawyer and a shark."

"The guy may try to sue you, too," Saint relayed, her voice taking on a matter-of-fact tone. "I'll call Talia now and get her on it."

"Don't worry about me," I told her. "You're the one that asshole tried to fucking violate. What the fuck was all that about? Does it happen a lot?"

"The premieres and organized events are more controlled because the photographers are cordoned off, but it's still crazy. It's the paps outside the nightclubs who are the worst, though. They're not regulated, so anyone can pick up a camera and follow me around, and there's nothing I can do about it, legally or otherwise."

I could feel Saint's frustration and hear the resignation in her voice.

My chest tightened as my thoughts flashed back to that asshole on the ground, trying to violate my woman's privacy and her body.

I'd been to LA before and had experienced how fucking sinister this town could be, but I never understood what a vulnerable position women like Saint were in with something as simple as going to an event.

What just happened was sick. That so-called photographer should've been on a fucking sex offenders register. Did he have a wife and kids? How would he have felt if somebody tried to do that shit to his daughter?

No woman should have to endure that bullshit. It was a stark reminder of the nasty shit that lurked behind the glitz and glamor of fame, and it made me realize exactly how much danger Saint and other women in the industry were in.

If something as simple as being photographed could result in that kind of abusive shit, I could only imagine how deeply being stalked must have affected her on the daily. Could you fucking imagine walking out of a nightclub or restaurant and having some guy get on his knees trying to get pictures of your fucking private parts?

Jesus.

The peal of my ringtone filled the car. I pulled my phone out of my pocket, saw who it was, and clicked to answer the call.

Saint's gaze darted toward me when I greeted, "Talia."

"Can't I leave you alone for five fucking minutes?" she screeched.

Pulling the cell away from my ear, I clicked the cell onto speakerphone and replied, "You could try leaving me alone for a few hours. Me and Saint need some sleep."

"Well, that's gonna be impossible, seeing as there are videos of you all over social fucking media having an altercation with the paparazzi. The fucks I give are negligible, Jacob. You could drag every one of those asswipes into a street full of speeding Mack trucks for all I care, but what I *do* care about is that you don't do it on goddamned camera. The pictures and videos are everywhere."

"You're shitting me," I muttered, glancing at Saint, whose face was starting to twist. "That fucking pap was trying to upskirt her, Tally. He was on the fucking ground trying to snap up her dress, for God's sake. He's a goddamned perv."

Talia sighed loudly. "I get it. The paparazzi are assholes when they do that, but you can't beat every photographer up who goes over-the-top trying to get a shot. I'm sure Saint doesn't want her panties plastered all over the World Wide Web, but better that than you in jail. Who'd protect her if you were behind bars? I'm not saying you have to let them get away with it; I'm saying, in the future, we go through legal channels. The record company has a law firm on retainer; it's about time we gave them something to do."

Saint let out a humorless laugh. "I wasn't wearing underwear, Talia."

Silence fell over the car.

"Did you hear me?" Saint prompted.

"Stop talking," Talia bit out. "I'm trying to think of all the ways I can ruin that fucking pap's life."

"Jacob was just doing his job," Saint explained softly. "Just like he was earlier with Jonny."

Talia went quiet for a moment, and I could almost hear the cogs turning in her head. "The cops may turn up at your place, Saint. If they do, call me immediately. Let them in and answer their questions, explain what happened, and don't leave anything out. Even the underwear thing. With any luck, I can get them to go back to the pap and try to pin him with some kind of sexual assault charge." She started murmuring to herself. "We could use this to our advantage. Saint's bodyguard is of such high moral standing that he won't allow some pervert to take advantage of his client. I can work with that, no problem."

"The guy was a fucking creeper," I retorted.

I felt Saint's shoulders tense up again, and I twisted my head to kiss her temple.

"I'll go through all the online footage and patch some shit together," Talia stated. "The other paps will be out to take you down, so their footage will favor the guy you dragged, but there's also phone footage from some of the Dischordium fans who were outside waiting to see the boys. I could ask Noah to go onto his Instagram page and ask if any of them would send in what they've got. I'll arrange a meet and greet to convey our gratitude."

"Thanks, Tally," Saint breathed.

"Remember. If the cops show up, call me. I'm too hyped to sleep, anyway. The guys from the security company are coming out, too, so I don't think you two will get much rest either." Talia sighed. "I've canceled your credit card, too, and your new cell phone should be with you by nine in the morning."

Saint smiled, shaking her head. "What would I do without you?"

"Live a phoneless, keyless, and broke life because somebody maxed out your credit card," Talia replied.

"Remember, keep me posted." And with that, the line clicked as Talia ended the call.

Despite the disastrous night, I chuckled. "I should take you to Virginia before we go to New York. You need some fucking peace from all this bullshit."

Saint's neck twisted, and she peered into my eyes. "Really?"

"I was joking, baby. Our home and base is an old hotel, which is great if you're a biker, but I'm not sure it's the kind of place you'll feel comfortable in. The guys are great, but they're fuckin' crazy, and we'd get zero privacy."

"Do you share a room?" she asked.

"No, I've got my own space, but I live communally. I keep meaning to look for places nearer town, but there's been no urgent need, and with my work, I'm not there all the time, anyway. Still, your pad puts mine to shame."

"I love my house," Saint mused. "But it's just a house. With all this stalker bullshit, it's lost its shine a little because I don't feel totally comfortable there anymore. It's made me realize that home is about safety and the people in it, not the environment." Her eyes held mine, and she smiled softly. "Home wouldn't be home without you."

"Baby," I murmured, my voice husky with emotion. I cupped her jaw and turned her face toward me, lowering my head to kiss her bottom lip and suck it gently until Saint's lips parted under mine, and her hands came up to rest lightly on my chest.

She pulled back slightly, and her eyes searched mine. "I missed you."

I kissed her forehead, feeling the weight of her words settle over me. "I missed you, too, baby. Every fucking day, I'd hear one of your songs on the radio and have to change the station 'cause I couldn't fuckin' stand how much I ached for you. Everywhere I went, I saw reminders of you, and they drove me insane."

She leaned up and kissed me softly, her hand going to my cheek, her thumb stroking gently across my stubble.

My gut was filled with a sense of fierce protectiveness for the beautiful woman in my arms.

I'd never let anything happen to her. Nothing would touch her when she was with me. Fans, photographers, even stalkers; none of them stood a fuckin' chance.

I'd burn the world down for Saint McClure, and if anybody tried to take her from me, they'd burn with it.

Chapter Ten

Saint

My thumb strummed my eight-string, my gaze studying Jacob, who lay naked and completely exposed on my white sheets, watching me languidly with his eyes half-mast.

He was so confident about his body, but then he had every reason to be. His skin was toned and tanned, his defined muscles rippling every time he moved. I loved the smattering of fine, dark-blond hair sprinkled across his pecs and the large tattoo across his collarbone in a semi-circle that read, *dream, achieve, believe* in sweeping, cursive script.

His shoulders and biceps were covered in tribal patterns, intricately weaved together, almost creating balance for the words on his chest. My eyes dipped to glance at the beautiful dreamcatcher inked into his ribs, probably my favorite tattoo of his because it was a protective symbol that reminded me of my guy's equally protective nature.

Jacob's aura filled the room, and I couldn't help but feel awestruck. Watching him relax into the sheets, his gaze lazy and unfocused, had a way of making everything feel lighter and lessened the weight of my own problems.

It had been a week since the Dischordium party, and we'd spent every waking (and sleeping) moment together. Getting to know Jacob was proving to be the happiest and most exciting time of my life. Every reveal warmed me, and every story brought us closer together. We talked about his family and my career. His military service and my days playing to audiences of four drunk people in a bar.

My fingers began to pluck at my eight-string, and with my eyes never leaving Jacob's, I began to softly sing the opening verse to "Rooms on Fire" by Stevie Nicks directly to him.

He propped himself up on one elbow, his gaze fixed on me with unwavering intensity, his eyes flicking over my face and body as if he wanted to drink me in and memorize the moment.

The emotion in the room grew along with the crescendo of the song as the words weaved around us.

A sense of peace settled over me. It was crazy how quickly Jacob had become part of my world, filling in the blanks I hadn't even realized were empty. I wondered how I'd gone so long without him because the thought of him not being beside me filled me with an ache that robbed my lungs of all breath.

I began to play softer, my voice almost a whisper as the song came to an end. Immediately, I went into the opening bars of "Landslide," but instead of singing, I asked, "Favorite album? Give me your top five."

"That one's easy, baby." He grinned. "*Dark Side of the Moon. Joshua Tree. Back in Black. Born in the USA*, and I'll cheat with the Eagles' *Greatest Hits*. It's still an album, right?"

I laughed softly. "It didn't take long to think about it. I love your choices, though I always thought *Off the Wall* was better as a concept album than *Dark Side of the Moon*."

He shifted on the bed, his gaze glued to where I was strumming on my guitar. "My dad used to listen to *Dark Side* with me. He'd take me out to his workshop, and we'd zone out to it for hours. My pop's a loud, confident guy, and he has all the chat of a Southern gentleman, but in those quiet moments, he'd just get lost in the music. I loved spending time with him but didn't get the album, initially; however, as I grew and understood more, Dad explained the thought process behind the record and how it's about the human experience in all its forms and how insane it is and ultimately, the shit we gotta do to get through it. Maybe it's not the music I love but the nostalgia and the moments in time those records represent." His warm eyes settled on mine. "I live for top fives. I've told you mine; now you tell me yours."

"*Rumors*"—I hitched a brow—"goes without saying because I love Stevie. *Hounds of Love. Legend. Hotel California*, and the *Dirty Dancing Soundtrack*."

Jacob let out a low chuckle. "*Dirty Dancing Soundtrack?*"

I nodded, thinking back to the time I first experienced it. "I used to listen to it in secret growing up. I saw the movie at a friend's house and became obsessed with the music. The dancers at the resort were so raw and free, and it was such a contrast to my life, which was so utterly manacled and repressed. I loved the movie's message, and I especially loved how, in public, Johnny Castle and the other dancers played by the rules and stayed in their lane, but behind closed doors, they allowed their true selves to emerge. It spoke to me on so many levels because that was my life, too."

Jacob shifted to his knees and took the guitar from me, gently placing it on the floor beside the bed. Then he tugged my hand and pulled me down to lie beside him, maneuvering me until we both faced each other, our noses almost touching. He placed his hand on my hip, his gaze holding mine, and his thumb stroking my skin. "Tell me."

"My dad's a church pastor," I informed him.

He gave me a tight-lipped smile. "And what did that mean for you growing up?"

"It meant no music, no TV, no friends or boyfriends. My social life was non-existent except for prayer meetings, church functions, and Sunday school. I wasn't even allowed to read unless it was the *Bible* or, at a push, religious-themed books, and even then, Dad vetted them."

Jacob nodded understandingly. "So, how did you become a rock star?"

"I had a teacher, Miss Hawkins, who played the guitar in music class one day, and I was mesmerized. At recess, I went to her and asked her to show me. I picked it up, learned three chords, and by the end of the week, was playing as if I'd been born to it."

Jacob smiled. "Maybe you were."

I smiled back, my memories making my eyes misty with tears. "I tried, Jacob, so fucking hard."

"Tried what?" he asked.

"To be what he wanted me to be."

He leaned forward and nuzzled my nose with his. "Baby. You can only ever be who you are."

I rested my hand on his. "I wanted to be a daughter he could love and be proud of, but I couldn't live like that. If I'd stayed, I would've been miserable because the instant I heard Solomon Burke singing "Cry to Me," something inside me shifted, and suddenly, my life wasn't enough. Music became my escape, my solace. It wasn't about Mom and Dad or the church. It wasn't even about me. In that split second, everything became about music."

Jacob's hand slid up my ribs and cupped my nape. "What happened next?"

I let out a short laugh. "I rebelled, or so Dad thought. I didn't mean to rebel, though; I just wanted to play guitar and listen to music. Miss Hawkins gave me that old six-string, and I learned it down to its bones. When Bryan Adams said, 'played until my fingers bled,' he was talking about me. I've guitar string scars that are ingrained into my skin, but they're also ingrained into my soul. Dad just stopped speaking to me one day, so I left. I had a thousand bucks in the bank that I inherited from my grandparents, and I got on a bus to LA."

"And the rest is rock 'n' roll history?"

I laughed softly. "I wish. Two hours after I got off the bus, I met Boomer in a coffee shop. He invited me to sleep on his couch, and that first night, I wrote "Born Again." We found Jonny, and then Talia came across our YouTube channel, added Sam into the mix, and the real hard work started."

His forehead furrowed as he studied me. "I've never heard anybody speak like you before. The way you use words and express yourself is like living in a song. It touches me somewhere deep, Saint. I dunno what to say around you sometimes 'cause you're so smart and eloquent; it's like your mind's in a different league to mine. You see beauty in things I don't look at twice. We don't make any sense what-so-*fucking*-ever, except when I'm with you, everything makes perfect sense."

"Jacob," I whispered, my throat thick with tears.

"I've never felt like this before," he murmured.

"Not even with—" I began to ask the question, but stopped myself mid-sentence. I still wasn't sure how comfortable Jacob was talking about his wife. The last thing I wanted to do was make him hurt, especially when we were being so vulnerable with each other. I needed him to trust that I'd keep him as safe emotionally as he kept me physically. Also, I didn't want to break the spell we'd weaved with our soft touches and heartfelt words.

If I could lie here, gazing at Jacob for the rest of my life, I'd count myself lucky.

"It was different with Allie," he explained softly, his eyes taking on a faraway look. "It was comfortable and easy. With you, it's thrilling, like I wake up excited for the day ahead 'cause I never know what I'm gonna get."

"Yeah," I breathed. "I know."

"I loved her," he murmured. "But I need you to breathe."

Heat hit the back of my throat. "Yeah," I repeated. "I know."

"Allie died of heart failure," he went on. "The postmortem revealed she had a condition called Long QT Syndrome. It prolonged Allie's QT interval, which led to a sudden heart attack. We didn't know she had the condition, and it had never knowingly affected her before. It came out of the blue." His forehead furrowed. "I was up in the air at the time on a surveillance mission. There was no way my commanding officer would or could have told me what had happened while I was airborne. I wasn't aware there was anything wrong until four hours after she was officially declared dead."

My throat burned. "I'm so fucking sorry, Jacob."

His fingers stroked the back of my neck. "You don't need to be, baby. I'm gutted I lost her, but I'm grateful to be here with you. My world stopped turning the day Allie died, then I looked into your eyes that night two years ago, and you made it spin again."

My heart fluttered at his beautiful words. "For someone who doesn't know what to say around me, you're doing a stand-up job."

Jake's chuckle was rough and deep. "Maybe you bring out the romantic in me." His hand lifted to the dip in my back, and he pulled me in until our bodies connected. His cock was hard, and I shivered at the sensation as he ground himself against me.

He leaned into my neck, his lips skimming my collarbone, his fingers lifting the hem of my tank, pulling it up my arms and over my head, leaving my breasts bared. "I can't get enough of you. Just when I think I've had my fill, you pick up a guitar and weave your magic. Never seen anything as sexy as you playing your guitar wearing just a pair of panties and a tiny little titty top."

I giggled at the tickling sensation from his stubble as it scraped across my neck. "It's not as sexy as watching you lie back naked with your arm flung over your eyes with that chest and all. You're hotter than Hades, and twice as bad."

His hand trailed across my breast, and my nipple pebbled in response. I let out a contented sigh and wriggled in his arms, my thighs clenching with need.

"You burn me up," he muttered. "I feel like I'm gonna spontaneously combust. Everythin' about you makes me hard. Even when you're bratty. Hell, especially when you're bratty." His teeth grazed the underside of my breast. "Never tasted anythin' sweeter than you, Saint McClure."

My toes curled as his mouth enclosed a nipple, and he sucked hard and wet before trailing kisses across my chest and drawing the other one between his lips. My head spun with need, and my skin burned for him, and going by the way heat rolled off him in waves, he burned for me, too.

My hand lowered to his cock, and I trailed my fingers across it, making his hips buck against my hand. "Touch me," he commanded, his voice rough and growly.

Wrapping my fingers around him, I began to pull and twist, adjusting the strength of my grip as I tugged.

Jacob let out a low moan, and he buried his face in my throat and sucked on the soft skin there.

"I love how hard you get for me," I whispered, stroking up and down.

"Jesus, woman," he rasped. "You're gonna make me nut." He pulled out of my hold and slid an arm under my leg, hitching it up and opening me good and wide. "Fuck!" he cut out. "Wrap."

He let me go, his arm going to his nightstand to grab a condom. I took the opportunity to wriggle out of his hold and slide down the bed until I was face-to-face with his big, hard dick.

Grabbing the base roughly, I took the tip in my mouth, then with a deep moan, I slid my lips down his length, sucking hard as I went.

"Jesus fuck!" he groaned, his hips bucking uncontrollably.

I gagged slightly but quickly recovered and began to suck up his length slowly until I reached the burgeoning head and swirled my tongue around it.

His hips bucked again, and the next thing I knew, I was being hauled up by the arms and slammed onto my back. He expertly sheathed his cock, and I licked my lips at the delectable sight. I could still taste him on my tongue, his scent all man and musky, with a hint of citrus and cedar from his Bleu De Chanel cologne.

Fucking hot.

He hovered over me, his eyes gleaming. "You gonna take it rough?"

I leaned up on my elbows and nipped his earlobe. "As rough as you can give it to me, Iceman."

With a groan, Jake came to me, and I spread my legs wide, getting ready to take him. My entire body heated, and my clit throbbed, nipples still peaked as he hitched my leg again from under the knee and held it high. "Sexy as goddamned fuck," he muttered.

I felt his cock nudge my opening, then his hips jerked, and he pushed inside, filling me up. He rooted himself to me, no inch spared, and ground his hips in a circular motion, catching my clit on the pass before pulling all the way out to the tip until I felt empty and slamming back inside again.

My pussy ached, it was so full of him, and he ground into me again, lowering his mouth to suck on my neck. Waves of pleasure ebbed through my body, my pussy pulsed, and my clit hummed every time the base of his hard, thick cock circled against it, giving me the friction I needed to start building to my climax.

Jacob hoisted my knees higher until they were almost flush with my chest, gaining access to go deeper than anyone had before.

He slammed his cock inside, then pulled out to the tip before thrusting hard again, over and over, until my eyes rolled into the back of my head and my walls clenched around him.

I got lost in the moment and in the force of the intense pleasure he was giving me. "Fuck... Jacob... yeah, baby, fuck me hard." My words were a chant, almost nonsensical, as I begged him to fuck me rough and to never stop.

My orgasm, when it came, was like a white-hot poker spearing through me, and I cried out into the room, every muscle on fire, the tendons in my neck straining as he bit down on my throat and sucked hard.

I cried out, "Don't fucking stop."

"Fuck yeah," he groaned. "Come on my cock, Saint."

I let out a keening cry as the waves of pleasure enveloped me. My fingernails dug into his ass, and I held on tight as he fucked me hard through my orgasm.

He let out a shout, and I felt his cock swell. Then warmth flooded me, and I felt a pulsing sensation as he filled the condom with his hot cum. His hips lost all rhythm, and he panted against my throat, his teeth scraping against my fluttering pulse as I came back to Earth with a satisfied sigh.

His pounding began to slow and soften until it became a gentle glide, and I felt the tension leave his body. He slumped down, releasing my knee, his hand going straight to my breast and cupping it gently.

Jacob lifted his head and stared down at me, his lips quirking. "You okay?"

I smiled like the cat who got the cream (because right then, that's what I was) and nodded enthusiastically.

"One of these days, I'll fuck you all night"—he checked the clock on my nightstand—"not just for forty minutes."

"I don't care," I whispered. "It's never been this good for me. I like how spontaneous we are. I love how we can be sitting, having a conversation, a deep one at that, and then you pounce on me like you're starving, and I'm your next meal."

"It's you and that guitar," he rumbled, his icy eyes softening. "You do things to me. You're like a beautiful songbird. Never believed in magic before; never had reason to. But you weave a spell on me that I never wanna break."

"For someone who says he's not romantic, you make my heart do somersaults, Jacob Irons."

His answering grin was full of mischief. "I've got a few good lines up my sleeve. You may be a songbird, but I'm a pilot, baby. I can take you to heaven and back."

Outwardly, I groaned at the cheesiness of his line, but inside, I melted.

His hands caught mine, and he dragged them up the bed until they rested beside my head. "Loved you then," he whispered. "Love you now. And I'll love you forever."

A rush of warmth spread through me, mingling with the desire I always felt when I was around him. My eyes filled with tears of emotion.

It was the first time he'd told me he loved me.

The first time anyone had where it was real, and not because I was performing on stage.

"I sing to thousands of people all over the world," I croaked. "But nobody ever saw me the way you do. Nobody ever made me feel so seen or so relevant. To you, I'm not Saint McClure, the rock singer; I'm just me, and you're just you."

He rolled us until we lay on our sides again, facing each other the same way we did before we fucked. "Nah, baby. I'm Iceman. Biker bad boy and bodyguard who's gonna corrupt my sweet, innocent girl and make her beg for my dick."

I giggled, storing that information in my head for future use.

"You gonna corrupt me, big, bad biker Iceman?" I asked softly.

He nodded, cupping my jaw before kissing me hard on the lips, and we began to make out again. My hand slid around to grasp his ass, and he moaned into my mouth. "Fuck, baby. How the hell am I hard agai—"

Jacob's phone pinged, and he froze briefly before releasing my lips and lifting his head. "That's a security notification," he cut out.

My stomach dropped.

Like a flash, he was up, grabbing his cell and checking the cameras. "Somebody's out back." He bent down to grab his jeans and stood up to pull them over his legs and ass. "Lock the door behind me and call Colt." He tossed his phone toward me. "My code's zero-eight-zero-one. Tell him what's happening and to lock in and get images. When you're done, call the cops." He pulled his tee over his head, then went to his dresser to rummage through the bottom drawer.

My eyes widened when something glinted in the lamplight, and I saw he'd pulled out a black handgun. "Oh my God."

He nodded to the phone in my hand. "Keep your shit together and make the call, Saint."

I stared at the gun, open-mouthed.

"Saint!" he barked. "Stay with me, baby."

Snapping my mouth shut, I nodded, cursing at my clumsy, trembling fingers as I fumbled with the phone.

A soft kiss landed on my head, and Jake murmured, "You'll be okay, baby."

I glanced up to meet his eyes, and my heart tugged painfully. "I'm more worried about you. Please be careful."

"Always." He pulled me up and toward the door, ordering, "Lock it after me," before pulling it open and disappearing.

After twisting the key, I looked down at the phone, my fingers shaking as I keyed in the passcode. It lit up in my hands, and I gasped at all the tech that had been programmed into it.

Going to his contacts, I looked for Colt's name and clicked on the number before pressing the speakerphone icon, all while trying to keep my panicked breaths steady. The phone didn't even have time to ring before the call clicked open, and a deep voice muttered, "Already on it. I got the security breach notification, too."

"It's Saint. Umm... Saint McClure?" My voice faltered because I didn't quite know what to say. "Jacob told me to call you."

"Hey, Saint," he replied. "I'm Colt, Iceman's MC brother, and I'm also an FBI agent. I've got eyes on your house, and I'm locking in and pulling up the cameras now to get more information. Are you okay?"

"Yeah," I confirmed in a low voice. "Nothing happened to us directly. I'm more worried about

Jaco—Umm... Iceman. He's gone down there alone with a gun."

"Ice knows what he's doin', sweetheart. Don't worry about him, you've got one of the best at your back. Feel me?"

"Yeah," I replied quietly, taking in the tapping sounds in the background as Colt typed on a keyboard. "I know."

"He's on the ground floor now. The intruder's in your backyard. He can't get inside the house, so don't worry." Colt paused, then said, "I'm a huge fan. My ol' lady, Freya, loves "Empty." It's one of her favorite songs. She makes me listen to it on a loop in the car."

I bit my lip nervously.

The last thing I wanted to do was talk about music, but I didn't want to seem churlish toward one of Jacob's friends, so I muttered, "Thanks." Keeping my eyes glued to the screen, I tried to focus. "I don't want to come across as rude, Colt, but right now, all I care about is Jacob's safety."

He chuckled softly down the line. "I know, sweetheart. Just trying to keep your mind off what's goin' on."

"What do I do now?" I asked, feeling utterly helpless. "Is there something I can do to help Jacob? I'm not the damsel in distress type, but I don't want to get in his way."

"Yeah, Saint," he replied gently. "You can stay put. Ice can't concentrate on taking down a perp if he's worried about where you are. I've got eyes on him, and our VP, Blade, is guiding him over comms. We'll get him through it. The most helpful thing you can do is stay safe and keep out of sight."

I nodded even though he couldn't see me. "You guys are like the A-Team or something."

Colt chuckled. "Yeah, I guess we are. Though none of us have been taken to military court for a crime we didn't commit."

"I always wondered what it was they were supposed to have done," I mused, starting to pace.

"They were accused of robbing a bank during a covert operation in the Vietnam War," he stated.

I stopped dead. "Oh"

"They were cleared of all charges by the end of the last series," Colt went on. "They were exonerated, got honorary discharges, back pay, and apologies."

"Wow," I breathed. "You know a lot about the A-Team."

"Used to watch the reruns when I was a kid," he informed me. "If a subject interests me, I find out everything I can about it."

"Are you on the spectrum?" I asked bluntly.

Colt chuckled before muttering a wry, "Probably. I obsess about a lot of shit."

"Yeah," I concurred. "Me too." I paused briefly before asking, "Is Jake doing okay?"

"So far, so good," Colt assured me. "He's already slipped outside, and he's got the jump on the intruder. Won't be long now."

The dragging minutes seemed like hours. I paced the room, biting my lip until it stung. Every second that ticked by increased my anxiety, and every slight noise made me jump until my nerves frayed like unraveling cotton.

After what seemed like an eternity, Colt's voice murmured, "It's clear. Iceman's apprehended the perp, and the cops are on the scene."

My shoulders slumped. "Thank God. Is he okay?"

Colt laughed softly. "He's fine. Dunno about the intruder, though. Iceman's trussed him up like a Thanksgiving turkey."

I couldn't help laughing at Colt's description.

"You feeling okay?" he asked gently.

"Yeah," I said earnestly. "Thanks."

"Stay put a bit longer," he advised. "Ice will be up to get you soon. The cops will probably want to take a statement from you both. I'll call my contact at LAPD and make sure they look after you."

I sighed my relief and murmured, "Thanks again."

"Make sure you get Ice to bring you for a visit soon. Freya's gonna be jealous as hell when she finds out I met you before she did, and she won't break my balls if I tell her she'll get to meet you soon. I'll let you go now. Tell Ice to call Prez with an update when the cops go, and you take care, Saint," he ordered before the call clicked out.

I sank down on the bed, tossed the phone on the mattress beside me, and dropped my head into my hands.

My thoughts immediately went to Jacob, and I wondered if he'd caught the person he'd been hired to protect me from. Weirdly, my stomach twisted at the thought. I mean, sure, I wanted my life back. The notion of being able to walk down the street without having to take security made my fears fall away for the first time in weeks.

But I couldn't stop my inner voice whispering, *What about Jacob?*

If he'd caught the man who'd been tormenting me, the job would be over, and he'd have to leave. During one of our many 'get to know you' sessions, we'd talked about his work and how one minute he could be protecting a diplomat or an actor, and the next, jetting off to a different country to mount a rescue. I was about to head to New York with the band to record the album, and I'd be there for a while, so there was no doubt we'd be separated.

The last time me and Jacob walked away from each other, everything imploded. I knew there were extenuating circumstances surrounding what happened, but it showed me that nothing in life was guaranteed.

I'd jumped head-first into Jacob in a way where I knew there was no going back, and I knew deep down in my bones that losing him again would ruin me.

Chapter Eleven

Iceman

I stood, legs planted a foot apart, and my arms folded across my chest, staring at the fucknut on the ground, hog-tied to within an inch of his life.

My lips twitched like a motherfucker as I listened to the cop rip him a new asshole like he was twelve years old and had just been caught stealing a candy bar.

"So," one of the cops, who had turned up, drawled. "You thought it was a good idea to come to the home of a celebrity at ten o'clock at night to serve her bodyguard with a complaint and a summons?"

"It's my job," a tight voice said from the direction of the floor.

The cop jerked his chin toward me. "And it's his job to hog-tie intruders who creep around his client's house like they're gearing up to rob the joint. Do you see my dilemma?" He shook his head exasperatedly. "You're lucky he didn't fill your ass with bullets. Did you know the owner of this house is currently being stalked, and everybody's on high alert?"

"Well. No," the guy muttered, his face flushing red.

The cop looked at his partner and shook his head again, his lips thinning. "Can you believe this clown?"

I rolled my lips together to stop myself from barking a laugh.

"Look, I'm just tryin'a do my job," the asshole whined. "The law firm offered me two hundred bucks to serve this dude. You know the law's on my side here."

The second cop's eyes narrowed. "What we know is that your job is to walk up the front path and ring the bell. You went around the back and were looking in all the goddamned windows without a doorbell chime to be heard. What were you thinking?"

The dude lowered his gaze, his face reddening so much it almost turned purple, and he mumbled, "I dunno."

The cop glowered. "If you don't start being straight with me, I'll keep those zip ties on you, haul you down the station, and book you for trespassing."

The guy shot me a glare. "Alright, alright. I just wanted to see Saint, okay?"

My head reared back. "Are you a pervert?"

"No!" he cried. "I'm a huge fan. That's why I took this job on. I thought I might be able to get her autograph and maybe a picture. Could you put a word in for me, man?"

I scraped a hand down my face. "Jesus Christ. I could've damned well killed you. Saint had to lock herself in her room, scared out of her wits because some imbecile decided to creep around her pad at night, uninvited, and you think she's gonna be all smiles while she poses for pictures?" My voice rose an octave. "You must be out of your goddamned mind!"

"Well, when you put it like that..." His words trailed off, and he had the good grace to lower his gaze, looking decidedly ashamed of himself.

One of the cops rolled his eyes and hooked his eyebrow at me. "We can arrest him for trespassing. There's enough video evidence to throw the book at him and make sure he thinks twice the next time he wants to perv on someone famous. If we do it that way, we'll need you and Ms. McClure to come down to the station and give statements, and it'll take up most of your night. Alternatively, we can drag him out of here and tell him he's not to come within ten feet of you or your client. That way, he can't serve you papers, and he'll have to go on his sweet way. And if he tries anything else, I give you my word that I'll lock him in a cell and forget he's there for a week or two."

"Wait here," I muttered, turning and prowling into the next room where Saint stood watching and listening. As soon as the cops arrived and read the guy his rights, I went upstairs to tell her everything was okay and to stop her worrying about what the fuck was happening downstairs.

The minute I spotted the guy peering into the windows from the video surveillance on my phone, I could tell he was no threat. Still, I wasn't about to take any chances with Saint's safety, and not only because I was assigned to protect her, but after the week we'd had together, she was also my woman, and no fucker touched my woman but me.

I walked into the kitchen and immediately saw Saint pacing by the door wearing denim shorts and her little bitty titty top. She didn't have a scrap of makeup on, and she still had sex hair from earlier when I gave her my cock and made her come good and hard all over me.

She was stunning.

Her azure-blue eyes slid to meet mine, and she beamed a smile that lit up every dark crevice inside me that Allie left when she died.

Good God above.

Beautiful.

"He's a dick," she announced, jerking her thumb toward the family room where I'd dragged the perp across the floor by the hair after hog-tying him.

"I know," I concurred. "But is he enough of a dick to make you press charges?"

"Probably not. Tell that asshole if he serves you because you pushed some prick who tried to upskirt me, I'll get him thrown in jail so quickly his head will spin. I'll also personally visit the prison they send him to and hire a burly fucker called Big Al to make him his bitch."

I threw my head back and laughed.

Saint's eyes turned molten, and she whispered, "God, you're fucking beautiful."

I prowled toward her, wrapped my hand around the back of her neck, and gazed down into her pretty face. "Funny that. I was just thinkin' the same thing about you."

"I can't believe our sex day was ruined by that twat," she grumbled.

I grinned. "Sex day?"

"Well. Yeah. Do you know how often I get enough time off to stay in bed all day with a hot bodyguard?"

I hitched an eyebrow. "Never before now, I hope."

"Exactly," she murmured, going up onto her toes and planting a soft kiss on my lips.

"You sure you don't want him charged?" I asked. "There's enough to get him locked up."

She heaved out a frustrated breath. "No, just tell the bastard never to come near me again."

I nodded, already mentally making plans to arrange for a few of the guys to fly out so we could dish out our own brand of justice. It would be hard for the dickwad to annoy my woman again if he had two broken legs.

I gave her nape a gentle squeeze and then released her, turning back for the door. "Okay, baby. Have it your way."

As I got to the threshold, my girl's melodic voice called out, "Thank you for looking after me, Jacob."

My heart swelled so big, it beat against my ribcage.

I craned my neck, locked eyes with my woman, and knew in that instant she was it for me.

We'd been together a week, and I knew she was always meant to be mine, the same way I knew our week would lead to another, then three, and eventually forever.

Everything that had happened since Allie died had led me to her, and I was done fucking around.

God only knew how we were gonna work it out, but Saint McClure was gonna be my woman, my ol' lady, and one day soon, she'd be my wife.

I was gonna plant babies in her and watch her nurture them. I was gonna comfort her when we took our oldest kid to their first day at school, then later wipe her tears away when we watched them graduate from college. I'd wipe more tears when one day they married the loves of their lives, then again when we held their babies for the first time on the day they made us grandparents.

I was gonna live a full and happy life with Saint McClure—soon-to-be Irons—even if it meant I had to sacrifice everything to do it.

Leaning back on the lounger, I cocked my knee, looked up at the stars, and muttered down the phone, "Found my one, brother."

Shocked silence ensued.

I grinned because I knew it was the last thing Hendrix expected to hear me tell him, but I had no fucks to give, and I also didn't give the first shit about his opinion or his judgment.

"Fuck me," Drix breathed. "Can't leave you alone for a fuckin' week." He sighed. "Colt likes her. He thought she was cute when they spoke. He liked that she kept a clear head, and he especially liked how much she worried about you. Dunno how professional it is that you do a job and end up with your dick in the client, but I can't lie; I had an idea somethin' like this would happen."

My mouth quirked. "Is that why you initially didn't assign me?"

"No, Ice. My reasons were honest. But at the same time, I knew it could go either way with you two. Your reaction to her was so extreme that there had to be a reason why, and it didn't take a genius to work out that you two would eventually either fight it out or fuck it out. Then I thought, however it went down, at least you'd get your head straight, and you could finally move on." He paused briefly, and I knew he was building up to something. "You okay with the Allie guilt?"

"Yeah," I assured him. "I think the birthday visit helped. It's hard to feel guilty when even Allie's folks are telling me it's past time to find someone else. Also, I've had a fuck load'a time to come to terms with it. Knew Saint was the one two years ago when I first met her, Drix."

"You're a dick for leaving it then," he muttered wryly.

I let out a quiet snort. "That's a fuckin' joke coming from you. The master of leaving shit alone."

"Anna was married," he said defensively.

"Yeah," I agreed. "Because you ghosted her."

"I fucked up royally," he admitted. "My woman won't marry me now. Says she's done it twice, and everythin' went sideways. She thinks gettin' married will jinx what we have."

I shrugged. "If you're happy, you don't need a ring."

"Same goes for you, Ice. You don't need a ring either."

I snorted again. "Fuck that. I'm getting my woman down the aisle ASAP. Sucks to be you."

Hendrix laughed softly. "Happy for ya, Jake."

His words made my gut warm. "Thanks, Jimmy. Happy for you, too." I cleared the emotion from my throat. "How's the club? Are we missing much?"

"Nah," Drix stated. "Everythin's quiet. My worries lie with the men more than the jobs."

"Don't tell me... Fender?"

"Yeah," he admitted. "And Blade."

My ears pricked up at that. "What's Veep done?"

"Got himself a woman," Drix explained.

"Well, it's about fucking time," I said wryly. "It's a good thing, right? Carina wasn't gonna wait forever."

"That's just it," Drix said dryly. "It's not Carina."

I sighed deeply and rubbed at the tension headache forming in my temples. "Fucking stupid dick."

"Yeah. I know, brother. Tried to talk some sense into him, but he's got a chip on his shoulder as big as fuckin' Texas. Says she's too young for him."

"There's an age gap for sure," I concurred. "But it's not like she's eighteen. Jesus, her daughter's a teenager, and Carina knows her own mind." I shook my head frustratedly. "How's she takin' it?"

Hendrix let out a short, humorless laugh. "Think she's given up. Anna reckons she's at the stage where she wouldn't take him now if he were gift-wrapped. Says she wants a man who wants her no-holds-barred like Benny did."

"Can't blame her for that, Drix," I pointed out. "It can't be easy to have all that chemistry with someone who keeps blowing her off. Her confidence must have taken a nosedive."

"You're right," he stated. "Blade's made his choice, and right or wrong, he has to live with it. Veep's big enough and ugly enough to take care of himself."

I chuckled softly. "Thought we were over all this angst bullshit when we left Wyoming,"

"Same," he responded.

"What's happening with Fender?" I asked.

He heaved out an audible breath. "Nothing. That's the problem. The kids are running wild. If it weren't for the women, they'd have no discipline at all. Addy's screaming for attention and even the boys are gettin' pissed with him. It's a nightmare, Ice. He can't even look at her."

"She's Ashley's double," I pointed out.

"Yeah, she is. But the kids' schools are even noticing now. Had Addison's teacher sniffing around the other day, checking on things. Anna asked me about approaching Fender to officially adopt her. She's fuckin' furious with the way he's neglecting his girl. She and Carina step in and step up, but Anna feels like she's crossing a line most of the time because Addie's not even related to her. She shouldn't be bathing the girl and doing all that personal stuff."

"Better Anna than nobody, Hendrix. Maybe you could couch it to her like we're all a big family, kids included, and you don't need to adopt Addie to care for her. Go with the whole 'it takes a village' concept. Fender obviously doesn't have an issue with Anna's relationship with Addie if he hasn't spoken up."

"Not sure he even cares, Iceman."

"He does. He's just lost in his grief. If anyone can get what he's goin' through, it's us." I felt a presence behind me, and I craned my neck to see Saint walking toward me wearing a short robe.

I held my hand out as she approached, tugging her onto my lap the instant she put her fingers in mine. My free hand went to her hair and stroked it back from her face, and I touched my mouth to hers.

"Gonna bring Saint to the hotel before we go to New York," I announced, shifting the cell phone slightly to allow Saint to tuck her head under my chin.

Her eyes lifted to meet mine, and she beamed.

"Anna and I moved into the house last weekend," Drix declared. "You two can take my suite while you're here if you like. It's at the top of the hotel, and nobody bunks up there apart from Dad, and he's cool. No fucker will bother you up there, except Diablo, maybe."

"Why the fuck would Diablo bother us?" I demanded.

"Apparently, he's a huge Saint's Rapture fan." Drix laughed.

Slowly, my eyes closed. "Oh fuck."

Prez laughed harder. "He'll make a fool of himself. You know he's got no chill."

I shook my head, smiling. "Luckily, Saint's got enough chill for the both of them. My woman will be sweet to him. She can't help herself."

Saint snuggled closer, tangling her legs with mine.

"Happy for ya, brother," Hendrix murmured.

"I'm happy for me, too." I cupped Saint's jaw and tilted her chin up until her eyes met mine again. "Gonna marry my girl and plant babies in her, and I'm doin' it soon."

I watched her face carefully, studying the nuances in her expression, but she didn't flinch or wince even slightly; she didn't seem shocked at all. In fact, I may as well have been talking about the weather because her lips curved, and she blew me a kiss before tucking her chin back into my neck and sliding a hand across my stomach, cuddling me closely.

"So, I guess we need a powwow when you get back," Drix deduced. "If Saint lives on the west coast and you live on the east coast. I'm pretty sure you don't want a long-distance marriage, so that means one of you has to relocate."

"Yeah," I agreed. "I'll talk to Saint about it, and we'll take it from there. There's no reason we can't have homes in two places. I'll build her a house with a recording studio in Virginia, and we can go between the two, depending on her schedule. I may have to cut back on jobs, but Colt travels the country with the FBI and still manages to keep up, even if it's remotely. No reason we can't do the same."

Saint glanced up and nodded enthusiastically, her azure blues dancing excitedly.

I grinned down at her.

That was fucking easy.

But that was one of the many reasons I'd fallen ass over heels in love with her. It wasn't a surprise that we were on the same page. Saint already told me in one of our many 'getting to know you' convos that she wanted kids, and she wasn't the type of woman to fuck around. My baby knew what she wanted, and she wanted it yesterday.

Perfect for me.

I leaned down and brushed my mouth against hers.

"How's the job going?" Hendrix asked. "We saw you fucking up that photographer on socials. Colt showed everyone. When Diablo saw that fucker try to upskirt Saint, he threatened to fly out there and chop a cock."

I busted out laughing. "Tell D I'll fly him out soon. Gotta couple of scores he can help me settle but chopping cocks off may be a little extreme."

A strangled noise escaped Saint's throat.

"Any movement on the stalker?" Hendrix asked.

"No," I muttered. "Nothing since the last lot of photographs."

"You think he's given up?" Hendrix asked.

I kissed the top of Saint's head. "What I think is that he's biding his time. I've no doubt he's been watching and seen me glued to Saint's side. Eventually, he'll cave and either try to go around me or through me. Either way, he'll fail."

I felt Saint's body stiffen.

"You and the boys are booked to go to NYC with the band when they start recording the album. When are you coming to Virginia?"

"End of the week. I need at least a few days in Virginia to sort my shit. Plus, I wanna start looking for a house or at least a plot of land."

I felt Saint smile against my neck.

"You know, me and Dad own plenty of land, Ice," Hendrix reminded me. "You can buy a plot and live on the river."

"Saint would like that," I said thoughtfully. "She loves the water. Okay, so it's not Malibu Beach, but it's still pretty. Could solve our problems."

"We'll talk when you get home," Hendrix assured me.

"Cool. See ya soon, brother."

"Later," he muttered, and the line went dead.

I dropped my cell phone on the table next to the sun lounger and wrapped my arm around my girl. "You warm enough, baby?" I asked.

"I am now," she replied softly, peering up at me. "You wanna get married quickly?"

I shrugged nonchalantly. "No point waiting. We both want babies and soon, and I won't knock you up until you take my name."

She held my gaze. "I need to keep my name for work. My management trademarked Saint McClure and Saint's Rapture. I can trademark Irons, too, but I'm not sure where that would leave me legally."

"Use McClure for work," I advised her. "But with everything else, use Irons. I want us and our kids to have the same name."

"Good idea," she murmured. "I'll talk to Talia, then patiently wait for your formal proposal." Her voice took on a teasing quality. "If you're good, I may even accept."

I laughed. "Baby. I'm not asking. Mark my words; by the year's end, you'll have my name and hopefully my baby in your belly."

Her eyes bugged out. "Jacob. That's four months away."

"Better hurry up and get that album recorded, then. Maybe we'll have a Christmas wedding." My lips curved into a self-satisfied smirk.

Her gaze was warm, her eyes soft. "So basically, I won't get a formal proposal. You've got everything mapped out, and I don't have a choice in it?"

"Pretty much," I answered, full of bravado. "I'll get down on one knee if you want, but even if you say no, I'll still slip a diamond on your finger."

Saint rolled her eyes like the brat she was.

I fingered the lapel of her silky robe, my finger dipping underneath to stroke her nipple. "I like this sexy little thing."

She shivered at the contact. "Thanks. I wore it for you." She leaned up and whispered, "I'm naked underneath, and hearing you talk about marriage and babies has made me all wet."

I groaned out loud.

Sexy as fuck.

"Wanna slip it off me and fuck me by my pool?" she asked seductively.

I let out a growl. "There's nothing I want more, baby, but that pervert fucker may be out there with a long-lens camera. Your body's for me and me alone."

Her hand came up and cupped my jaw, her beautiful eyes darting between mine. "You better take me to bed then, Jacob. Your woman needs a good fucking."

I didn't need to be told twice. I did an ab curl to a sitting position, hauled ass off the sun lounger, and then reached down with both arms and scooped Saint into them.

She let out a surprised squeal. Her hands slid up my chest, and she linked her fingers around my nape, staring into my eyes as I carried her into the house.

And I proceeded to give my woman a good fucking.

Chapter Twelve

Saint

I felt it, the wrongness in the air. It was as if the atmosphere had turned thick and heavy from a miasma of darkness settling over us like a blanket in summer that was too hot and suffocating.

Jacob had gotten a phone call a few minutes before. He'd looked at the display and snatched his cell up before biting off a curt, "Be right back," then gone out into the yard to talk.

The way he paced up and down the side of the pool indicated a few things. First, he was angry but trying to keep it locked down, probably for my benefit. Second, Jacob always spoke in front of me. He never hid anything and often told me to go into his phone to get a number or to start a call for him if he was driving or in the middle of something. Which led me to believe he was worried about me hearing his conversation, which also meant he was trying to protect me.

Something had obviously happened, and he was trying to get ahead of it before he told me. I may have only been with Jacob for a short time, but I knew him inside out.

It wasn't difficult to deduce that the stalker had made a move, and Jacob was not happy at all.

"Your man, he seems upset," Catalina, my housekeeper and second mother, pointed out.

Absentmindedly, I watched her spray the countertop with cleaner before wiping it down. She pushed back the lock of dark grey hair that had fallen out of her bun and began to scrub at an invisible spot. "He never takes calls in the yard." My gaze turned back to fixate on Jacob. "We don't hide things from each other."

"Men and women need *some* secrets, *Mi Santa*. It's not good to know everything. *Mujeres* need some mystery in their men, or where is the romance, huh?"

I couldn't stop the knowing smile that curved my lips because one thing Jacob and I had an abundance of was romance. Not even a weirdo-stalker vibe could kill that. I'd been romanced to shit over the last couple of weeks, and not in a cheesy pick-up line kind of way, but in a lingering look, whispered words way that made my skin tingle and my blood pump hard through my veins.

I glanced at her bustling around my kitchen in her beige slacks and pretty shirt with ruffles on the sleeves. "Can I do anything to help?"

"Make coffee," she threw over her shoulder at me. "And not the weak stuff the cat peed. Heat up some *Café de Olla*." She glanced outside, then back toward me again. "Your man looks like he needs it."

I went to the fridge and pulled out the container of coffee Catalina had brought with her, and my eyes almost rolled with pleasure as I caught a whiff of its cinnamon, spicy scent. I placed it in the microwave and set the timer, leaning back on the counter as I watched it turn.

"I'm going to miss your coffee," I murmured softly. "Are you sure you can't come out to New York for a while?"

Her dark brown eyes caught mine, and she gave me a smile. "*Mi Santa*," she breathed. "I cannot. *La bebé...*" Her warm eyes held mine. "When everything settles, and my girl is in a routine with *mi nieta*, maybe I can try."

Catalina's daughter was due to give birth to Cat's first granddaughter in a few weeks. Having grandchildren to spoil made her happy and dulled the pain of losing her husband, Carlos, the year before.

I stepped toward her and took her hands in mine. "I'm sorry, Catalina, I shouldn't have asked. It was selfish of me."

She moved in for a tight hug before pulling away and waving a hand through the air. "Bah! Nonsense! You have *corazon de oro*." She clicked her fingers, trying to find the words. "How you say? Ahh, yes. Heart of gold. Mi Bianca still cries with the money card you gave her for *la bebé*." She lifted a hand to stroke the hair back from my face and breathed, "*Santa* by name and *Santa* by nature."

I gave her big eyes. "I wish someone would tell that to *mi padre*."

"Bah!" Cat exclaimed loudly, waving her hand again. "His loss. Men are sometimes stubborn and stupid. Even mi Carlos acted like a fool sometimes, and I had to"—she tapped her foot hard on my tiled floor, acting out what she was trying to say—"stamp my foot down."

God. I loved this woman.

"I'll miss you when I'm away," I murmured.

Her smile was warm. "You'll see me soon, and we can do FaceTime. Mi Bianca showed me how, and it's easy. You can see *mi nieta* when she comes." Her eyes lifted over my shoulder, and her face took on a brusque-like quality. "Jacob. You like *Café de Olla*?"

He pushed the bi-fold doors half closed behind him and walked straight toward us. "Love it. Diablo's mom makes it for us when she visits the clubhouse. It's fuckin' awesome."

She clicked her tongue, shooting him a glare as the microwave pinged. "Language, Jacob. And who is this Diablo? Diablo is the devil, no?"

He grinned. "Exactly."

Her face softened, and she took out the plastic pitcher and ordered, "Cups, Jacob."

He stretched to open the door to the cupboard above her head and grabbed a few out, placing them on the counter. "Anythin' else you need?"

"Just your words," she demanded. "What made you angry on the phone? Is it *ese idiota*?"

He reached out for me, grabbed my hips, and lifted my ass onto the countertop before standing between my legs and cupping my face gently. He stared into my eyes and murmured, "There was another envelope on the porch this mornin', though this one was left at the front door and not around back."

"Jesus." My eyes darted between his. "Why didn't you tell me?"

"Didn't open it. Called Talia, who arranged for it to be couriered to the detective dealing with your case. He's coming over soon to talk to us. Now that I know what was in it, we can discuss our next steps. You wanna see what the fucker sent, or do you want me to tell you?"

I stared up at him.

"You can handle it, baby," he murmured, touching his lips to mine. "Hand to God, Saint, nothing will touch you while I breathe air."

My life was fucked up. I had a weird guy sending me weird gifts and making weird threats—a fact that had exacerbated the band's need to hire bodyguards—but still, I believed every word Jacob said.

Nothing *would* touch me while he breathed air.

I knew it down to the core of me.

"Okay," I agreed. "I wanna see."

His arms slid around my waist, and he leaned down to kiss me. "That's my girl."

My belly fluttered.

He pulled out his phone, went to his photo app, and clicked on an image before enlarging it. Then, he held the phone up for me to see.

I peered closer. "Is that a funeral wreath?"

He nodded.

My chest tightened. "Is that his way of threatening to kill me?"

"No, baby. Look." He pinched his fingers onto his phone screen and enlarged the photo even more.

My eyes went straight to the writing on the 'in sympathy' card accompanying the flowers, which read,

Saint,

Sorry for your loss.

My eyes narrowed on the image. "I don't get it."

"This came with it, too," Jacob said, his voice lowering. He fiddled with his phone again and clicked on another image. That time, it was a photo of me and Jacob. We were walking hand in hand down the street. I recognized the clothes I wore from the day before when Jacob had taken me to the gym with him. We'd just finished working out and were heading back to the car. My face was turned toward Jacob's, and I was laughing at something he said. Jake was looking ahead, no doubt scanning for threats, a small smile playing around his mouth.

But what chilled me to the bone was the fact that the stalker had completely blacked out Jake's eyes, and a big red cross had been angrily scrawled over his face.

A cold shiver ran from the top of my spine to the bottom, and the strangled gasp that left me was loud enough that Catalina rushed toward me. "*Santa.* What's wrong?"

I pointed to Jacob's phone and demanded, "Show her!"

"Baby," Jacob murmured, handing Cat his phone. "It's fine. It's good. It shows he doesn't mean you any harm. Just me."

My eyes slashed toward his, and I screeched, "Are you fucking crazy?"

His fingers wrapped around my nape. "I'd rather the target was on my back than yours, Saint. It's my job to keep you safe."

"No!" I snapped, watching Cat scroll through the pictures. "It's not your job anymore. You're more to me than that."

"Saint," he murmured more calmly. "I don't mean it's my job as your bodyguard; it's my job as your man. What the fuck is this guy gonna do to me? I'm trained in every fighting discipline and every type of combat there is. I can fly planes, I can handle a car like a racing driver, and I can fight and shoot like a professional because that's what I am. The goddamned government gave me a license to kill, and that's what I'll do, baby, no thought, no hesitation. I'm gonna be okay."

My chest felt fractured inside, like somebody had split me open and scooped out the contents. "If anything ever happened to you—"

His fingers squeezed the back of my neck. "Shh. Nothing's gonna happen. I'll wear a vest and take extra precautions. We're going to Virginia tomorrow. The club's got better security than Fort Knox, and the town's so small that any stranger who shows his face will stand out. Colt's team is putting together a completed profile, and we're closing in. In a way, I hope he does show so I can put a stop to his bullshit, and we can get on with doing everything we talked about." He held my face in his hands, his icy eyes boring into mine. "It stopped being about the job for me the first night I was here. I wanna build a life with you, and by doing so, I'll protect and love you unconditionally. I'll go to sleep lying next to you every night for the rest of my damned life, knowing our souls are tethered."

"Jacob," I whispered huskily, my eyes shining with all the emotions his words had brought out in me. "I'm gonna put that shit in a song."

He busted out a laugh before resting his forehead against mine. "I wouldn't expect anything less from my songbird."

My heart melted. "What's your MC like?"

He lifted his head from mine and cocked an eyebrow. "Fuckin' crazy."

I grinned and breathed, "Awesome."

Catalina's voice floated across the kitchen. "Are you hungry, Jacob?"

He reached around my body and picked up his coffee cup. "Well, I dunno, Cat. Depends if you're making tamales."

She beamed at him. "You're a good boy who loves his food."

"Love *your* food," he corrected her.

She beamed even brighter.

"Especially your tamales," he added.

"Did *tu madre* make you tamales, Jacob?" she asked. "Is that why you love them?"

Jake's face twisted into a smirk. "No, Cat. My mom's idea of cooking was throwing a frozen pizza in the oven or picking up a McDonald's on the way home from work. Pop-Tarts for breakfast and chips and dip for dinner were the norm for me growing up."

Her brown eyes grew wide. She rested a hand across her chest and exclaimed, "*Dios mío*."

Jacob laughed. "Ma couldn't cook, but Dad could. He made the good stuff. He barbequed most nights, and to this day, Pop's gumbo is legendary."

Cat's hand shifted to her heart, and she murmured, "*Gracias a Dios por eso.*" Then she gave Jacob a knowing look and announced, "*Mi Santa* makes good tamales. Your babies won't have to eat Pop-Tarts."

Jacob looked a little shocked. "You cook?"

I shrugged. "Yeah, a little. Cat taught me a few things."

"Cat's a fucking revelation," a dry voice said from the doors. "Are you making tamales, babe? My stomach feels like my throat's been cut."

I turned to see Talia stepping through the bi-folds, sniffing the air appreciatively. "Is that *Café de Olla* I can smell?"

Cat gave her an indulgent smile. "Take a seat. I'll fetch you some."

Talia heaved her huge bag from her shoulders, dropped it onto the countertop, and slid onto a stool. "When are you gonna leave Saint and come to work for me, Cat?" She made a pouty face. "I wanna wake up to *Café de Olla.*"

"I'll never leave *Santa*," Cat said breezily, pointing a finger at Talia. "And you are too messy and have too many men." She shook her head disapprovingly. "Every time I bring you food, I see a different boy. One in and one out. Every day it's different."

Talia grinned. "What can I say? So many men, so little time."

"These modern girls," Cat grumbled. "You need a good boy who'll give you many babies."

"What I need is a good, big, hard d—"

"Talia!" I barked, cutting her off. "What are you doing here?"

She chuckled, throwing Catalina an apologetic wink. "The boys will be here any minute. We need a band meeting to discuss the latest development with weirdo stalker." She gave a little shudder. "That photo was creepy as fuck."

I glanced at Jacob, who was leaning on the countertop, sipping *Café de Olla* without a care in the world.

"*Hombre loco*," Cat announced, opening the fridge to pull out a packet of beef. "Crazy man."

The sounds of laughter and footsteps drifted in from the backyard, and Sam and Boomer appeared at the doors.

"Morning!" Boom sang.

"*Hola, hijo,*" Cat called out. "*Café de Olla?*"

Boomer held his arms out and ran toward Cat, enveloping her in a bear hug. "Cat. I love you."

"Jonny's taking a swim," Sam informed the room, jerking his thumb toward the pool just as I heard a loud splash.

I rolled my eyes. "That asshole better be wearing swim shorts this time."

Jacob's gaze hardened, his neck craning toward the glass doors.

"Bah!" Cat exclaimed. "Jonny J shows off." She emptied the packet of beef into a frying pan, shaking her head exasperatedly. "Always with the *pene*."

Talia barked a laugh.

I chuckled.

Sam approached and flung his arm across my shoulders, pulling me in for a hug. His eyes softened as he studied my face. "You look pretty today, Saint. How are you coping with the whole photo thing?"

A low growl cut through the kitchen, and the air froze as Jake's deep voice rumbled, "You wanna stop touching my woman, brother? Maybe take a step away?"

I peered around Sam's body to see Jacob looking furious.

My throat worked.

"Just bein' friendly, Iceman," Sam drawled, but still, his arm left my shoulders, and he stepped back. "Saint and I are old friends."

For a split second, I thought Jake's head would explode.

"We go way back," Sam insisted.

"How about you be a friend who doesn't put your arm around her from now on?" Jacob bit out.

Talia chuckled, looking on with interest.

Sam held his hands up defensively. "You've got nothing to worry about. Saint and I tried but decided to stay as friends."

All my breath left my lungs, and suddenly the air felt like it had been sucked from the room.

"Come again?" Jake said, his tone deceptively quiet.

My heart sank.

"It was once," I blurted out. "Years ago."

"Wait," Boomer interjected. "Did you two...? He glanced at Jacob, and his words faltered when he saw my guy's murderous expression. "Fuck," he muttered under his breath.

Talia laughed.

Jacob glowered at Sam. "Stay the fuck away from my woman," he snarled.

Cat smiled approvingly. "I like this. *Un hombre debe ser un hombre*. A man must be a man. Mi Carlos would be a big, jealous lion too." Her smile widened, and she repeated to herself, "*Un hombre debe ser un hombre*."

Jacob's stare slashed to mine, and I felt the chill hit me from three feet away.

Sorry, I told him with my eyes.

His lips thinned, but one corner of his mouth hitched slightly.

Inwardly, I breathed a sigh of relief.

Oops.

"You better delete your Raya profile," Boomer muttered. "Or your dude will have an aneurism."

Another growl hit the ether.

"Thanks for that, Boom," I snapped sarcastically.

"Yeah," Jacob cut out. "You'd better delete your fuckin' Raya profile."

"Never once have I had a date from Raya," I announced.

Talia brought her hand up to her mouth and coughed, "Liar."

"Am not!" I wailed.

"I thought that was how you met Hunter," Boomer interjected.

"No," Tally interrupted. "I introduced Saint to Hunter."

Boomer nodded slowly. "Right."

"Will you guys stop talking about my dating life in front of my boyfriend?" I demanded, eyeing Jacob's angry, flushed face. "He's about to spontaneously combust. He doesn't know you well enough to know what assholes you are when one of us gets a new partner."

"He better get used to us," Talia said. "He'll be stuck with us in Virginia and then New York."

Jacob's icy eye beam rays suddenly became more powerful. He glared at Talia and snapped, "What?"

My body froze.

A slow grin spread across her face. "We're going to Virginia with you. I thought a few days staying in a nice hotel on the Potomac River would be fucking awesome."

Jacob's stare never left her. "You're not coming with us."

"I am," she argued. "So's Boom, Jonny, and Sam. It's already arranged. The boys' bodyguards want to spend some time at the club before we head to New

York, and we all need protection from the weirdo, creepy stalker, so I thought, two birds, one stone."

Jake folded his arms across his chest. "Hendrix won't agree to it."

A grin split her big, fat mouth. "Your prez already did."

Jacob's face fell, and I thought for a second he was about to cry, but instead, he turned on his heel and stalked out of the room.

Cat watched him go, and she slowly turned her head toward Sam. "See what you did? You never make a man like that jealous. You're lucky he didn't take his gun out and shoot you." She began to mutter under her breath, "*Chicos estúpidos.*"

Sam's smirk was all the answer I needed, and my eyes narrowed on him in disbelief. "You did that on purpose."

"Not on purpose exactly," he muttered, his stare avoiding mine.

"That's a shitty thing to do, Sam," I snapped. "How would you like it if I did that to Jolie?"

Sam shrugged. "It's over between us. She dumped me."

My jaw dropped. "So you thought what? That you'd spread the misery? Well, it's backfired because how the hell can you come to Virginia now? Jacob doesn't even want to be in the same room as you."

"Oh, come on," Boomer interjected. "It's not like he's been a virgin in the last couple of years. Gambit's been telling me about the Speed Demons' club girls."

Talia sat up straighter. "Club girls?"

"Club girls?" I echoed.

"Girls who hang around the club and fuck the brothers," Sam explained.

Bile rose through my throat.

Cat let out a gasp, pulled her rosary from around her neck, and brought it to her mouth.

Talia's grin widened. "Bikers have groupies, too? Awesome!"

At that moment, the bi-folds opened, and Jonny J wandered in completely naked, with water dripping from his body and his hand covering his junk.

He cleared his throat. "Did I hear somebody mention groupies?"

I looked to the heavens and let out a deep sigh.

Fuck my life.

Chapter Thirteen

Iceman

It was chilly in this dang car.
In fact, my nuts had been freezing since the day before, when I'd ticked Saint off by walking out of the kitchen to stop me from ripping asshole Sam's head clean off his goddamned neck. I didn't expect my girl to tell me the gory deets about every sexual partner she'd had over the last two years, but I did expect her to inform me about any that hung with us.

At her house...

Every damned day.

The reason my nuts were freezing was that Saint hadn't gone near them since that particular convo. But it wasn't because I basically told Sam (in so many words) never to touch my woman again—though, according to Saint, that shit was bad enough.

No, the reason my woman hadn't made any contact with any part of my anatomy was because of dickwad Gambit, the big-mouthed fucker.

I mean, why would he tell Boomer about the club whores?

Why?

It wasn't a state secret, but civilians didn't understand the reasoning behind the club girls.

Not only did our men have needs, but they also had *needs*. It wasn't as simple as just getting off; moreover, the boys—in our club in particular—needed release. They needed help to sleep and relax. Hell, they needed help to function. It was necessary for them, and sex helped them do it in a way where they didn't need drugs to get their dopamine moving through their bodies.

It wasn't the most efficient coping mechanism, but it was still healthier than taking prescription medication when there was a danger that the men could develop an addiction.

However, my argument came crashing down when Saint pointed out that sex could also turn into an addiction. The other part that came crashing down was that I didn't actually have PTSD; I just really fucking liked sex.

So yeah, Saint wasn't talking to me, and it was making things tense for everyone except Boomer, who kept looking between us and grinning. He seemed to thrive on awkward silences because the fucker sat in the backseat of the club's GMC Yukon on the way to the hotel, picking his guitar, grinning, and shaking his stupid head at the shitty atmosphere.

Lucky for Sam, he was in the other car with Ghost, Trick, and Jonny J, so he wasn't in danger of being decapitated—for now—though I meant every word I said to him the day before. He needed to stay the fuck away from Saint because I was already hanging by a thread, and if he made one wrong move, I knew that thread would snap.

The girls and Boomer were in the back of the Yukon chatting, so I took the opportunity to catch up on club business with Blade, who'd picked us up from the airport.

Talia had taken one look at Veep and smirked appreciatively.

I got it. He was a mountain of a man, and even I could appreciate the handsomeness of the dude. He was dark-haired, tanned, and had piercing blue eyes that saw straight down to any mischief in your soul. He could look at a man and assess their intentions from the get-go, which was a talent that came in very handy, not only during his military career, but also when it came to controlling a club full of men.

Veep turned his blinker on to maneuver the car off the I-95 toward Arrowhead Point and side-eyed me from the driver's seat before asking, "Doghouse?"

I jerked a nod and rolled my eyes.

His lips twitched, and he muttered, "Whipped."

I jerked another nod and proudly said, "Yep."

"Can't wait for Church," he cut out under his breath. "This one's gonna be good. Ice, the unbothered, is suddenly very fucking bothered. And there was Diablo thinking that Saint McClure was gonna be the next and last love of his life."

"Hendrix mentioned he's a fan," I said dryly. "Never saw that one coming."

"Why?" Blade asked. "Saint's Rapture's music's cool as shit, and your girl's beautiful. A lotta the boys are excited to meet them. Even Wyoming has..." His words trailed off, and he let out a quiet *harrumph*.

A chill ran down my arms.

Slowly, my head turned toward him, and I asked, "Wyoming has what?"

He took a left and drove down the lane that led to the hotel. "You're about to find the fuck out."

As he said the words, the hotel came into view, and my mouth fell open at the sight before me.

Going by the sheer number of bikes and trucks parked outside the hotel, the entire club had turned up to meet and greet. The steps leading up to the hotel were packed full of people sitting and enjoying the afternoon sun. They'd probably been there for hours, judging by the volume of empty beer bottles taking up the surfaces.

"They're here," a voice screeched, and my head reared back when I saw Sunny and Kady Stone run out of the hotel doors holding a huge white banner with the words 'Welcome Saint's Rapture' emblazoned across it in red paint with the smaller words underneath declaring, 'We love you.'

"What the fuck?" I muttered under my breath.

"Word got around," Blade explained, his jaw ticking as he rolled his eyes. "Told Prez it's a security risk, but he couldn't exactly turn the mother chapter away, could he? Breaker, Atlas, and Abe are here, wives and kids in tow. Cash's ol' lady has come too with that hellion son. Oh, and Tristan turned up, though in fairness, he was planning on visiting Anna anyway."

The roar of Saint's laughter inside the car cut through the moment, and I breathed an inward sigh of relief that she was taking all this bullshit in the manner it was meant, even though it was clearly the work of lunatics.

Blade glanced back at her approvingly. "You've got some fans."

Saint busted out another laugh before replying, "Clearly. Just as well I brought my guitar."

Even Blade—who hardly smiled—grinned widely as he drove the SUV into one of the spots close to the hotel that had clearly been reserved for the guests of honor.

I jumped out of the car and pulled the back door open, helping Talia out. Saint followed closely, and I took her hand as she stepped out of the SUV, glancing behind her as the car containing Jonny and Sam pulled up behind.

"You okay?" I asked.

She shot me a frosty look. "Depends. Are any of your fuck buddies there?"

I shot a look at Tia, Heather, and Arizona stood in a huddle. "Well..."

Saint let out a huff.

"Baby," I murmured, pulling her closer. "Don't be like that. Two years ago, I thought you'd fuckin' ghosted me. Do you think for one minute I would've gone elsewhere if I knew what had happened? Jesus, you're all I've thought about for two years. Looked for you in every woman I've come into contact with and found them all lacking in every way. Sex is sex, but with you, it's more, so please don't get it twisted."

Her lips pursed, but at least she didn't pull away that time. Instead, she put her hand in mine, nodded toward the crowd, and said, "In that case, I guess you'd better introduce us."

One side of my mouth quirked, and I pulled her into my side, sliding an arm around her waist until my hand rested on her hip. "Come on. It's time to meet the family." I guided her toward the hotel, taking in all the excited chatter and expectant faces.

Hendrix walked down the steps to meet us, baby in arms, Anna by his side, and a sardonic smile across his face. "About fuckin' time," he drawled as soon as we were within earshot. "These assholes have driven me bonkers all morning."

Saint's eyes went to the crowd, and she blushed.

"This is Hendrix, Anna, and little JT," I announced, turning to my woman. "Guys, meet Saint."

Anna stuck her hand out. "Hi!"

Saint dropped my hand and waved Anna's away before pulling her in for a hug, murmuring, "Jacob's told me so much about you, and yes, it's all good."

I puffed my chest out proudly because that was my woman all over. No airs or graces, and no diva behavior. Just down-to-earth, good old-fashioned joy to be here, meet new people, and put them at ease.

"As you can see, Saint doesn't stand on ceremony," I told them.

Hendrix took in the scene. "Just as well 'cause I give it five minutes before some fucknut says somethin' stupid to her."

Saint pulled back from Anna and moved toward Hendrix, smiling down at little JT in his arms. "Same," she concurred. "My drummer's an asshole, too, but he's a sweetheart when you get to know him." She shot Jonny a wry look and then added, "Eventually." She pulled a hovering Talia into the circle. "This is Talia, my manager and best friend."

"Welcome," Anna said, nodding toward me. "Can't wait to get to know the woman who's settled this one's ass down."

Saint laughed melodically. "He's not so bad." She dropped her voice as if she were sharing state secrets. "You just have to learn how to use sex as a weapon."

Anna burst into a laugh. "I hear ya, sister." She threaded her arm through Saint's and pulled her up the steps toward the other women. "Come meet the girls and Tristan."

Saint looked around and gave me big eyes, grabbing Talia's hand and pulling her along with them as they chatted.

I watched my girl go, and I knew pride shone from my eyes.

In one fell swoop, Saint had made everyone fall in love with her, and not with the rock star they saw on a late-night chat show or performing at an awards ceremony, but with the real person.

"We've got Church in an hour," Hendrix informed me.

"Has something happened?" I asked.

"No, but the profile's in, and we need to talk about it. Colt's also uncovered a few things we need to discuss." His gaze slid toward Boomer, Jonny, and

Sam, who'd been greeted by a few of the guys and were chatting with them, along with Gambit, Trick, and Ghost.

My curiosity was piqued by the way his stare went straight to the boys. "Need to show Saint our room, get the band and Talia settled in, and then I'm all yours."

"Anna and Tristan have been briefed," he informed me. "They'll look after Saint and Talia; make sure they're good while we're in our meet. Also spoke to Cass and Rockabye, who'll keep watch, too. Not that I think they'll even get a look-in. Seems to me your woman's already making an impression."

I looked up the steps to see Saint leaning down to listen to Kady gab excitedly in her ear with a huge smile on her face. Saint gave the young girl a tight hug before pulling back and laughing with her about something.

"Fuck me. They'll be kidnapping her and taking her back to Wyoming at this rate," Hendrix said, a warning tone in his voice. "They're all starstruck. Had to send Diablo on a weird-assed errand; he was getting so wound up about meeting Saint that he was losing his mind."

My lips tipped. "Still can't believe he's a fanboy."

"You should've seen his face when he found out you and Saint were together. Thought he was gonna start bawling." Hendrix's stare fell on my face, and he nodded slowly as he took in my happy expression. "Good to see you happy, brother."

I shrugged. "Good to be happy, brother." I clasped his shoulder, looking down at JT, who slept soundly in his arms. "If someone told me a year ago that you and I would both be wifed up, you with a baby too, I would've gone out and brought the first straitjacket I could find for them."

Drix's face flushed, and he murmured, "Don't tell these morons, but I think I might have found a way to get Anna to marry me."

My teeth flashed. "What the fuck are you up to now?"

He leaned down to touch his mouth to TJ's little forehead and declared, "Our convo about taking Addie in led us into a deep and meaningful powwow about adoption. I looked into it, and it turns out you've gotta better chance of being accepted by the agencies if you're married." His face split into a wide grin. "I reckon I've cracked the code."

My chuckle was deep. "You're a sneaky fucker."

He turned to look at the women, who were about to disappear inside the hotel. "A man's gotta do what a man's gotta do. Want her ring on my finger, want my last name replacing hers, and I want a shit load of babies running around the place. Locking my woman down legally is my top priority. I'm not saying every day's moonlight and roses, Ice; hell, some days it's more like weeds and thornbushes. But there's nobody else on this planet I'd wanna do this with, even when times get tough. Especially when times get tough."

"I know what you mean," I concurred.

"I know you know what I mean, seeing as you confessed how hard you've fallen on the phone not two days ago. Why d'ya think I'm talking to you like a lovestruck fool and not the others? Could you fuckin' imagine the shit I'd get ripped outta me if I shared all this dewy-eyed, simpering slush with those ass clowns?" He sniffed up through his nose like a fighter about to get in the ring with an opponent double his body weight. "I gotta rep to protect."

"And I gotta band to sort out and a woman who, after a five-hour flight, no doubt wants to freshen up," I relayed, heading toward the steps.

Hendrix and JT fell into place beside me. "Got Gopher to move your shit into my room. You're ready to rock and roll," he said as we ascended the steps to the hotel.

"Thanks, brother, but I'm not sure I'll need it. Going to New York soon, and then, who the fuck knows?"

"You're not leaving the club, Iceman. Already had some ideas I wanna run past ya that'll keep ya busy."

I twisted my neck to look at him, my curiosity piqued once again. "Shoot."

"I will after you get your shit done, and I hand my boy off. He's due a feed, and Iris wants to do it. Promised her she could, seein' as she misses out on a lot with him." His voice dropped low. "Plus, between you and me, I think she needs a break from Wilder."

"Mother Theresa would need a break from that little shit," I muttered as we hit reception. "He puts me off having kids."

Hendrix grinned. "I think he's funny."

"I think he's a fucking scream, bro, but I'm not sure I could live with his antics day in and day out."

Hendrix looked down at his boy, and a soft look fell across his face. "Ours won't be like that." His eyes lifted, and he added one hope-filled word, "Right?"

My mind was filled with images of the club, the work, the club whores, the Friday night fights, and all the other crazy shit that happened. I thought about Blade umming and ahhing over Carina, then my mind drifted to Fender's grumpy moping and how Diablo ran around threatening to chop cocks off, then went and slept in a room filled with jars of body parts lit up like a goddamned Christmas tree.

I turned back to Hendrix, and God help me, did him the biggest solid I could, even though it involved lying through my fucking teeth.

"It's okay, bro," I assured him. "I'm sure our kids will turn out normal."

I knew I'd done the right thing when I saw his shoulders relax and the look of slight panic fade from his face, even though in my head I heard Allie's laughing voice whisper one word.

Liar.

"So," Colt began, his stare fixating on me across the table. "They've delivered the profile. You ready?"

I shifted in my seat and leaned over the huge round table with the Speed Demons' patch burned into the center. "Go for it."

My club brother picked up his iPad and began to tap. Within seconds, the walls of Church lit up with a graph of lines and squiggles, all centered around a picture of Saint and one word spelling out 'stalker.'

"Jesus," Diablo muttered. "That looks complicated as shit."

"Not really," Colt stated. He tapped on his device, and the graph turned into a list with headings and subheadings. "It's just the way the team set it out. Remember, when they're profiling, they need room to add thoughts and even gut feelings sometimes. You should be able to see it clearer this way."

I scanned the list, trying to take it in as Colt started talking through the bullet points.

"He's young, between twenty-eight and thirty-six, and he has a history of failed relationships. He's social but finds interacting difficult, though he probably hides it well by overcompensating and being the friendliest guy in the room. To everyone, he seems like a great person, but the mask slips now and again, and he expresses bouts of anger or resentment. Stalkers are fueled by different things, but we think this guy has a few of the classic triggers. He desires his target and even thinks he's in love. He also has a distorted sense of entitlement, which we think is a toxic personality trait, but it could also be because he's got money and power. Basically, he thinks he's a catch. If the woman he pursues doesn't welcome his advances, he'll eventually turn what he thinks is romance into threats. However, he always justifies it to himself by blaming the victim for their lack of encouragement."

"So, he's got an inflated sense of his own self-importance?" I asked.

Colt nodded. "Exactly. The profilers also believe Saint's met her stalker. It could be somebody she knows, a fan she met in passing, or an exec-type whose hand she shook once at an industry party. The language in the notes conveys a sense of familiarity. This isn't his first rodeo, either. He's definitely done this before, which should make it easier to run through the list of men Saint comes into contact with. His behavior's too obsessive for it not to be a compulsion."

Something pinged in the back of my head. "How well could they know her?"

Colt shrugged. "It ranges. The profile can't pinpoint it, but they've definitely met."

"Does anyone you already checked out fit the profile?" I enquired.

He nodded. "I've got a few hits. The first one is Braden Hunt."

"Where do I know that name from?" Hendrix asked.

My gut twisted. "He's Dischordium's manager."

"He is," Colt affirmed. "Braden's also a hothead, entitled rich boy who's had a complaint made against him from an ex-girlfriend who accused him of stalking her. I dug deeper, and the charges appear to be bullshit made-up ones. She was pissed he ended things with her and turned out to be vindictive as fuck. Still, we can't rule it out."

"I've met Braden a few times, and I can't see it," Hendrix interjected.

"I'm sure people said that about Ted Bundy, boss," Colt responded. "I'm not saying he's guilty; I'm saying a lot of his shit fits the profile, but then I'm sure a thousand men we know do, too."

"Maybe we should bring Carbine into the fold," Blade suggested. "Ask him to keep his eyes peeled."

I jerked my grin in assent. "Agreed. Carbine may be in a rock band, but in his heart, he's still a Demon and loyal with it."

"I'll talk to Cash after Church and get him to approach Carbine," Hendrix offered. "I think it would go down better coming from his prez."

We all murmured our agreement.

Colt's stare met mine across the table. "Why did you ask about the perp's closeness to Saint?"

I held his gaze. "It was just something that happened last week, and it resonated with me when you mentioned bouts of anger and resentment. Jonny lost his shit with Saint, and it came out of nowhere."

Our tech guy began to tap on his iPad. "Jonny Jensen, aged thirty-one, born in San Diego, an only child to Derek and Lindsay. Moved to LA when he was twenty-five to be a session drummer. Joined a couple of bands after the first year, but they never amounted to much, then he joined Saint's Rapture and hit the big time. He's a party boy, exhibitionist, who likes the limelight." Colt's stare narrowed on the screen. "No criminal record apart from one pap altercation a year ago, which was settled out of court, but it looks like his records were sealed when he was seventeen."

I leaned forward. "Can you get into them?"

Colt rolled his eyes. "Gimme a minute." His fingers flew over his iPad as if they were on fire. He paused a couple of times, waiting for the device to catch up with him. Images began to flash up on the screens. A police report first, then a hospital admission form, and finally, a grainy mugshot.

"Jonny was arrested for attempting to break the terms of a restraining order served on him by an ex-girlfriend. He was accused of harassing her and her new boyfriend. The judge took pity on him and ordered him to complete an anger management program rather than give him a custodial sentence. Jonny's dad's a partner in a law firm in San Diego and managed to get the case sealed." His lips thinned. "Obviously, it's not what you know; it's who you know."

Hendrix grunted. "So he's got a history of not handling rejection well? Plus, his dad's loaded, so that fits the entitlement part of the profile. We all know lawyers are a special breed. Some of 'em think they *are* the law. That could've rubbed off on his boy."

"Seems that way," Colt confirmed. "Though I have to point out, this happened nearly fifteen years ago, and he's been clean since. It could've been a one-off sitch."

I thought back to the day Jonny snapped at Saint. The venom in his tone shocked me, and the way he called her a cunt. At the time, it was explained as him coming down from a high, but after hearing Colt go over the profile of Saint's stalker, alarms were wailing in my head.

"So what do we do about it?" Gambit asked.

Hendrix bit the inside of his cheek, deep in thought. "Nothing for now. The clubhouse has got cameras everywhere, and we make sure Saint is never alone with Jonny."

"I don't like it," I murmured.

"Neither do I," Diablo agreed.

A surge of heat hit my chest, and my nostrils flared. "You know that Saint's *my* woman, right?" I asked, turning to the SAA. "I've been protecting her just fine for the last couple of weeks, *brother*."

His cheeks flushed red.

"Iceman," Hendrix said quietly. "Don't take your shit out on the wrong person. I get it's frustrating, but D's just worried."

The surge left me as quickly as it had reared up, and I slumped back in my chair. "Sorry, D," I muttered. "I think the pressure's getting to me."

He nodded. "S'okay."

But I could tell he was hurt by my outburst.

"Come outside with me after, brother," I offered. "I'll introduce you."

His forehead furrowed. "You don't have to."

"Yeah, I do, bro. There's no man in the club I'd rather my woman be around or be protected by than you. Brave as a fuckin' lion and a heart bigger than anyone I know." I grinned. "You're a mouthy fucker too, but the good outweighs the bad by far."

The boys chuckled, and to my relief, Diablo laughed along, too.

I shot him an apologetic smile.

He grinned back and gave me a chin lift.

My shoulders relaxed, but the nagging feeling in my gut persisted, and a sense of dread made my chest clench.

Threats were coming from all angles, and I knew something was about to go down; I could feel it in the air that I breathed because it contaminated my lungs every time I inhaled.

In a way, I wanted the stalker to bring it on because the sooner I could shoot him in the head, the sooner all danger would pass, and Saint and I could get on with our lives.

I just hoped that when the dust settled, everyone I loved was still standing.

Chapter Fourteen

Saint

"This place is *awesome*!" I squealed, standing up to wiggle my ass in time to the gorgeous Rihanna singing how she found love in a hopeless place. I shoved another five-dollar bill in Heather's G-string, then, circling one arm in the air, lasso-style, I yelled, "Twerk that ass!"

My new friend, who was dancing on the table in front of me, shimmied her hips in my face and gushed, "I can't believe I'm dancing for *Saint McClure*. I'm such a huge fan."

"Woo hoo!" Talia bellowed from a few feet away at the bar. "Shake it, girl."

I looked up to see my other new friend, Kennedy, strutting across the bar top before doing a sexy hair flip, and I gave another loud whoop when my new BFF, Sunshine, danced behind her and did a high kick before shimmying her shoulders.

"Do you want another drink, hon?" I called up toward Heather.

"Yeah, thanks, babe," she said gratefully. "Dancing's thirsty work."

I danced over to the bar where Talia was in conversation with some guy who had just approached her.

"Hey, beautiful, I'm Rockabye," I caught him croon. "Can I get you a drink?"

She looked him up and down with interest, then sighed disappointedly. "No. I better not. Drinking's bad for my legs."

He looked at her, his forehead furrowing. "Why? Are you allergic? Do they swell up or something?"

"No," she replied ruefully. "They spread."

Kennedy, who at that moment was strutting past Tally atop the bar, stared down at her for a split second, then let out a loud cackle.

I busted out a laugh.

"Jesus," Rockabye muttered, his face heating. "Bitches are crazy."

Kennedy roared so hard she almost fell off the bar.

My other new friend, Sophie, wandered over with my other new friend, Tristan, who I'd been told was a hair genius. He'd already announced that he couldn't wait to get his hands on mine and Talia's hair.

"What's so funny?" Sophie asked.

Kennedy wiped a tear away, doubling over at the waist, and shrieked, "They spread!" She laughed so hard that she swayed precariously.

"Whoaaa!" I exclaimed, jerking my hands up to help cushion her blow in case she fell. As I moved, I saw two more hands appear beside mine, except they weren't small and soft. No, these hands were big and tanned, and the perfectly muscled arms they were attached to had sexy veins meandering under the skin. Plus, one of the fingers proudly displayed a black-and-silver wedding ring.

My neck twisted left, and my eyes met golden ones that danced with humor. "I've got this, babe," the beautiful man who was Kennedy's husband rumbled from deep within his chest. "Come on, Kitten, before you fall."

I sighed like a schoolgirl with a crush (though to be fair, there was no *like* about it—I definitely had a crush), and then I sighed again as I watched the beautiful man reach up to tag his woman's waist and pull her down from the bar before tucking her safely into his arms, bridal-style.

Kitten?

Gawd!

My poet's soul squealed in delight.

I *loved* these men.

And I *loved* this place.

It was *fucking awesome*.

And the club girls were *so nice*!

My gaze met Gopher's (my other new friend, who'd been making us these amazing cocktails, which he'd named Ol' Lady's Ruin). Apparently, Ciara, the bar manager, was away visiting family, but I was sure when she returned, we'd be great friends too because everyone here was just so dang *nice*!

Jacob needed to get to it and look for a house or land for us because I could see myself spending a lot of time in Virginia. LA had been getting old for a while, especially with the whole stalker thing.

I loved New York, and we always recorded there, so I planned on talking to the band to see how they felt about relocating our base there from LA. I knew Jonny loved NYC, and Boomer wouldn't care either way. It was Sam who'd be affected the most, as he lived at his dad's compound in Montecito. *Anyhoo*, either way it would be fine. We were only a five-hour flight away, and Jacob had a fucking private jet anyway, so... *Go me*!

I pointed at Gopher and cried out, "*Ruin* me, biker boy. In fact, *Ruin* me times two because Heather wants to be *Ruined* too."

A slow grin spread across his handsome, all-American-boy face, and he jerked a nod. "Two Ol' Lady's Ruins comin' right up."

"Awesome!" I exclaimed just as a deep voice sounded from beside me.

"Hey, babe."

I twisted my neck right that time to see a young guy of about eighteen eyeing me up. "Hi!" I cried, sticking out my hand. "I'm Saint."

His surprisingly full lips curved, and I knew this kid was going to break some hearts in his time—he probably already had.

"Know who you are," he rumbled from his chest just like Kennedy's man had moments before. He took my hand and squeezed, jerking his chin toward Breaker and Kennedy, who by then were smooching and dancing along to the music. "Thanks for helping my mom out there. She gets a bit carried away."

My eyes widened. "You're Kennedy's son."

He puffed his surprisingly large chest out. "Kai Stone."

My eyebrows snapped together. "Wait. You're Kady's twin? But she's only fifteen."

He puffed his chest out a little further. "I look older than my age. Everyone says I'm mature."

"You are," I agreed. "I thought you were about eighteen."

His eyes lit up. "Really?"

I smiled and nodded. "At least."

He stared at me with his lips parted slightly and his golden eyes soft.

My eyes flicked over his pink, flushed face. "Are you okay, Kai? Are you coming down with something?"

"No," he squeaked, then cleared his throat. "No," he said, voice deepening. "I'm cool."

I shot him one of my dazzling smiles and watched curiously as his eyes glazed over again. "Anyways,"— I jerked my thumb toward Tristan, Anna, and Sophie, who were squealing as the song morphed into an old Usher tune—"I'm gonna go dance with my new friends. Catch you later?"

He shook his head as if he was coming out of a daze and rumbled, "Yeah, babe. Catch ya later." Then, with his cheeks pinking even more, he turned and sauntered away.

My gaze followed, and my eyes widened in surprise as they caught on my new friend, Sunshine. Her gaze was also following Kai, except hers seemed dark with displeasure as she stood with a hip popped and her hand jammed to it, scowling at his back.

I was about to walk over and ask her if she was okay when a sweet voice announced, "Sunny's in love with Kai."

I jumped a mile high before turning to see Kady standing there.

My hand went to my throat. "Jesus. You scared the life out of me."

She smiled apologetically. "Sorry, I was just saying, Sunshine's in love with Kai."

"Awww. That's so sweet," I gushed.

"Not really," Kady announced. "He loves her, but he won't be her boyfriend because she's family. He says he loves her like a cousin."

I winced, my eyes sliding back to Sunshine, who looked fit to be tied. "Well, it's legal, I guess."

Kady laughed. "Doesn't matter. Kai won't; plus, he's got all his honeys to juggle. He has different girlfriends who made the cut to be one of his honey squad. Sunshine won't put up with that because she says she's a strong, independent woman, and she doesn't need no man bossing her and giving her lip." Kady leaned in. "The boys at school all ask her out, but

Uncle Bowie says she's not allowed to date until she's fifteen, and even then, no car dates, so she keeps them dangling on her string to make Kai jealous."

I resisted the urge to laugh and instead sucked back a mouthful of the cocktail Gopher had just placed on the bar for me while I took in Sunshine's extremely pretty face and her arresting huge, grey eyes. "Tell her not to worry. When she gets older, she can date all she wants, and believe me, by then Kai will be older too, and he may appreciate a strong, independent woman."

Kady nodded sagely. "That's what I said. Let Kai play the field and have his honeys. He'll leave eventually anyway to enlist in the Army like our dad did. If she waits for him to grow up, she can grow up at the same time, and when they come back together, they may both be ready."

"That's very good advice," I told her softly.

She smiled. "I'm good at giving advice."

I took in her face, which was equally as pretty as Sunshine's. "What about you? Have you got a boyfriend?"

She shook her head. "I don't care about boys. I only care about my music." Her eyes settled on mine, and she asked, "Have you met Taylor Swift?"

"Yeah, at an awards show," I confirmed. "I wouldn't call her a friend, and I'm not in her squad, but we say hi when we see each other. She told me she loved "Empty"."

Kady's eyes widened. "I can't wait to pursue my music."

"What do you play?" I asked.

"Piano and guitar, and I sing, too. Mom and Dad get me private lessons, but they said I'm not allowed to go to LA to pursue my dreams until I finish college."

"So kill two birds with one stone," I suggested. "Go to a performing arts college in LA. That way, you can go to auditions and even try your hand at session work to get some experience. I could hook you up with some people."

She let out a loud squeal and her hands flew to her mouth, and she breathed, "Really?"

I nodded. "This isn't a nepotism thing, though. I can hook you up, but you have to impress the execs and producers enough to get the gig. I can't control that. And I agree with your parents that you have to stay in college while you do it."

"Noah said the same," Kady explained. "He's the lead singer of Dischordium. It was Noah and Hendrix who played guitar with me growing up and taught me all the cool stuff."

"That bodes well," I assured her. "Noah's a great guitarist."

She beamed. "Yeah, and so's Hendrix." Her voice dropped. "I think Drix was hoping he could jam with you and the boys, but he's too embarrassed to ask because he said you probably get hassled all the time, and he doesn't wanna be a fanboy 'cause the brothers will rip him a new one."

"How about everyone with a guitar goes and grabs them, and we can all have a jamming session together when the guys come back from their meeting?"

Her eyes rounded, and she clapped her hands excitedly. "Oh my God! I'll get Mom to video us. Wait until I show the kids at school!" She leaned in and gave me a one-armed hug. "Thank you so much! I knew you'd be brilliant when they said you were Iceman's ol' lady. He's so cool."

I laughed at her obvious joy, my heart warming as I took in her happiness. "Yeah," I agreed. "He is."

She jerked her thumb toward reception. "Gonna go get my guitar."

I nodded, smiling after her as she went.

"She feels things," a voice announced roughly.

I craned my neck to see Kennedy's husband staring after his daughter. "She's special," he went on. "I dunno what it is, but all her life she can feel whatever you feel."

"Empath," I stated.

He grinned at me, his eyes catching mine. "Yeah."

My belly wobbled.

God, he was so fucking handsome.

"It comes with having a poet's soul," I told him. "It's what makes her musical—she feels what most people can only dream of."

"You sound like you have experience in that," he stated.

"So do you," I shot back.

His eyes leveled mine. "Maybe. I'm not a musician, though."

"You don't have to be a musician to have a poet's soul." My head tilted. "Breaker, right?"

He nodded.

"Kady just told me how desperate she is to go to LA," I pointed out. "She has a poet's soul but also a courageous one. She wants to live her life on her terms."

"We've been approached by her music teacher. Kadence is gifted; she can look at a sheet of music and know it by heart, and she can hear a song and immediately play it by ear perfectly. I don't doubt her talent, but I worry those LA sharks will chew my baby up and spit her out. Want her to have a childhood and go to college, and experience all the normal rites of passage she should. LA will still be there after, and if she's as good as they think, she'll make it."

"Yeah." I nudged his shoulder with mine. "And luckily, now Kady knows someone who has a house on Malibu Beach where she can stay while she's auditioning and making connections. Someone who knows a lot of people in the business who'll look out for her and guide her right. Plus, she has Noah Hart, who's like a brother to her and who'll wring the neck of anyone who tries to take advantage. She'll be okay."

He dipped his chin, holding my eyes. "Thank you."

"If Talia hears Kady play as well as you say she does, she'll go after her," I warned him. "It may feel soon for you, but Tally will respect your wishes and just keep her finger on the pulse with Kady for now. She's a great manager. She's trying to build her agency and wants to gather real talent and make sure they're supported in the right way."

He jerked his chin toward Tally, who was whooping it up with Tristan and Heather to the music. "You mean the ballbuster who nearly made Rockabye cry?"

I grinned. "That's her."

His shoulders visibly relaxed. "Kady could do worse."

I took a big swig of my drink. "These cocktails are fucking *awesome*."

"Fucking lethal more like. Kitten's wasted, and she can handle her booze."

"She's a great dancer," I told him, glancing at her enviously as she strutted around with Anna and Tristan, shaking her ass.

"She was dancing the first time I ever saw her," he murmured, his eyes taking in his woman and softening so beautifully that it made my heart tug. "I was a young soldier on leave before I had to deploy to Afghanistan. She was a Vegas stripper; the best one in town and the headlining act. I saw her show, and she blew my mind. Then, I met her at an all-night diner where we talked for hours, and afterwards I took her up a mountain to see the sun rise over Vegas." Emotion filled his face, and there and then I saw the poet's soul shining from his eyes. "I've loved her ever since."

The back of my throat burned, and I croaked, "You just inspired me."

His gaze fell over my shoulder, and he nodded in the same direction. "Boys are back in town."

I glanced over my shoulder to see Jacob with Hendrix and the other officers sauntering through the doors from reception.

Jake spotted me immediately and made a beeline for us. He grabbed my hand and tugged me close, and bent his neck for a kiss, murmuring, "You okay?"

"I'm great," I assured him softly. "Gopher created a cocktail for us."

His stare fell on Kennedy and Sophie, who were doubled over laughing at something hysterically, and he grinned. "So I see."

"I'm a little drunk."

His eyes darkened slightly, and a wolfish grin fell over his face. "Excellent."

"I may have told Kady that me and the boys would jam with her, Hendrix, and anyone else with a guitar."

He threw his head back and laughed, and in that moment, I loved him with all my poet's soul, and I knew I always would.

Jacob's eyes fell back on me, and he dipped his chin to look deep into my eyes. "Can't wait."

I smoothed his hair back from his face, wondering how I had never realized how dark my life was before him. He lit me up completely.

"I love you," I whispered.

He grinned. "How much?"

I smoothed my fingers over his dark blond brow. "If you can't see I love you soul deep, then you're not paying attention."

His smile faltered, and he rasped, "Baby," before bending his neck again and softly touching his mouth to mine. He lifted his head. "Where's your boys?"

"A group of the girls led them off about twenty minutes ago."

Jesus," he muttered. "They didn't waste any time." He pressed his forehead to mine. "Want you to meet a few people."

I smiled brightly and sang, "Okay," then I jumped ten feet in the air when someone barked, "Yo!"

Craning my neck, I saw a behemoth of a man standing behind me. "Hi!" I squeaked, clearly more drunk than I thought, because I followed it up with, "You're a big boy."

A slow cocky grin spread across his face. "Sure am."

Jacob's growl was low.

I pulled out of his arms and held my hand out. "I'm Saint."

He looked at me with his incredibly long-lashed, brown eyes and blushed profusely. "Diablo."

"Oh, hi!" I gave him a low wave.

"Howdy," he replied in a timbre so deep that it reminded me of Khal Drogo. "Big fan."

"You're such a sweetie-pie!" I exclaimed, glancing at Jacob. "Isn't he sweet, Jake?"

"Fuckin' peachy," my man muttered.

Diablo blushed again and stared down at his boots, before lifting his eyes to look through those amazing lashes at me. "Got all your CDs. Wondered if you'd sign 'em before you leave. Mi mamá loves ya, too. "Empty" is one of her favorite songs."

"I love that!" I cried, then I lowered my voice. "Has anyone ever told you that you've got beautiful eyelashes? In fact, you're very good-looking."

Jacob grunted from beside me.

Diablo's face burned scarlet, but he beamed a smile. "Do you like Christmas lights?"

My eyes rounded. "I love Christmas lights."

He grinned. "Me too." His face turned a slightly more normal color. "Someone just said you're gonna jam later." His eyes lowered to the ground again, like he couldn't meet my gaze. "I play a bit."

"You should jam with us, too!" I exclaimed.

He looked crestfallen. "I'm not very good. Probably wouldn't be able to keep up."

I touched his shoulder. "Go get your guitar. I'll go over a few chords with you before we jam, and I'll also make sure we keep the songs simple. If the others want to play fancy stuff, they can, but you can just strum the chords. Our jamming sessions aren't about perfection, they're all about fun."

Diablo's face stretched into a huge smile. "I'll go get it."

I gave him my killer grin. "Good."

He turned to go but faltered slightly. "Nice to meet you, Saint."

I clasped his huge, solid shoulder and squeezed. "You too, Diablo."

"Friends call me D," he grunted.

"Then D it is."

He gave me a loose salute with two fingers, then ambled away, leaving me to step back into Jacob's arms. "He's a sweetheart," I announced.

"He's an asshole, but he's a little bit in love with you, so it's all good." Jake picked up my glass and sniffed the contents. "What the fuck did Gopher put in this?"

"Vodka, sparkling wine, pineapple juice, and a few other things I can't remember."

He chuckled. "Why's it pink?"

"That's Sunshine's fault," I admitted. "Gopher asked what we wanted in it. Sunny said it should be pink because it's her favorite color." I leaned forward and lowered my voice. "And did you know that Sunshine and Kai have a love triangle going on? He's got a harem of honeys, so she flirts with the boys at school to make him jealous, even though she's a strong independent woman and doesn't want him anyway until he's been in the Army and grown up some." I gave him big eyes.

He laughed. "That's Wyoming for ya. The stories I could tell ya are crazy." He leaned down and nuzzled my nose with his. "Me and you are fuckin' boring compared to those drama-filled fuckers."

I deadpanned. "Well, we had a two-year separation. I wouldn't call it boring."

"We reconnected and had talked it out within days. No miscommunication, no bullshit. I told you where I was coming from, and you did the same. No fighting, no angst, and no daytime soap opera bullshit. Job done."

"No thanks to you not telling me about the club girls," I said dryly. "Oh, Heather's lovely by the way, haven't had a chance to talk to the others, but we had a chat and she's very sweet."

"They're okay," he acquiesced. "We did have a couple'a bitches in our midst, but we kicked 'em out. Hendrix won't have nasty shit goin' down at the club, and neither will Anna."

"I love it here," I announced.

Jacob's fingers curled around the back of my neck, and he touched his mouth to mine. "I'm glad."

"Relocating to Virginia won't be a hardship. I feel safe here with you."

His eyes crinkled with his smile, but still, he seemed wary. "We need a quick chat, Saint."

My stomach dropped slightly at his expression. "What's happened?"

"Nothing. It's just we found some shit on Jonny and Braden Hunt. Historical issues with ex-girlfriends. Did you know about it?"

"Braden, no. I don't know him well at all. Is he even capable of that kind of crazy? He seems so together."

"According to the profile, he hides the crazy well," Jake confirmed. "Remember, we're not dealing with an everyday Joe here, baby." He sighed, his icy eyes boring into mine. "What about Jonny?"

"Yes," I admitted. "Look, Jonny swore us to secrecy at the time, but he was honest about everything. He told us when he joined the band in case Talia dug up shit from his background. He was open about it; he said he was young and stupid and fancied himself in love. She cheated and dumped him, and he went off the rails. He has anger issues and, as far as I know, got therapy, but I think all that's fallen by the wayside recently."

"How recently?" Jacob asked.

I shrugged. "I dunno. Maybe a few months ago."

"When you started getting the letters and gifts," he pointed out.

A sick feeling jolted through my stomach. "I never thought of that."

"We'll keep an eye on him and never leave you two alone. The entire place is covered with cameras, and there are men around all the time. Stick with me, and when I have to go off and do something, you stay with Diablo, Hendrix, Blade, or Gambit. They're the brothers I trust the most, and they're fuckin' deadly. The good thing is, Jonny admitted to you he went off the rails, but the stalker justifies everything he does in his own head. Jonny fits a lot of the profile, but that part doesn't ring true. I'll talk to Colt about it and see what he says. In the meantime, we stay vigilant."

His protectiveness made my heart swell.

I pressed my face to his chest and let the comfort of his body melt away all my worries and anxieties. It was crazy, but in a way, I just wanted the stalker to make a move. Living in limbo was beginning to take its toll. I was walking on eggshells constantly, and it was starting to have an effect on my mental health.

Jacob must've read my mind because he tilted my chin with his finger until our gazes locked. "Love you, baby," he whispered. "I'll die before I let anything happen to you."

His words sent a cold shiver down my spine, but internally, I shrugged it off. Jacob was a professional bodyguard, and he knew what he was doing. I just had to do what he told me and play it smart until whoever was tormenting me slipped up. We could ride it out, and we would overcome our challenges; we just had to keep the faith.

The alternative didn't bear thinking about.

Chapter Fifteen

Iceman

The beer flowed, and the party raged on.
Saint downed an ungodly amount of the cocktails Gopher poured like a professional, but then, she was a rock star, so of course she could handle her booze. Sophie couldn't keep up, and she had her two young girls, so she and Atlas bowed out early, along with Abe and Iris, who valiantly put Wilder to bed, which was good of them considering the kid was a lunatic.

Cara, Kennedy and Breaker, and Tristan stayed along with Anna and Hendrix. Will took JT upstairs to his room for the night, but honestly, he needn't have bothered; the kid could sleep through a hurricane.

Eventually, the boys in the band came back with the club girls under their arms, and everybody looked mighty satisfied with themselves. Saint asked if they wanted to jam, and they agreed, so everyone who wanted to play went off and got their guitars and instruments. Harmonicas and even a banjo made an appearance, so everyone was set.

Kady and Diablo sat on stools next to Saint, while Hendrix set up a couple of mic stands next to the Saint's Rapture boys. Trick had a fucking fiddle in his hand and took his place among the players along with Rockabye, K9, and a couple of others.

A lively discussion ensued about what songs they were gonna play. Saint suggested tracks that were guitar-driven, seeing as that was the predominant instrument within the group, and everybody agreed.

Saint wanted to hear Kady sing, so they settled on a 10,000 Maniacs song that the kid could sing and play from memory, because it was one of Kennedy's favorites.

Saint bent down to watch Diablo position his fingers on the fret, then helped him move them around, talking him through the transitions.

"The intro's easy, honey," she began. "A, D, G, D." They began to discuss terms like Dsus4. I started to zone out, mainly because I didn't have a fucking clue what they were talking about. Somehow, my attention turned to Jonny J, whose gaze was fixed on Saint while she taught Diablo the chords he'd need. A soft look moved across his face as he studied them, and my stomach clenched with unease.

I suspected Jonny's expression mirrored the same one on my face when I looked at my woman, but in all fairness, she was acting cute with my club brother by taking him under her wing. Saint was a little drunk and a lot chatty, and she kept whispering things to Diablo that made him laugh, I assumed to put him at ease.

I fucking loved that about her. To her mind, it was never about her; it was always about the other person and how she could make them feel at ease around her. She wanted everybody to treat her like everyone else and never looked down on people, including Diablo, who was a good, decent guy, but also a little loopy, as evidenced by the human body parts he kept in his room.

When he first came to the club, he was an oddball who never quite fit in, but he was still loyal to the core and held a love for the brotherhood that couldn't be denied. I suspected that it was the fact that he kept a degree of separation from the men that convinced Hendrix to give him the Sergeant at Arms patch.

An SAA needed to discipline the men and keep them in check. The social cues that Diablo either missed or ignored set him apart from everybody else. Plus, he was a big, tough motherfucker who could beat the fuck out of most of the men with one hand tied behind his back, so that helped Drix in his decision-making process, too. D acted the fool, but was a lot more calculated than people gave him credit for. He took risks but only when he was certain he'd get away with it.

I'd always wondered what happened to Diablo to make him tick the way he did. He didn't go to therapy sessions and never spoke to anyone about his Army career, which by all accounts was a prestigious one. At night, you could often hear some of the guys wailing and fighting their demons in their sleep, but never D. He seemed at peace with himself and his past.

I didn't doubt he'd talk when he was ready, but until then, Diablo seemed happy in his own crazy and weird world of chopping off people's body parts and storing them in jars filled with embalming fluid that he lit up like Christmas decorations.

Fucking lunatic.

My stare flicked back to Jonny, noticing he was still fixated on my woman. Possession reared up inside me, and I almost got up out of my chair to tell him to put his eyes back in his head, and his tongue back in his mouth, because he was panting after Saint so hard. What stopped me was the hand that rested on my shoulder as a presence took the chair beside me.

"He's a little bit in love with her, but he'd never go there." Talia's voice was low, so only I could hear her when she relayed, "Now look at Boomer and Sam."

With my pulse racing already from the way Jonny was looking at Saint, my eyes slid to the other two men, my heart jolting when I saw the exact same soft expressions on their faces as they glanced over at Saint while she gave Diablo a crash course in guitar playing.

"All three of them are a little bit in love with her," Tally murmured. "Boomer won't ever go there; he's like her brother, and honestly, I'm surprised Sam did, seeing as he has no patience and hates rejection in any form. Those boys made a pact between themselves when the band first got together that they wouldn't pursue anything with Saint because, more often than not, when it comes to bands, romantic entanglements don't end well." She glanced at me, giving me one of her rare smiles. "They were right. I don't know of one band romance that survived past the second album. Music heightens emotions, and when you add on the crazy schedules, the groupies, the party lifestyle, and the exhaustion, it's damned near impossible to make it work. Still, it doesn't mean you have to do it alone. Sometimes, a person"—she smiled—"*the* person comes along who you'd give it all up for in a heartbeat. Except, if that person is truly the right one, they'd never allow you to." Tally nodded toward Saint, who had settled back in her chair to make sure her guitar was tuned. "She'll offer to do that one day, and maybe, for a while, it may seem like the perfect solution. You're gonna get separated because that's the nature of the beast, or she'll get papped at a weird angle with another guy that looks like something it isn't. Shit will happen, and rather than lose you, she'll offer to walk so she can keep you. But have no doubt, she'll waste away if she does. One day she'll wake up and it won't be Saint anymore, at least not this version of her."

"You shouldn't judge me by other dude's standards," I advised her.

"So, what happens when the separations become too much?" she challenged.

My eyes slid to meet hers. "I leave the club. *I* give it all up for *her*."

Her eyebrows drew together thoughtfully, and she studied me. I could almost see her mind ticking over behind her eyes, "I've never witnessed anyone look at another person the way you look at Saint. It's like you're drawn together every time you're in the same room. It warms my cold, dead heart."

I chuckled. "Good to know you've still got one."

"Oh, don't you worry. It's still there." She smiled wryly.

My eyes fell on my woman, and my lips curved as I studied her laughing with Kady and Diablo. "She saved me. I fell hard the night we met, and I never forgot her. Reconnecting and sorting our shit made me realize that she's my missing piece of the puzzle. I'm gone for her again, hook, line, and sinker, but I'm determined that we're gonna fall in love right this time."

She cocked her head slightly. "That's very... poetic."

I nodded to where Saint and Kady giggled with their heads together. "She's the poet, and it inspires a side of me I never knew I had. She brings out a softness that, before, I always thought was a vulnerability, except I don't anymore. I see it now; you can't find light without casting shadows."

She turned back toward the band. "That's pretty profound."

My throat thickened with every sliver of emotion in my soul. "It's the way I feel."

A huge smile spread over Talia's face. "Protect her."

My gaze went back to my beautiful woman. "Always."

"She'll die for you."

I took a swig of my beer and placed it back on the bar. "I'll never let her 'cause I'll die for her first."

Talia squeezed my shoulder again. "Good."

The bar stool beside mine scraped across the floor, and I turned to see Breaker deposit a very drunk Kennedy on it. He grabbed the one next to it and immediately pulled it close to Ned's before he sat down and wrapped his arms around her.

Kennedy looked at me and Talia with glazed eyes before announcing, "I'm lit."

"Everyone's drunk, babe," I assured her. "Right about now, you're one of the most sober ones in the room. Saint's so wasted that she's a little bit in love with Diablo the cock chopper, and even Talia's all up in her feelings."

"It's those fuckin' cocktails," Breaker rasped, shooting Gopher, who was serving someone down the end of the bar, a glower.

Kennedy waved a hand dismissively. "Oh, stop pretending like you care, golden boy. You know I get dirty when I'm drunk. You don't fucking complain then."

My ears pricked up.

Breaker's glower turned into a wolfish grin.

Talia laughed.

Three hollow taps sounded from Jonny J as he thwacked the wood on his acoustic guitar, and Boomer immediately came in strumming the opening chords to a song I recognized but couldn't place.

After a beat, Saint nodded to D, who began to strum his guitar, though not as fast as the others— for every four chords Boomer played, D only played one— but it seemed to fit. Then Kady came in, adding another layer of sound, followed closely by Saint and Sam. Hendrix soon joined in, and by the time Kady began singing, everybody was strumming the chords to the track, and the room was filled with the sounds of guitars.

The hair on the back of my arms stood on end.

It was cool as fuck.

Kady closed her eyes, her sweet and surprisingly husky tone filling the air as she leaned her mouth so close to the microphone that it almost became an extension of her. I smiled at the way she felt the music the same way Saint always did.

My woman sat back with a knowing smile on her face, giving Kady her moment. The only time she sang was to harmonize and elevate Kady's performance, and my heart flipped over with pride for my incredible woman.

This was an everyday thing for Saint, but to Kady, it was a dream come true, and the fact that my girl gave the kid a moment she'd remember for the rest of her life filled me with so much respect for Saint that my heart swelled with it.

"What song's this?" I asked Kennedy in hushed tones.

"These are Days," she replied distractedly, grasping Breaker's hand as she gazed at her daughter in awe. "It's pretty, right?"

"Real pretty," I muttered, taking in the words that conveyed how we should all live in the moment and appreciate life in all its glory.

It suited Kady and her voice perfectly.

Talia sat forward, her stare glued to the kid, then she glanced at Breaker. "She's yours, right?"

My brother smirked. "She is. Kady's also fifteen years old and too young to have the pressures of a music career on her shoulders."

"I get it," Talia announced. "Respect it even, but she won't always be fifteen, and I need to point out that if you try to stop an artist making art, they wilt. There are ways you can let Kady be who she is, but still control the outside noise. I can help you and her with that. But don't waste her potential. She won't thank you for it. Let her be who she is and let her do what she needs to do. She's got a good family and a solid foundation, so as long as she has the right people around her, too, she'll be okay."

Breaker and Kennedy glanced at each other.

"We'll talk before I leave," Talia told them.

Breaker pushed a deep breath out, but he nodded, almost resigning himself to the fact that Talia made perfect sense.

Kady's voice soared above the guitars, and goosebumps trailed down my arms.

Jesus, I knew the kid was good, but this was something else.

My stare slid to Saint, and my mouth hitched again when I saw the light dancing in her eyes as she grinned at Kady encouragingly.

I hadn't fucking smiled this much since I was a goofy teenager. She brought something out in me I hadn't ever experienced before, a kind of freedom and lightness that made me feel like I was walking on air.

She had something about her that moved me, and a grace that humbled me. Saint McClure should've been a bitch, but instead, she was an angel.

Something pinged in my mind, and I leaned closer to Talia to ask her the question that had been on my mind since the night Saint had played with Dischordium. "Why doesn't Blue De Santis like Saint?"

She rolled her eyes. "Blue De Santis is an arrogant asshole who thinks women should drop their panties for him whenever he walks into a room." Her eyes came to me, and she cocked a questioning eyebrow. "Can you see Saint dropping anything for him?"

I almost laughed at the thought. "No."

Iceman

Her eyes went back to Kady. "Men have come a long way in the last hundred years, Iceman, but Blue De Santis is still stuck in a time period where he thinks if a woman doesn't want him, she's either frigid or a lesbian. Frankly, he's an asshole."

"So he tried his shit with Saint?" I asked.

Her lips thinned. "Blue tries his shit with everyone. The problem is, he's hot as Hades, so he usually gets away with it."

"Good to know," I muttered, storing that shit away for future use.

She chuckled just as the song reached a crescendo. All the guitars played together in such perfect synchronicity that even the odd bum chord couldn't spoil the magic they weaved as they strummed the last chords.

A loud roar went up, and immediately, Saint began to strum another set of chords, these ones sharper than the last. She counted down, calling out the sequence and nodding to Diablo and Kady, who joined in, closely followed by the others as they began to play the opening bars of one of our favorite songs called "We Are the People."

The notes seemed heavier when Saint played the chords. The tune was a dance track, but I liked it because it fucking rocked; plus, Saint was good at dirtying it up to make it more my taste. The dazzling smile she threw my way conveyed her joy, and I knew she was playing this one for me because it was a favorite.

It was Sam who leaned forward and began singing the words in a surprisingly tuneful voice. You could tell he was no singer, but he carried it well, all the same, and when Boomer and Saint came in on the chorus to sing the harmonies, it sounded fucking awesome.

The momentum of the song built, the sound of guitars crashing through the air, causing vibrations that hit me down to my bones. It was easy to get caught up in the feeling of it all, and when Saint's eyes locked with mine, her expression full of fire from the hard edge of the song she played, I found myself getting caught up in her, too.

She made me feel everything with just a look, and I wondered how it could be that I'd gone through the last twelve years not really getting close to anyone, and then along came Saint, and suddenly, connecting was easy.

We just fit. Sometimes it was chaotic, other times it was peaceful, but it always felt right because being around Saint made me feel softer and brighter. Like I'd woken up from hibernation and was ready to meet the sun head-on after a long-assed sleep.

She was pure beauty, and that was exactly what she brought to my life. I thought after Allie passed that I was destined to be alone. I thought nobody else could compare, but that was my first mistake because it wasn't about comparisons. It was about letting the person you loved and admired be themselves, as well as accepting and celebrating everything about them.

Allie was Allie, and I loved her to my bones.

Saint was Saint, and I loved her to my soul.

It wasn't more or less; it was just different. Loving Saint didn't stop me from missing Allie, but missing Allie also didn't stop me from loving Saint.

Time had moved on, and thankfully, so had I.

Now, it was all about letting go of the past and living again.

The song began to wind down, so I turned to Gopher and jerked my chin, watching as he came sauntering over before ordering, "Get me a Coke for Saint, brother."

"Sure you don't want a cocktail?" he inquired, smirking slightly.

"I want a cocktail," Kennedy piped up.

"Me too," Talia declared.

Breaker grinned and whispered something in Kennedy's ear that made her giggle. "On second thoughts, I'll leave it," she said decisively. "I'm going to bed soon."

Gopher shook his head, smiling before going to the fridge and grabbing a bottle of Coke, popping the cap, and placing it on the bar. Then he set about making Talia her cocktail.

The brothers clapped and cheered as the song came to an end. I craned my neck to see Saint pull her guitar strap over her head and lay her eight-string down gently on the floor beside her chair, then I waited for her approach before holding the bottle out for her to take.

She gave me an appreciative kiss on the cheek before grabbing the bottle and taking a sip. "Just what I needed."

I took her hand and pulled her against me, my arm sliding around her waist. "That was cool," I told her.

"I know, right?" Her eyes danced. "I love jamming sessions, especially with such a range of different people. I get so used to performing with the boys and putting pressure on myself to never miss a note that I forget how freeing it is to let go and just enjoy the moment."

I gazed down at her, taking in her obvious joy. "It sounded awesome."

"Yeah. I love it." Her eyes jerked to the side where Talia spoke to Kennedy, then back to me. "What did Tally think of Kady?"

Gopher turned up the music, and I leaned down to speak into Saint's ear, giving the lobe a gentle nibble while I was down there. "I think Talia's already planning the first album."

"I knew it." My woman laughed, sliding her hands up my chest and linking her fingers behind my neck. "I just hope she doesn't try to force it. Tally means well, but she's a bulldozer. A Mack truck has more subtlety. I worry she'll go at a hundred miles an hour and make Breaker and Kennedy back off more."

"Breaker won't let her, and he seems set on what he's comfortable with. He wants Kady to experience life the way she should, and it doesn't include drugs, booze, celebrity parties, and life on the road."

"Life on the road can be awesome," Saint corrected. "Though not so much when you're all sleeping in one car because you got stiffed by the venue you just played at and you can't afford a hotel."

I laughed.

She looked around at the old hotel ballroom that the club now used as a bar and social space, her eyes warm with admiration. "Do you know how amazing this place is?"

My gaze skated around the room. "I take it for granted now, but seeing it through your eyes makes me appreciate it again. When we first moved in, we were like kids in a candy store, but over time, we got used to it."

Saint leaned up to whisper, "You should take me on a tour, Jacob. One that finishes in the bedroom."

My lips tipped up. "Now?"

She laughed softly. "No time like the present."

I didn't need to be told twice. It had been a couple of days since we'd fucked because of our club whore argument, so my cock was already kicking like an NFL quarterback at the mere prospect of being inside my woman.

Grabbing her hand, I led her out of the ballroom and into the reception area, but instead of taking her upstairs, I headed for the doors outside.

"Where are we going?" she asked, her tone playful as we passed a group of brothers drinking beer and shooting the shit outside by their bikes.

It was dark, except for the lights from the hotel. The forecourt was lit up too, and the moon shone through the trees, casting its glow on us and lighting my way as I pulled her around the back of the building.

"Gonna show you something I've been working on," I told her, leading her by the hand toward the new auto shop. I pulled my keys from my pocket and unlocked the doors before tugging her inside the building.

It took a minute for my eyes to adjust, but the light from the moon shining through the windows illuminated the space. I walked across to the control pad and hit a few buttons, which triggered a couple of the side lights on the walls.

"Come here," I demanded gently, taking her hand again and leading her to another door at the back of the room. This one opened easily, and I pulled her through, telling her, "Welcome to my lair."

She giggled, then looked around, the smile dying on her face as her gaze caught on the drawings and designs pasted on the walls.

I leaned down until my mouth rested on the shell of her ear and murmured, "This is *my* version of music."

Saint dropped my hand and walked over to the board full of drawings of bikes attached to it.

"I started working with Bowie over at the Wyoming chapter," I explained. "He designs customized bikes. Loved the work, and I loved the creativity, so I started experimenting."

Saint looked around wondrously at the images. "Jacob. These are incredible."

"I dunno about that," I began, but she twisted her head and skewered me with a look.

"Are you crazy? These are beautiful." She turned back to the drawings, lifting a finger to touch one. "Look at this, baby. It's fucking stunning."

"Yeah," I murmured, my chest warming as my eyes went to her ass. "It is."

"Why didn't you tell me you drew this stuff?" she asked.

I shrugged. "Just did."

"These should be in magazines." Her attention got caught up in the artwork of a tribal design I'd recently completed. "The colors are amazing, and your ideas are so original. I'm no expert, but I haven't seen anything like this before."

I walked over and looked at the drawing I'd finished just before I went to NOLA. It seemed so long ago, even though it had only been weeks. "That one's for Blade's new bike."

"It's wonderful." Her eyes met mine, and her lips curved seductively. "You're so fucking sexy right now, *Iceman*."

My dick punched against the zipper of my jeans.

I loved it when she called me by my road name. It was fucking hot.

Her hand went to her pocket, and she pulled out a hair tie.

"You wanna go, baby?" I asked, my tone low and husky with need. "You want your biker man to take you to our room and fuck you until you pass out?"

She sifted her fingers through her hair before pulling it into a high ponytail and tying it up securely. "No," she murmured, her eyes widening innocently. "I want my big, bad biker to drop his jeans for me right here, and right now." Her beautiful, puffy lips pouted prettily. "I wanna suck your big, hard cock."

Chapter Sixteen

Saint

Something about being here in Jacob's space and seeing his heart and soul pasted up on that board did funny things to me. My thighs shook, and heat built in my core.

I didn't know if it was the booze, the environment, or just being around my hot biker man, but suddenly, I wanted to play.

Slowly, I moved toward my man, my hands going to the hem of my tee, and I pulled it up and over my head, tossing it somewhere behind me.

Jacob's grin lit up the room, and my nipples tingled, not just from the cool air in Jacob's workspace, but also with the knowledge of what I was about to do to him.

"I wanna suck big, bad, biker cock," I told him huskily, flicking the buttons of my jean shorts open and sliding them down my legs, making sure to take my panties with them before kicking them off. "You wanna give my face a good fucking, Mr. Biker?"

"Gonna fuck your face and then your tight cunt," he vowed in a low raspy, sexy as all hell voice.

I widened my eyes innocently, my hands going behind my back to unclasp my bra. "Please be gentle with me," I purred coquettishly, throwing my bra in the same direction as my top, leaving myself completely bare. "I'm so small down there, you'll hurt me."

"Hell no," he muttered, his eyes roaming my naked body. "Gonna rough up that little pussy."

"Oh no," I whispered as I approached, falling to my knees in front of him. My eyes lifted to meet his as he loomed above me, his hands going straight to his belt buckle and undoing it. Then, he unbuttoned his jeans, shoving them down his thighs and took his hard cock in hand. "You want this?" he rasped.

I nodded, keeping my eyes wide and innocent as I stared up at my man. "If I suck your cock good and swallow your hot cum, will you hold off on fucking me? I'm so tight down there, I'm scared you'll rip me apart."

His cock swelled even bigger at my words. "Lick it," he ordered.

I obeyed and stuck my tongue out, lapping him from root to tip, my eyes never leaving his.

He groaned, his stare hooked on my mouth and what I was doing to him. I kept going, lapping him gently as if he were my favorite flavor of ice cream.

A drop of pre-cum appeared at the tip and I moved my way up, taking the head in my mouth, and sucked hard.

He grunted.

I released him, pulling my mouth back slowly, and internally cheering when a tiny string of pre-cum, which was still connected, stretched before it fell down my chin.

"Fuck me, you're hot," he muttered, his eyes blazing.

I went back in and devoured his cock. Opening my throat as wide as I could, I took his big, beautiful length as far as I could handle without gagging. My hand went to the root, and I gently worked his balls while bobbing up and down his length and sucking him like a lollipop with my eyes still glued to his.

"Baby," he rasped.

I moaned around his dick, and he hardened even more in my mouth.

"Sexy little bitch," he muttered.

I moaned again, his words making my pussy flood with moisture.

Sucking Jacob was one of my most favorite things to do. He was large but not ridiculously so. His dick was velvety soft and smooth, with the hair around the base neatly trimmed and groomed. His cock was thick and straight, and I loved tracing the fine veins that ran the length of it with my tongue. He tasted of clean soap and Bleu De Chanel, and I fucking loved the traces of it that he left on my sheets, and even more amazingly, my skin.

I released him with a pop, and watched as his hard dick bounced against the abs on his stomach. My fingers wrapped around his length, and I slowly started jacking him, twisting my hand while also altering the tightness of my grip as I stroked him from balls to tip.

Jacob's fingers wrapped around my nape, and he forced himself back inside my mouth. I hummed around his dick again and he threw his head back and moaned, "Fuck, baby." Slowly, he pumped his hips back and forth, driving deeper down my throat but never uncomfortably so. "Take that cock."

I hollowed my cheeks and sucked hard, and his nostrils flared.

Strong hands grabbed under my armpits and dragged me to my feet. Jake's mouth smashed down on mine and our tongues tangled while his hands went to my hips and he lifted my ass onto his desk.

There was something so fucking hot about me being naked apart from my white sneakers and Jacob being fully clothed. My hands went to his cut, feeling the smoothness of the leather under my fingertips, and my pussy clenched with need.

He pulled back. "Hot little bitch," he rasped. "You and your sexy little games."

My eyes went wide and innocent again. "What?"

"Don't even go there with that innocent act."

"I can't help it if I love that big, hard cock of yours," I told him breathily.

"You're gonna know all about my big, hard cock in a minute," he vowed, his molten eyes on fire. "Gonna use it to ruin your tight little pussy."

"What you gonna do, you big, bad biker?" she whispered, her eyes rounding until they were huge and seductive. "You can't fuck my pussy too hard. It's too big to fit inside without hurting me, and I'll have to miss college cheer tomorrow."

He let out a long grunt, then spread my legs, folding my knees up until my heels rested on the edge of the desk and my pussy was completely exposed to him.

He ran his fingertips over the inside of my thighs. "You want me to make you come?"

"Yes please, Sir," I said breathily "But please don't fuck me. You're too big. I just want you to make me come."

His finger slipped inside, and he started to fuck me, his thumb dragging over my clit and circling it.

I gasped at the sensation, and my hips bucked.

"That's it, you sexy little slut," he muttered. "Clench those fingers with that tiny little pussy."

I gave my walls a squeeze. "Can you feel how tight I am, you big, bad biker?" I murmured. "You'll tear me up if you fuck me too hard. I won't be able to walk tomorrow."

"Fuck," he muttered, his fingers sliding in good and deep. "Baby."

That was when I knew I had him. His eyes flared and he dragged his fingers from inside me and gripped the base of his cock. "You want this?" he demanded.

"No. It'll hurt me," I insisted. "I'm too tight to take it all."

"Well, you're getting it," he growled, lost in the fantasy. "Gonna tear that pussy up with it." I felt the tip nudge against my core, then I cried out as he guided himself inside me before thrusting deep.

My fingers linked around the back of his nape, and I circled my hips with him inside me and whispered, "Feel how wet my little pussy is for you, Mr. Big, Bad Biker?"

He groaned and proceeded to fuck me hard until I squealed.

He buried himself to the root until he bottomed out and groaned, "Baby."

"You're so big," I said with a moan. "So fucking hard."

Jacob's eyes dropped and he watched himself fuck me. "Look how fucking hot we are."

My gaze lowered and my walls clenched instinctively as I watched his glistening cock disappear inside me over and over again.

"Fuck. Fuck. Fuck," Jake chanted, his cock slamming into me. His fingers reached down, and he pressed on my clit, rubbing it hard as he pounded my cunt. His jaw clenched, and I saw a muscle tick in his cheek as he kept grinding into me. "You're so fucking tight, baby."

His fingers kept working my clit while the other hand lowered from my nape to pinch my nipple. My pussy contracted hard as my orgasm began to build, and my head dropped back as my eyes swept over his face, examining the way his eyebrows pulled together in concentration as he drove harder into me.

He was so fucking beautiful that he made me ache inside.

My hips bucked. "Baby. Don't stop." I felt his fingers press against my clit and my cunt squeezed. Heat pooled in my core, and then I cried out as my climax hit me like a tidal wave.

"Fuck, I'm gonna blow." Jacob thrust hard inside me again, but he didn't pull back; he stayed deep and circled his hips, biting out, "Jesus."

His words triggered something, and my orgasm intensified. My pussy contracted uncontrollably, and I rocked my hips, chanting, "Yes. Yes. Fuck me."

His hand gripped the back of my neck, angling my head toward him until our faces were close, and he ordered, "Mouth. Now."

Our lips connected, and I groaned my pleasure into his mouth. My cries mingled with his loud grunts, and I felt my pussy flood with his cum. Pressure exploded in my core, making my nails dig into his neck and back, my hips bucking uncontrollably as I rode his long, deep strokes until eventually, I started to come back down.

Jacob's hips jerked, and he emptied himself into me, his grunts and groans filling the room.

My hand reached his balls, and I stroked them gently as his body jolted, his movements completely out of control. The muscles in his neck were corded with the strain of his orgasm until finally his eyes opened, locking with mine, and he let out a long, low growl.

He leaned forward, half against me, half against that table. "You broke me." He laughed softly as his fingers wrapped around mine and he pressed them against his pounding heart. "Can you feel what you do to me, Saint McClure? Do you know you brought me back to life?"

"Jacob," I whispered, my throat burning with emotion.

"It's not just about the physicality of us, baby," he went on. "I fell in love with your soul, and it only took one look. I never even needed to touch you to know you were mine."

Tears sprang to my eyes as the beauty of his words dug deep.

"Can't fucking wait to have everything with you, Saint. Can't fucking wait to see you walking toward me in a white dress, with my diamond sparkling on your finger. Can't wait to give you my name and my babies, and to show you how much I adore you every day for the rest of my life. You make my world better just by being in it."

My eyes welled with tears, and I felt one spill over and track down my cheek.

Jacob thumbed it away, his eyes never leaving mine.

The intensity behind his stare burned into me, and I knew I'd never love another man the way I loved him. It wasn't just the things he said that melted my heart; it was the complete absence of irony or embarrassment. He didn't care about anyone else's opinion, and he wasn't concerned about what anyone thought of him, his brothers included. Jake's love for me was loud and proud, and he didn't care who saw it. He may not have possessed a poet's soul, but he possessed an artist's one, and I loved that about him.

It was becoming clearer every day that if I didn't have Jacob, I wouldn't have anything worth living for. The music, the fame, and the fortune wouldn't mean anything without him by my side. He was my muse, and if my muse disappeared, so would all the beauty in everything I did. The best songs on the last album were penned from our one fleeting night. I could only imagine what a lifetime spent with Jacob would inspire within me.

"I need to get you inside before you freeze to death," he murmured.

"I'm always warm when I'm with you," I whispered.

Jacob grinned. "You fucking blow my mind. Who the fuck plays slutty cheerleader? You, that's who. You're full of surprises."

I laughed softly. "Did you like that?"

He lifted one eyebrow. "Did you feel how hard I came, baby? Thought my head and my dick were gonna explode at one point. I've filled you with my cum."

"Just as well we got our tests back." I giggled.

"Babe," he muttered. "You think I wouldn't have a wrap on me? If there's one thing I've established in the last few weeks, it's that I've always gotta be prepared when it comes to you." He slid his arms around me, and I lifted my chin to meet Jacob's soft kiss, my heart flipping over in my chest.

"I love your road name by the way," I told him when he pulled back. "Why Iceman?"

He grunted a laugh. "My old chapter reckoned I've got a look of Val Kilmer from the old *Top Gun* movie."

I cocked my head. "I don't see it. I thought it was because your eyes are icy blue."

"Nah. Those boys wouldn't go that deep, but you're right, it is a cool name, so I wasn't gonna look a gift horse in the mouth. A few of the others that were suggested weren't so cool, so I took it and ran."

I put on my slutty cheerleader voice. "You're such a big, bad biker."

He glanced downward and I followed his gaze to see his cock twitching again.

I choked out a laugh.

"Jesus Christ," he cut out good-naturedly. "What the fuck am I gonna do with you?"

I laughed harder.

His hand cupped the back of my skull, and he leaned down to kiss me. "She keeps me on my toes," he murmured against my lips.

"You better believe it," I said back.

Jacob's lips moved over mine insistently, and I marveled at their strength, but at the same time, their softness. Nobody had ever kissed me like he did—full of feeling and intensity. Just like everything Jacob did, he did it with meaning and gave it his all.

He pulled back, his eyes hooded as he took in my expression, which I knew conveyed how visibly he affected me. "Come on, beautiful. Let's get to bed. Wanna take a shower and spoon my ol' lady."

My eyes followed him sauntering across the room to retrieve the clothes I'd tossed when we played our little game. When he turned back to me, his eyes were soft and languid, probably from the force of his orgasm, and all tenseness had left his body.

He looked younger, boyish even, and my belly swirled with the knowledge that I did that. I took away his stress, and even if it only lasted until morning, it was worth it.

Jacob dipped and threaded my panties back over my sneakers, followed closely by my shorts. He lifted me from the desk, placing me gently on my feet, and pulled them over my ass. Then he grabbed my bra and tee and dressed me as if I were a child.

I nodded down at his still semi-hard cock he hadn't tucked away, and gave him an exaggerated, cheeky wink, "You sure you want that to go to waste?"

He burst out laughing and pushed his dick back inside his fly before zipping up. "Upstairs, shower, bed, then we fuck again. In that order."

I saluted him. "Yes, Sir."

He grinned, shaking his head as he gazed down at me with so much love in his expression that my bones quivered. "Maybe that could be our next game." He tucked a lock of hair behind my ear. "Lieutenant and new recruit."

I lit up from the inside, but on the outside, I just nodded approvingly. "Niiiice. Maybe I've been a bad, bad girl and put the rest of the recruits at risk, and you have to punish me for it."

His hands went back to his fly, and he adjusted his crotch. "Fuck me. You carry on with this shit and I won't last until we get upstairs. You're gonna be the fucking death of me, Saint McClure." His face descended, and he kissed my neck.

My body shivered from head to toe. "I love you," I whispered.

Jacob lifted his head, nuzzled my nose with his, and muttered, "Love you, baby." He took my hand and led me out of the office and back into the workroom of the auto shop. Then he hooked his arm around my neck and pulled my body into the side of his so snugly that his forearm hung down over my chest.

Something sparked inside my belly, warming me. The scent of Jacob's cologne washed over me again, and I sent up a word of thanks to God for bringing this beautiful soul into my life because he'd made my heart open again.

All my life, I'd felt like I wasn't enough. Not sweet enough, not obedient enough, and certainly not religious enough. Jacob had flipped that on its head, and I knew now I *was* enough, and I always would be, because he saw something in me that made it that way.

Nothing could take this or him away from me; I wouldn't let it. Whatever happened, I'd fight. I'd kick, scream, and claw to keep Jacob by my side. I'd give up anything and everything for him, and the reason I'd do it happily lay in the knowledge that I knew he'd do the same for me. But the real joy came from the fact I'd never have to, because he'd never ask.

I wasn't stupid; I knew it wouldn't all be moonlight and roses, and I also knew we'd have challenges to deal with because that was life and it threw curve balls all the damned time. Navigating the world was hard, but navigating it with Jacob was going to be my honor and my privilege.

And I couldn't wait to get started.

He made me so fucking happy.

We slipped out of the auto shop, giggling like schoolkids who'd secretly sneaked into the janitor's closet for a make-out session.

Jacob pulled me to face him, his hands resting on my shoulders, and he pressed his forehead to mine. "Wanna go for a ride tomorrow?" he asked. "Want you on the back of my bike where you belong."

I almost squealed with delight. Instead, I bounced on the balls of my feet excitedly and breathed in the style of Chandler Bing, "Could you *get any better*?"

My man chuckled, his grip on my shoulders tightening as he pulled me in and touched his mouth to mine before asking, "My songbird likes motorcycles?"

"I've never been on one." My gaze locked with his, and I took in the icy blue eyes I loved so much. "But I do know that as long as I get to hold onto you, I'll love it."

He turned me to the side, his beautiful big bicep cuffing me to his side again as we headed around the side of the hotel. "Come with me. Wanna show you somethin'."

"I've heard that before," I replied drolly, laughing along with his chuckle as Jacob pulled me around the front of the building and up onto the hotel steps. His feet faltered and he dropped his ass onto the top stair, pulling me down to sit across his lap before gently turning my face toward his with his forefinger.

"I'm gonna show you the last piece of me," he murmured. "The one piece you haven't seen yet. I'm gonna do this here before we go inside because it doesn't belong in our room with us, but it's still an introduction that needs to happen before I let it go for good."

My eyebrows pulled together curiously, and I watched as he reached into the inside pocket of his cut and retrieved his wallet. Flipping it open, his fingers went inside, and he pulled out a couple of small photographs.

"Saint," he said, his voice suddenly husky with emotion. "This is Allicent."

My sharp intake of breath was audible. "Jacob..." I began, but my voice trailed off when he held up the first picture.

"This was her on our wedding day," he explained gently, holding the small square image out.

With trembling fingers, I took it from him, and pulling in a deep breath, I braced and turned the picture to study it.

A pretty blonde woman smiled up at me. She wore a long, white, capped-sleeved dress, and her pose was exaggerated, as if she were pretending to be a model.

"I sneaked that photo just before the ceremony," Jacob told me, his voice soft. "I wasn't supposed to see the bride before the wedding, but I didn't care. I waited for her bridesmaids to leave and then broke into her room and made her kiss me before she headed out to the church."

I laughed. "That doesn't surprise me about you, Jacob."

"Her dad caught us, but I swore him to secrecy. It cost me a two-hundred-dollar bottle of whiskey." He chuckled. "Most expensive kiss in history."

I smiled down at Allie Irons. "She's beautiful."

"She was," he agreed. "I loved her until the end of her life, and I will until the end of mine. But I'm *in love* with you. Allie was incredible, but I'm not holding onto her anymore. I'm holding onto you."

"You didn't need to do this," I whispered. "I don't expect you to switch your feelings for Allie off. If you were the kind of man who could, you wouldn't be the right one for me."

"I know," he assured me. "But I think I needed to do this for myself. I wanted to show you the last hidden piece. I wanted you to see everything, even the painful, raw, ugly shit that isn't easy or pretty. Now you've got all of me, baby; the good, bad, and everything in between. Allie was a big part of helping to shape me into who I am today. It's because of her that I'm here now, heart open and ready for you. She made me that way."

Throat burning, I slotted the image behind the other one, taking a look at a slightly older but still beautiful woman, except that time she wore jeans and a tight, pink tee and was looking to the side of the camera. A small smile played around her lips, and she seemed to be deep in thought, her long, blonde hair streaming out to the side as a gust of wind caught it.

"That was two weeks before she died," Jacob rasped. "That photograph fucked me up for a long time because she looked so alive. All along, she had a ticking time bomb in her chest, and we didn't know about it. How can that be, Saint? How can anyone be so full of life, then two weeks later, drop down dead?"

I tilted my head, resting it on his shoulder.

"For years, it stopped me from getting serious with another woman," he continued. "Because I knew how goddamned precarious life could be. I was so fucking scared of running headfirst into the same scenario, to find a woman full of love and life and then lose her because of something I couldn't control. So I resisted and shied away from making connections. There was one woman I felt a spark with before you and I fucked it up on purpose; knew exactly what I was doin' but did it anyway. Canceled a date with her and fucked a club whore instead." He laughed self-deprecatingly. "I did it under the guise that I knew my club brother liked her and wanted to stand aside for him, but I was lying to myself. Can you believe that shit?"

"You were just protecting your heart," I pointed out.

"Yeah," he agreed with a smile. "And it all worked out for the best. She's happily married, and just over a year later, I saw you backstage at a gig and fell head over heels in love at first sight. If I'd have gone there with her, I would've had to end it when I met you, and that shit would've gotten messy."

"Life has a habit of turning out the way it's meant to," I stated.

He turned his head and murmured, "Yeah," into my hair.

Emotion grabbed my throat and squeezed.

"Time to go upstairs," he muttered, glancing behind him just as I heard the hotel doors open and then slam shut.

I craned my neck to see a dark figure at the door with the lights shining behind him, effectively casting his body in shadow. An uneasy feeling hit my chest, and without thinking, I grabbed Jacob's hand.

"I've been looking for you," a familiar voice rasped. "You disappeared, and I got worried. I went all over the hotel. Even checked your room. Someone said you might have gone down to the gym, so I went there and took a wrong turn and ended up in Colt's office."

I smiled at him tentatively. "You've found me now. You okay?"

Sam stepped forward, and his face came into view. His eyes went to Jacob's before swinging to me and looking at me accusingly. "There are cameras in there. I fucking saw you."

My forehead furrowed. "You saw me what, Sam?" My heart beat a little faster as I took in the wild look in his eyes and the unnatural twist to his mouth.

His expression was manic, almost tortured, and his voice had an eerie whine when he spat, "I fucking *saw you!*"

Jacob's hold on my hand tightened, and he muttered, "Cameras everywhere."

"Yeah, *cameras*," Sam yelled, his strange, maniacal stare never leaving mine, and he screamed, *"How could you? How could you let him do those things to you?"*

My blood ran cold.

"Sam," I began gently, trying to keep my voice low and calm. "Jacob's my boyfriend. I'm sorry you saw what you saw; it wasn't meant to be witnessed by anyone else, but what we do is our business." Slowly, I dropped Jake's hand and went to stand on the step, but Jacob was already halfway up, his arms outstretched as if he was trying to appease a rabid animal.

"Was it you who sent the stuff to Saint's house?" he cut out.

Sam's crazy stare slashed to Jacob, and he whined, "They were gifts. She was mine and then she met you and you fucked her over. I got it, you saved her from that pig who hurt her, and she was grateful, but that's all it was, a gratitude fuck. I got it, I did. But then she pulled away from me again." His eyes swung back to mine, and he took a step towards me. "I was trying to court you, send you little gifts to show you how much I love you."

Bile rose in my throat.

Jesus, how did I not see this? Looking at him, seeing him like that, it was so obvious.

It suddenly dawned on me how hard it was to scrape him off after I spent the night with him, and how insistent he was that we give it a go, even though I gently explained it was a rebound thing, and I never meant to hurt him.

I should've known.

Memories flashed through my head of me and Sam in bed together, and nausea filled my stomach. God, he was so clingy after that, so insistent, such a pest.

He even fit the profile. Someone I knew, and who could access my schedule. Rich, entitled, and used to getting his own way. Sam was a nepo kid whose dad was loaded. His mom left when he was a baby, and he was raised by nannies along with whichever woman his dad was married to at the time. Because of that, he was socially awkward and found it hard to connect.

My heart dropped, and the sick feeling in my stomach intensified.

I should have fucking known.

"You let him touch you," Sam ranted, his face twisted and ugly. "I see the way he touches you all the fucking time. It's disgusting the way you can't keep your hands off each other, and always with your tongues down each other's throats all the fucking time, touching, touching, all the fucking time. I wanted to be that for you, but he took you away, and you let him." He sucked in a breath. "I saw him touch you. I saw *everything*." Sam took another step toward me, his face contorting with rage.

Jacob took a step toward Sam. His outstretched hands dropped to his sides and clenched into fists. "Get the fuck away from her," he snarled.

"Fuck you," Sam roared, raising a hand in my direction.

I saw the glint of gunmetal in the moonlight, and then it was gone because Jacob's body was there, shielding me, and suddenly I couldn't see anything apart from his chest as he crowded me.

"No, Jacob," I screamed, but I was drowned out by the deafening bang that ripped through the air.

A burning pain spread through my shoulder, and suddenly I was fighting for breath. Winded, I fell to the ground at Jacob's feet just as another ear-splitting shot rang through my ears.

My eyes slashed up to Jacob's face, and my blood turned to ice when I saw the blank look on my beautiful man's face.

His eyes lowered to mine, shocked and filled with pain. "Bab—" he gargled, but choked on the word, and my eyes widened, horrified as blood erupted from his mouth and he fell to his knees, his entire body swaying.

I let out a piercing scream and dived for him, the burning ache in my shoulder completely forgotten. All I could feel was the pain in my heart as it seared through my body while I cradled Jacob's head in my arms.

Shouts went up and two more gunshots rang out, but I didn't look at what was happening, I didn't care because in that moment all I could see was Jacob's precious blood pumping from his chest, its sticky warmth coating my hands. The burn of heartbreak razed through my lungs, and I screamed again, my wail filling with heart-shattering agony as I sat, looking on helplessly while the love of my life bled to death in my arms.

Chapter Seventeen

Hendrix

The scream sent a chill down to my bones.

It sounded like an animal's wail, and I shivered because whatever helpless creature was out there, it sounded like it was in pure agony.

Anna's face whipped to face me as we walked past reception, and she asked, "What was that?"

My body jerked as two gunshots exploded from outside, and I froze for a split second before turning to my woman and resting my hands on each side of her neck, angling her face so she looked me directly in the eyes.

"Go get Sophie and Atlas," I ordered, injecting urgency into my tone. "Then go to Dad and whatever happens, stay upstairs with JT."

"Jamie—" she began, but I cut her off with a shake of my head.

"Don't argue with me, Freckles. Just go."

She jerked a nod and turned away to rush down the corridor, where thankfully the guest rooms were situated.

I headed for the doors, and taking a deep breath, I squared my shoulders, preparing myself to walk outside, all the while telling myself to brace for what I was about to see.

The last time there was a shootout here, Daisy and Ace were involved, and my heart began to pound at the prospect of seeing his smug face again. When it came to that asshole, anything was possible, and although I didn't think he'd have the guts to show up at my place and say his shit with his chest, he was usually involved when trouble came knocking.

I was so convinced I'd see Ace that when I got outside, my body locked when I was confronted with the absolute fucking bloodbath on the steps of my hotel.

Sam Grady, the bass guitarist for Saint's Rapture, and a client, lay on his back with half of the skull he had left tilted at an angle, with the one eye that hadn't been blown off staring vacantly at the moon.

Another scream went up, and my head jerked down the steps to see Diablo trying to drag Saint away from Jacob, who lay on the floor, unmoving.

"*No!*" she shrieked. "*He needs me. Let me go!*"

"I need to see to him, Saint," Diablo bellowed. "I need room. Let me help him."

My throat closed up from the lump that formed there, and my brain short-circuited, my mouth opening in horror as I suddenly clocked the pools of blood dripping from the steps. There was so much that it had left a metallic scent hanging in the air, and it made my stomach churn. Even Saint was covered in the stuff. It was on her clothes, her face, even in her hair.

Diablo suddenly spotted me, and he bellowed, "Sam shot Iceman. Get help."

My chest twisted.

What the fuck did he mean, Sam shot Iceman?

What the hell was going on?

At that moment, Saint managed to wriggle from D's hold, and she raced toward Iceman, skidding onto her knees and throwing her body on top of his, chanting, "No. No. No. Baby, please wake up, please." She lifted his head so gently and so reverently that I could've cried. Instead, I gulped as she cradled Ice in her hands, sobbing, "Jacob, baby. Please wake up. Please don't leave me, baby. I need you."

"Jesus," I rasped. My mind began to race, and I knew I had to pull my shit together, I just didn't know how. I'd been to war, and I'd witnessed shit like this before, worse in fact, but seeing my best friend so unexpectedly laid out like that was screwing with my mind.

My fingers clenched and my jaw locked as I strode toward my brother with my heart in my mouth and my thoughts in tatters.

By the time I got to Ice, Diablo was already there, pulling Saint off him again.

She screamed again, but then suddenly, all the fight left her, and she turned and buried her face in Diablo's chest, sobbing her grief out.

Horrified, I stared down at my brother's dark blond hair, which, by that time, was stained with his own blood, and I just wanted to puke.

A familiar voice suddenly barked, "What the fuck?"

I looked up to see Atlas and Sophie racing toward me. My brother immediately took out his gun, looking around for possible threats. "Have we got a shooter?"

"No," Diablo barked. "Sam shot Ice. I shot Sam."

"Fuck!" I scraped out, my brain suddenly coming back online. I kneeled down beside Sophie, who was preparing to start CPR on Ice. "What can I do?"

"Looking at the trajectory of the entry hole, I think a bullet hit his lung. I'm gonna have to crack his chest open. I need a clean room where I can operate."

"Diablo," I roared. "Get Gopher to prep a medical room and then call Bones and Freya. Need Blade out here too."

"Already here, boss," my VP shouted as he raced down the hotel steps.

My eyes fell on Saint, who was wrapped around Diablo like a spider monkey. "Get her in the bar and get a whiskey down her. I need to know what the fuck's gone on."

He nodded and pulled Saint from Diablo's arms, crooning gently to her as he tried to soothe her wracking sobs.

She began to struggle again. "I'm not leaving him," she screeched. "I'll tell you everything, but I won't leave Jacob." Her tear-streaked and bloody face turned to me. "Sam's the stalker. He was going to shoot me, and Jacob dived in the way. He saved my life."

"I came out and saw it all," Diablo confirmed. "By the time I'd pulled my weapon, Ice was already down."

"Jesus," Blade muttered.

"Don't make me leave him, please," Saint implored. "He needs me."

I moved toward her, my throat contracting with grief.

But I had no choice; I had to keep my shit together. I had to be a fucking Prez while my best friend bled out yards away from me. My eyes flicked down her body, taking in her blood-stained clothes. "We need to sort you out, Saint. You're covered in his blood."

Her eyes dropped to her clothes, and she looked at her hands as if she'd never seen them before. "I don't care. It's his blood, so I don't care."

I took in Saint's stricken expression and her tear-streaked face, covered in my brother's blood. She looked like she'd stepped out of a horror movie, and I knew Iceman would go crazy if I left her in that state.

"I'll strike a deal with you, Saint," I offered, my voice urgent. "Let us clean you up while Jake's in surgery. He needs help. Sophie's a doctor, a good one. She'll sort him."

Her eyelids drooped, and her hand went to her shoulder as she slowly nodded.

A group of men appeared and, between them, gently hoisted Iceman up and carried him inside the hotel. I took the opportunity to slide my arm around Saint's waist and gently lead her after them, murmuring softly as we went. Every step felt like a mile, and the weight of what had happened pressed down on my shoulders like an oppressive blanket I couldn't shake off.

Saint held onto my cut with bloodstained hands, her hiccups jerking her entire body. She was obviously in shock at what she'd witnessed, so when we finally reached the entrance and she stumbled, I didn't think anything was amiss.

"Saint," I muttered, holding onto her tighter. "You okay?"

My blood ran cold as her feet faltered and she fell to her knees, and I called, "Saint?"

Heart pounding in my chest, her body turned deadweight, and I lowered to the ground with her, trying to shield her head from bouncing off the concrete as she let out a pained moan.

"She's bleeding!" somebody shouted, and suddenly Freya was there, pushing me out of the way while she dropped to her knees and murmured soothing words to Saint as the woman's eyes fluttered closed.

Freya began to check her vitals before running her hands over Saint's body, looking for wounds. After a few seconds, she announced, "GSW to the shoulder. She's losing blood."

"I didn't see her get shot," Diablo argued. "Just Ice."

"Well, she did," Freya confirmed. "The blood's hers as well as Iceman's."

My heart dropped, and my chest clenched.

"Get her down to the med wing," Freya ordered. "I need to take a look and stem the blood flow."

Diablo stooped and picked Saint up, tucking her into his huge arms bridal-style. "Let's fuckin' go!" he shouted, striding through the hotel doors after the men carrying Ice.

My eyes caught on Freya, who ran after them, and I heaved out a breath, running a hand through my hair. I couldn't stop one question from running through my brain.

What the fuck's going on?

Chapter Eighteen

Bones

Shifting my bike down a gear, I leaned left and took the turning for the lane leading to the hotel. My back wheel spun slightly, and I corrected my speed to slow down as I pulled up outside the clubhouse.

I was off my bike in seconds, then turning toward the hotel, I removed my helmet, dropping it to the ground as I raced toward Diablo, who waited for me by the entrance.

"Status report," I ordered, falling into step beside him as we hurried down the corridor toward the medical wing.

"Iceman's in surgery now, Sophie's operating. Freya's got Saint. Both have GSWs; Saint took one to the shoulder, and Iceman took two to the chest. Sophie thinks Sam shot Iceman in the back, and it ripped clean through him and into Saint. Both are in a bad way, though Iceman's worse. He crashed as the guys took him down. She thinks the bullet hit his lung."

"Traumatic pneumothorax," I muttered under my breath.

"Soph said the same thing," he concurred.

"What about Saint?" I asked.

"Freya's got her," he confirmed. "No exit hole to be found, so the bullet's still in there. Freya's main worry is that Saint lost a lotta blood. We thought it was Iceman's at first, the crazy bitch was all over him, screaming that she wouldn't leave him alone, but then she passed out."

"Adrenaline's a powerful thing," I pointed out. "Seen similar shit on the battlefield."

He nodded, then for the first time ever, at least in my presence, he gave a small piece of himself away. "Same."

Approaching a door to one of the theatre rooms, I pushed it ajar, stuck my head around it, and barked, "How you doin' in here, Doctor Stone?"

"I've retrieved the bullet," she informed me, her golden eyes never leaving the open wound she was working on. "The patient's stable. She had a small internal bleed that I patched up. Her vitals are steady."

My eyes flicked around the room, taking in Gambit, who stood opposite Freya in scrubs and a face mask, holding a Yankauer Suction Tube.

"You need me?" I asked.

"No," she replied. "Iceman needs you more. Can you send Gopher in, though, please? I could use some help closing Saint up. Gambit's done a great job, but I'd feel happier with a medic."

Gambit looked up at Freya and said in his clipped English accent, "I don't wanna leave her. Ice would want me to stay and make sure she's okay."

"You can stay, honey," she assured him. "But you don't have to help me operate."

Gambit breathed an audible sigh of relief, and his shoulders slumped. The poor guy wasn't into this at all, and I almost grinned at the green-tinged pallor of his face as he watched Freya's fingers deftly move while she inserted the Blake Drain into Saint's shoulder.

I couldn't help the wave of pride that washed over me.

Freya Stone had come to me three years before as an intern with a lot of enthusiasm but not much knowledge. Over time, she'd blossomed into an excellent resident and a talented surgeon, who wasn't scared to get stuck into all the serious stuff.

I was confident she had everything under control.

My chin dipped. "I'll be next door if you need me."

"Got it," I heard her murmur in reply before I closed the door with a soft *click*.

My head whipped around as the door opposite flew open, and Gopher came racing out. He saw me, and the angry twist to his mouth slackened. "Thank God you're here. We need blood. Now!"

Quickly, I ran through all the matches for Iceman in my head. My eyes fell on Diablo, who stood sentry at the mouth of the corridor with his arms crossed over his massive chest.

"Need to hook you up, D," I told him, pulling my phone out to call Prez while my mind raced through all the names of the men in the club, along with their blood types—information I'd had memorized since the day I joined the Speed Demons.

He answered on the first ring. "What do you need?"

"You, Trick, Will, and Picasso," I barked. "I need your blood. It's gonna be vein to vein, so I want you all scrubbed in and clean as a whistle."

"On it," he muttered just before the line went dead.

I started for the bathroom, calling over my shoulder, "Get D cleaned up. Then I want you to go in and assist Freya."

"Yes, Sir," Gopher replied.

Within minutes, I was washed up, scrubbed in, and heading through the doors to the operating room.

It was fucking bedlam.

Sophie sat astride Iceman with her hand inside his chest, manually massaging his heart. There was blood everywhere, including on her, but the determined glint in her eye that I caught when her face whipped around to throw me a glare made me smile inwardly regardless.

"Where the fuck have you been?" she demanded.

Oh, and did I mention? Sophie Woods was one ballsy bitch.

"I literally got out of surgery forty minutes ago," I told her, heading toward the table where Iceman lay. "In that forty minutes, I did a half-hour bike ride in half the time it should've taken me, checked on our other patient, organized a flow of blood for Ice, and scrubbed in."

"Lazy fuck," she muttered.

I barked a laugh. "Do you ever give it a rest?" I asked good-naturedly.

"No!" she clapped back. "I don't. That's why Iceman's still alive, so stop your yapping and start stemming the internal bleed that I can't patch up 'cause I'm too busy performing open cardiac massage to keep my friend's heart fucking beating in his goddamned chest."

"Alright, alright." I moved toward the bed, picking up the suction tube and using it to clear away the pool of blood in his chest so I could take a look.

"I've plugged the hole," Sophie told me, "But he's got a bleed that I didn't have time to locate because he crashed. Plus, I'm running out of extra blood, fast."

I jerked my chin in Diablo's direction, who stood back watching the scene, his eyes glued to Iceman's white face. "Come here, bro, and hold out your arm. Gonna do a vein-to-vein transfer. Do you know what that is?"

A small grin lit across his face. "Yeah, Doc. I'm familiar."

"You squeamish?" I asked.

"You seen my room?" he shot back, coming to stand beside me and holding his arm up.

I rolled my lips together to stop myself from laughing. Instead, I concentrated on making an incision in Diablo's vein and slipping a tube through. Quickly, I set up the blood transfusion, and after a few minutes, watched as D's life force flowed into Iceman.

Immediately, the angry beeping of the heart monitor began to slow, and I watched as Sophie carefully climbed off Iceman's chest.

I cocked at eyebrow at the other doctor. "Did you teach Freya that move?"

She shrugged one shoulder. "Not teach exactly, but she's seen me do it. I'm small in stature, Bones. I can get better leverage on a body by straddling it than leaning over it. The first thing I learned in trauma surgery was to do whatever it took to gain the advantage." She picked up the suction tube and cleared away the new pool of blood that had appeared beside Iceman's lung.

I reached up to the surgical light head and angled it slightly to the left of the organ. "Right there," I murmured, pointing to a tiny tear on the side of the tissue. "There's your bleed."

Sophie's fingers moved deftly as she worked. It took a few minutes to stem the blood flow, then she inserted a chest tube to remove any excess air before checking the site again.

"Looks clear," she murmured. "Not gonna close him up though. Not until we're certain that we don't have to go back in."

I nodded my approval before turning to Diablo, who remained standing beside Iceman while his blood dripped into the brother. "How you doing there?"

"Good," he replied nonchalantly.

For a second time, I rolled my lips together.

This dude was a trip. Blood and innards everywhere, and he just stood around, taking it all in like he was watching a fucking Hallmark movie.

Goddamned lunatic.

My heart dropped as a loud beep sounded from the monitor. I looked up and cursed under my breath as the alarms began to screech a deafening wail.

"BP's dropping," I called out.

"On it!" Sophie muttered, lifting the sheet she'd just placed over Iceman so she could examine the gaping hole in his chest. "We've got another bleed." Her stare lifted to meet mine, and I watched her shoulders tense tightly. "It's like playing whack-a-mole. The minute we plug one, another appears."

My gaze held hers. My chin dipped, and I leveled her with a stare. "It's gonna be a tricky motherfucker. This is Iceman, so you know the asshole's gonna put us through the goddamned wringer. You ready for this?"

Sophie's jaw clenched determinedly, and her lip curled while she jerked her head in a decisive nod.

Picking up the suction tube, I took a deep breath to calm my thudding heart before placing it inside my brother's chest. "You better hold on, Stitch," I bit out, focusing my mind on the vast job ahead. "It looks like we're in for a fucking long night."

Chapter Nineteen

Diablo

The low beep of the heart monitor pulsed through the room, providing us with constant reassurance that Saint was alive.

The sound should have been annoying, akin to the drip, drip, drip of water torture, but instead, it was everything I needed to keep my heart settled and my mind intact.

My eyes drifted over to the other two chairs, where Boomer and Jonny slumped with their shoulders hunched, and their eyes red and bloodshot with exhaustion and a few tears.

It was hard to believe it had been twenty-four hours since the shooting. It seemed like the day had passed in the snap of my fingers, but then, I hadn't stopped. I'd shot dead the bass player of one of the biggest rock bands in the world, and life had taken a turn of crazy that put my brand of lunacy to shame.

I shifted my gaze to Talia, who was curled up asleep in a chair.

For the last twenty-four hours, she'd had to deal with record companies and the press. The label had held a press conference and everything had gone fucking loopy. It seemed that the bass player of one of the biggest rock bands in the entire world being shot dead after trying to kill the lead singer he'd been stalking, along with her handsome bodyguard boyfriend, was hot news.

It was morbid shit, made more so by the fact their first album, which was eighteen months old had shot back into the Billboard and streaming charts at number one, blowing all competition out of the room—*excuse the pun*.

Talia's eyes fluttered open and she sighed, shifting her ass on the chair to get more comfortable. "I wish she'd wake up," she murmured.

"The drugs are keeping her under," I reminded her. "Sophie said, the longer she sleeps, the more she heals, which means she'll feel less pain when she eventually does open her eyes."

"I've got a bad feeling," she stated emphatically. "What if it's not the meds keeping her under. What if something's wrong?"

I leaned toward her and placed my hand on his shoulder. "She's gonna be okay. They got the bullet out, and there's no lasting damage. Saint just needs to heal."

Talia nodded slowly, her eyes never leaving Saint. "Why don't you go get some rest? I've had a nap. I can stay with her for a while."

I sat back in my chair and folded my arms across my chest in a stubborn move. "Not leaving."

Talia's head swiveled to me. "Why?"

"'Cause I'm SAA," I explained. "It's my job to make sure she's safe. Iceman's on life support, but he's got his folks and half the club with him. I'm staying with Saint, not only because Ice would want me to, but also because *I* want to. She was patient with me, took her time, and taught me guitar. She never dogged me, and she was kind. She's my friend and she needs me."

In the dim light, I noticed a glint as Talia's eyes filled with tears, but she blinked them away, murmuring, "Fair enough."

"Gonna teach her how to shoot when she's better," I went on. "She won't be in that position again. She asked me to help her the night Sam"—I paused—"when it happened. Gonna buy her a nice gun that's not too heavy that she can keep in her purse. What's her favorite color?"

Talia smiled and muttered, "Icy blue."

My lips hitched. "Should've figured."

We sat in silence for a while, our stares glued to Saint but our thoughts somewhere else.

"Are you okay?" Talia asked.

"Yeah," I scraped out. "Just thinkin' about what happened and wonderin' if I could've done somethin' more."

She twisted her body to face me. "Don't take that on. You saved their lives, D. There was nothing that anyone could have done. We couldn't have known that Sam was the goddamned stalker. He was clever and masked it. If anyone should have worked out what he was up to, it was me. Nobody could've saved him."

My face twisted.

"No, Diablo," she insisted. "Get it out of your head. If you hadn't killed Sam, he may have fired off more shots and killed them both outright. Let it go, please. Neither Ice nor Saint would want you to mope over this. You did your best and you did the right thing. Stop taking this shit on."

One side of my mouth tipped up. "You've got it a bit twisted, Talia. I don't care about killing Sam. My issue is that I should've done it sooner. I wish I'd come out and seen it go down, then maybe Ice and Saint wouldn't be stuck in hospital beds fighting for their lives."

Her lips curved.

"Should've looked after my club better." I leaned forward with my elbows to my knees and bent my neck to rub away the tension there. "Should've killed him sooner." As the words left my mouth, the door cracked open, and Breaker appeared with Kennedy, who was holding little Kady's hand.

Kadence's blue eyes hit mine, and she shot me a sweet smile.

I smiled back.

"We've come to check on her," Kennedy murmured, guiding Kady over to where Saint lay out completely still on the hospital bed. "My girl's been worried."

Talia got to her feet and jerked her thumb toward the door. "Gonna get some coffee." Then she turned and exited the room.

Kady tagged Saint's hand and looked at her with sad eyes. "Saint's cold," she said quietly, turning to Breaker. "Can I warm her up?"

Dude dipped his chin, his eyes boring into his daughter's pretty face. "You up to it?"

"Yeah." She smiled brightly. "I'll spend an hour with Saint and then go see Iceman. He's got too many people with him right now, but once they've left, I can concentrate."

My forehead creased questioningly. "What's she talking about?"

Kady's eyes met mine, and she said, "You know. You feel it, too."

My eyes narrowed on her.

Breaker helped Kady onto the bed beside Saint and took her sneakers off for her. Then the kid lay next to Saint and snuggled into her body.

"Don't overdo it, Kady," Kennedy ordered gently. "You know it wipes you out. Just sleep. That'll be enough to make her warm again."

Kady snaked a hand over Saint's stomach and laced their fingers together. She smiled up at her mom as Kennedy unfolded a blanket and placed it over her before she closed her eyes and settled in.

My skin prickled, and I felt the room around me warm almost immediately. It reminded me of a time when I was a kid of about eight and my mom got sick.

Ma was strong and healthy, but one time she got the flu, and there wasn't anyone else around to look out for her. She shivered with the cold so bad that I ended up getting into bed with her to try to warm her up.

It must have worked 'cause she was better by morning.

Kady's eyes opened suddenly, and she beamed at me.

A sense of camaraderie passed between us, and I grinned back at her before murmuring to Breaker, "Is she okay?"

He nodded, his eyes never leaving his daughter. "She's fine."

"It's been a fucked up couple of days," I pointed out.

He let out a short laugh. "You Virginia boys are fucking crazy."

"What? Like you're not? I remember a time not so long ago when we had to come and help your Wyoming chapter defend your club against an evil rival biker club and a mayor who was taking local girls and putting them in a trafficking ring."

Breaker smirked. "True. But I had to come and help your prez rescue his pregnant woman from her evil drug-dealing husband, so I think we're even."

I chuckled. "Never a dull moment."

He nodded. "Yep."

My stare went to Saint, looking so tiny and vulnerable in the bed that it brought a lump to my throat. "I hope we get a quiet few days. Not sure my nerves could stand much more of this."

Breaker shrugged, his eyes still glued to Kady. It seemed the kid had fallen asleep. Her breaths came evenly, and her chest rose and fell in a relaxed rhythm.

"Doesn't matter what happens, you'll cope," he assured me. "You've got no choice, Diablo. You've chosen a life full of missions and adventure, and along with that comes something that makes you vulnerable in some ways but also makes you stronger than you could imagine."

My head tilted, and I asked, "What's that?"

Breaker glanced at me, his golden eyes soft. "Brotherhood, friendship, the club. You'll do anything for them, and when you meet your woman, your 'one', you'll fight tooth and nail to keep her safe and happy. You'll die for her, just like Ice was prepared to."

The hair on the back of my arms stood up as my mind went to all the jars in my room, lit up all pretty and cute on the shelf. My baby trophies.

There wasn't a woman in this world likely to accept that. I had compulsions and needs that not even a mother could love, which was why, even though my ma adored me for who I was, I still wasn't sure she could grow to love that side of me, too.

"Don't think it's gonna happen for me, dude," I argued gently. "I'm not the settling down type."

Breaker glanced at Kennedy, who rolled her eyes before turning back to me and muttering, "Yeah, brother. That's what they all say."

Chapter Twenty

Saint

My eyes fluttered open to darkness, the smell of disinfectant, and so much warmth that my skin tingled with it.

There was no confusion, no muddled brain, and no doubt about what happened. I knew it hadn't all been a dream, and I was one hundred percent aware that I was in a hospital bed after Sam—who'd been stalking me for months—shot me and Jacob.

The only thing I didn't know was how long I'd been here; though, going by my stiff muscles and aching limbs, it had been a while.

I turned my head to the side and saw blue eyes.

But they weren't the icy ones I desperately loved. These eyes were a pretty shade of cornflower blue.

"You're warm now," Kady announced gently.

"Hey," I croaked, my voice husky from lack of use. I tried stretching my lips over my teeth to smile at her, but I just ended up grimacing as my mouth was so parched.

Slowly, Kady sat up, and that was when I sensed movement from the corner of the room. I turned my head a little further to see Diablo leaning forward and Breaker leaning back in his chair, almost lounging.

"How long was I out for?" I asked.

"Two days," Diablo replied softly.

I opened my mouth to ask the next question, but the words burned my throat because what if the answer wasn't what I wanted to hear?

Diablo gave me a closed-mouthed smile. "Iceman's still alive, but he's in critical condition. Hendrix called his mom and dad up from New Orleans. They're in with him. He got hit twice. Once in the side of his stomach, the other time in his chest. The chest shot nicked his lung and went straight through him and hit your shoulder. You lost a lot of blood; had to have three blood transfusions. He's still out of it."

The wave of sorrow that hit me was debilitating. I closed my eyes, the pain in my heart almost too much to bear. "I'm glad he's not alone," I whispered.

"Neither of you is alone," Diablo corrected me, then said pointedly, "You've both got family with you."

The door clicked open softly. "Evening!" a deep, sexy voice called out as one of the most handsome men I'd ever seen walked into the room. He approached my bed holding an iPad and wearing a white doctor's coat and a sexy grin. "Good to see you awake, Saint. I'm Doctor Locke, but the brothers call me Bones." He dipped his chin to study my face. "How you feeling?"

"Like I've been shot in the chest," I murmured.

The doctor choked out a laugh.

He got me.

"Not too soon then?" I asked.

Bones took the chair beside the bed and helped Kady down from beside me. "Just wanna check your blood pressure." He leaned over me, lifting my arm so he could hook a cuff onto it before clicking a button on the small white machine attached.

"When can I get up?" I asked. "I need to see Jacob."

He checked the reading on the machine and removed the cuff from my arm. "Now."

My heart leaped, and I breathed, "Really? I expected an argument."

"Nope," he said, popping the P. "If Diablo or Breaker don't mind carrying you in, you can go see him now. Word of warning, though. You'll be meeting the parents. His folks are in with him, too."

"Can I stay with him?" I asked. "He may wake up if I'm there, and I want to stay close in case he needs me."

"Yep," Bones told me. "He's hooked up to tubes and monitors, so you gotta be careful, but you can stay in there with him."

"Help me up?" I asked.

Bones took my elbow and gently pulled me until I was in a seated position. Once I'd had a drink of water and used the bathroom, somebody produced my short robe, and I slipped it over my PJs.

Breaker and Kady went to get Kennedy, and my stare fell on Diablo, who stood sentry at the door. His face was stoic, and his stubble was a few days more than overgrown. I could tell he'd been in the same clothes for days because of the blood stains on them, but he was still one of the most beautiful sights I'd ever seen.

"How do I thank you?" I croaked, blinking away the moisture welling in my eyes. "There aren't words."

"Guitar lessons," he replied.

I went to chuckle, but the movement pulled at the stitches in my shoulder, so it came out more like a choke. "You're on." I smiled when I'd recovered. "I owe you everything."

He hitched an eyebrow and lowered his chin. "You don't owe me shit. We're family, and family sticks together."

"You're gonna make me cry," I whispered. "You beautiful, beautiful man."

His cheeks flushed red, and for a second, he looked almost embarrassed by my compliment. "Don't get all schmaltzy on me, Saint. For fuck's sake, last time I looked, I don't gotta vagina, so stop with the slushy shit. Did my job, though I'll argue day and night that I was a bit late to the party. Still, you and Iceman are here, and if there's a God, he'll wake up soon."

"There is a God," I announced. "Because people like you exist."

He flicked his hand out. "Bah. Stop with the bullshit. At this rate, you'll make me grow a pair of tits."

I smiled and carefully touched my fingers to my heart before touching them to my mouth and blowing a kiss his way.

He smiled, his white teeth flashing through his beard, and he shot me a wink.

"You gonna carry me to my man?" I asked.

"Yeah," he rumbled. "But I gotta wait for Bones to give me the green light first."

My eyes closed. "I can still see him coughing up blood, D. I can still feel the fear and the helplessness." I opened my eyes again and they welled with tears. "If I lose him, I may as well die, too."

Within seconds, Diablo was sitting by my side, and his arm slid around me. "He's gonna be okay. I'm not gonna lie and say it's not bad 'cause he's got a collapsed lung. Not gonna dress it up pretty for ya, Saint, 'cause you need to prepare yourself. They lost him a few times in surgery, but he pulled through, and it's because of you. He's fighting to come to you."

"They lost him?" I breathed.

God, I felt sick.

"Not gonna lie to you, woman," he bit out. "Got too much respect, but you need to get prepared before you go in that room. Once you're in there, no tears, no whining, you be strong for him; you be the ol' lady he needs. You lie there, whisper in his ear, and tell him to wake the fuck up. You tell him you'll battle every demon in Hell to bring him back to you. Don't let him fall, don't fucking allow it. If you wanna cry, do it now and get it outta your system before we go in, 'cause once we're in there, it's time to fight."

Diablo's words hit me in the chest.

He was right. Jacob had fought to keep me alive; he'd taken a bullet for me and almost sacrificed everything because he loved me.

Now it was my turn to fight for him.

The door opened, and Bones appeared. "You want to see him?"

I nodded eagerly, and within seconds, I was up in Diablo's arms, and he was carrying me out the door. Chairs were lining the corridor, filled with bikers. Men in leather cuts even sat on the floor with their backs against the wall as they waited for news of their brother.

Murmurs of greeting and well wishes went up, and I caught sight of Gambit and Trick standing together with their backs to the wall.

"Tell the lazy bastard to wake up, Saint," Trick called out in his hybrid Irish accent.

Chuckles went up, and I tried to smile too, but my heart wasn't in it. I just needed to see Jacob, to hold him, and tell him I was there and that I loved him.

Whatever happened, I needed him to know that.

It was weird because I thought Jacob's room would be deathly silent with machines beeping and an atmosphere you could cut with a knife, but as Diablo carried me over the threshold, we were met with soft laughter.

My wide-eyed stare slashed toward the bed, greedy to catch sight of Jacob. I sucked in a sharp intake of breath when I saw my guy laid out on his back with a breathing tube down his throat. My pulse began to pound with the sudden, desperate need to get to him, to touch him and let him know I was there.

I took in the older couple sat by his bed, and then I was met by icy-blue eyes identical to Jacob's and I almost lost my shit. Instead, I took a fortifying breath and murmured, "Hi. I'm Saint."

"Oh my God," the woman breathed, her hands flying to her mouth. "Look at her, Doug. She's perfect." She launched off her chair and rushed toward me, taking my hand and walking with me as Diablo carried me toward the bed.

"I'm Kathy, Jake's mom, and this is his dad, Doug," she said excitedly. "We're so happy to meet you."

Diablo stooped down to place me gently on the mattress beside Jake, then he straightened to his full height and folded his arms across his chest.

I turned to Kathy, taking in her pretty face and Doug's obvious similarity to Jacob. "I wish we could've met under better circumstances."

"He's gonna pull through, darlin'," Doug rumbled. "Jake's a stubborn mule as well as a fighter."

I turned back toward Jacob and gently smoothed my fingers over his temple.

His skin was surprisingly warm, but the sickly grey transparency of it made my heart ache. Jacob's brow was smooth in sleep, and he looked impossibly handsome. I yearned for his eyes to flutter open and pull me into the icy-blue depths that I'd written into a hundred songs during the years since we met.

"Has there been any sign of him waking up?" I asked.

"No," Kathy said softly. "But that's good. Both Sophie and Grayson think the way forward is to keep him in a medically induced sleep to allow his body time to heal. They'll give him a couple of days and wean him off the medication, and if he doesn't wake up himself, they'll put him back under for a few more days."

"So, it's a waiting game?" I asked.

"Yeah, darlin'," Doug murmured, leaning forward to inspect my bandaged shoulder. "And how are you doin'?"

"Good, thanks to Jacob," I responded nervously. "I'm sorry. It was all my fault. He got hurt because he was protecting me."

Doug held up a hand to silence me. "Don't wanna hear that bull. You never shot him, Saint, that asshole did and he was seriously whacked. Neither of you could've known. Plus, he was paid to protect you, and Jake's the kind of man who takes his responsibility seriously."

"He would've protected her anyway, Doug," Kathy snapped. "He's in love with her." One eyebrow lifted, and her lips pursed into an angry line. "Don't listen to him, Saint."

"Didn't mean it like that," Doug grunted.

"You never do," she clipped. "But you still always manage to put your foot in it."

He rolled his eyes at me. "See what I have to put up with? It's like living with a fucking Banshee."

"I can't *believe* you, Douglas Irons," Kathy bit out. "We met Saint thirty seconds ago, and already you dropped an f-bomb. What must she think of us?"

"It's okay, Kathy," I assured her. "I've been known to drop an f-bomb here and there myself, and my manager, Talia, well, she drops one every other word."

"See, woman?" Doug muttered. "Saint says fuck, too."

Kathy's eyes turned to slits. "Douglas Irons!"

His mouth stretched into a lazy grin, and he looked so much like Jacob that my heart flipped over. The urge to touch him washed over me again, and I turned to my guy and snuggled closer, resting my hand on his blanket-covered stomach and inhaling the scent of his skin. Light as a feather, I ran my fingers up the blanket, past the huge bandage stuck across his torso, and cupped his heart in my hands.

"Wake up, baby," I whispered. "Please wake up."

My eyes lifted to his, and I held my breath, waiting for a sign. But it didn't come.

The machines kept beeping, Kathy and Doug kept bickering, and my throat filled with tears.

"Stop bustin' my balls, woman. It ain't the time or the place," Doug muttered.

"I'll bust 'em alright," Kathy warned. "You've a mouth like a sewer."

My hand pressed lightly on Jacob's heart, and I wished more than anything that he could wake up so I could bust his balls. I would've given anything to bicker with him like an old married couple. It would've been beautiful.

A loud screeching noise began to wail like a siren, and the *beep, beep, beep* of Jacob's heart monitor rose to a shriek.

My neck twisted to see Diablo rushing out the door, shouting for Bones, who after a few seconds, came rushing into the room with Freya and Diablo at his heels.

"What's happening?" I cried, looking on in horror as Bones pulled out his stethoscope and checked Jacob's heart.

His stare flicked over me, and he ordered, "Get her out of here."

"No!" I wailed, but before I could cling to Jacob, Diablo had scooped me into his arms and he carried me out into the corridor on the heels of Jacob's parents.

My heart cracked apart. "No! Please help him!" I begged

Diablo put me on my feet, tucked me close to his chest, and rumbled, "Let 'em do their jobs, Saint."

Bones glanced at Freya, jerking his chin toward the door and barking, "Privacy."

Freya came to the door and smiled at me sadly. "We'll take care of him, I promise," she murmured, slowly closing the door and blocking Jacob from my sight.

Tears welled up in my eyes, and I stared at the door in shock.

What the hell just happened? Jacob was fine, peaceful even, then all of a sudden he wasn't. Suddenly, it hit me. This was serious. Jacob was in a really bad way, and with all my money, fame, and connections, there was nothing I could do about it.

I let out a small sob and dug my fingernails into the heel of my palms to stop myself from doing what I really wanted, which was to scream the waiting area down.

No, no, no.

Jacob had to be okay.

I couldn't lose him.

Chapter Twenty-One

Hendrix

"The cops turned up again this morning," I barked, turning to Colt. "Can you not get them off my back?"

All the officers—barring Iceman, D, and Bones—were in Church. I'd called an impromptu meeting to talk about what happened with our brother, the job, and what we could've done differently to stop the shit from hitting the fan.

I didn't blame my boys for what happened. We were a team, and I was in charge of it. If anything, the buck stopped with me. What we could do, however, was talk about where we went wrong and discuss ways to plug the gap so it wouldn't happen again.

Colt reared back slightly. "One of the biggest rock stars in the world was shot dead by one of our men, Prez. There's gonna be questions and media attention. The cops are under pressure to come up with answers and do it in a way where there's no comeback. We've got nothing to hide. D acted to save Saint and Iceman after Sam shot them. It was clearly self-defense. We're camera'd up to the asshole, and the cops have access to the footage. Just let them investigate so they can close the case, and we can all move on."

I scraped a hand down my face. "Are Sam's asshole father's lawyers still sniffing around asking questions?"

"So what if they are?" he threw back. "They found the room with all those pictures of Saint he took over the months. They've traced the stalker's pictures of Saint back to a camera they discovered in his dad's compound."

My hand went to grip the back of my neck. "It's a shit show."

Blade leaned forward. "Agreed, Prez, but in this case, I can't see how we could've done anything differently. Ghost stayed with Sam and didn't pick up on any bad vibes. He also didn't have access to the room Sam used to keep his weird shit in. The profilers smashed it, but we weren't told about Saint's previous relationship with Sam because she wanted to keep it quiet. I get it, I'm not blaming her either. I just think when we look at the big picture, we can see our hands were tied."

I heaved a breath out and slumped back in my chair. "I know, Veep. Nobody's to blame. I'm just worried about our brother, is all."

Murmurs of agreement went up around the table.

"How was Ice last night, Son?" Dad asked.

I tipped my head back. "Better. The first two days he didn't stop coding, but he's stabilized now."

"That's good, right?" Pyro asked.

"Yeah," I agreed. "But Ice isn't out of the woods. Bones reduced his meds 'cause I think even he's getting worried, and he wants to see if Iceman comes around. He wants an idea of what he's dealing with." I looked around the table at my brothers, noting the two glaring absences.

Bones wouldn't leave the medical wing, and rightly so, and Diablo wouldn't leave Saint. Our cranky sergeant at arms had appointed himself her bodyguard and keeper, at least until Iceman woke up. He liked her, though it wasn't a romantic thing. Saint and D had bonded when we jammed, and she helped him with his guitar. The way she did it earned her his respect, and whether she liked it or not, she had a friend for life now, along with a protector.

"What are we gonna do about all the press camped out at the end of the lane?" Trick asked. "They're trespassing on our land and taking photographs of the place. It's not only a security risk, but also a total pain in the ass."

"Thought they'd have moved out by now," Blade muttered.

"Must be a slow news week," I pointed out. "But to be fair, Sam was a fucking guitar icon."

"Sam was a fucking pervert," Gambit corrected.

"Amen to that, brother," Dad concurred, his tone lowering as he asked me, "How's Saint doing?"

"She's the definition of putting a brave face on things. Diablo's making her keep her shit together. Every time she starts to break down, he pulls her outta that room and gives her a talking to. She cries, but she does it with him and not in front of Kathy and Doug, and certainly not in front of Iceman."

"She's a fucking trouper," Gambit interjected. "Trust Iceman to find a woman who's talented, adored the world over, loaded, sweet, funny, and a strong bitch to boot."

"She loves the bones of him," I murmured. "I'll never forget the sound of her scream when Ice got shot. I thought it was an animal that'd been wounded in the woods. It cut through me. Felt her pain like it was my own."

Dad smiled sadly. "He loves her to the bones, too, and that's a good thing, Son. There's nothing in this world worth fighting for more than the love of a good woman."

I gave Pop a nod because that was a statement I could get behind.

"Gonna cut it short," I told the boys. "Wanna get down the med wing in case Iceman wakes up. Any other business?"

"Nothing that can't wait, Prez," Blade replied. "Go see to our brother."

My fingers reached for the gavel resting by my right hand, and I banged it into the sound block.

Chairs scraped as we all got to our feet and started for the door in silence. Gambit got there first, opened it, and ushered everyone through.

My boots hit the corridor and faltered, because there stood my Anna in all her glory with our boy in her arms, waiting.

Without a word, she walked toward me and transferred JT into my arms and then fitted herself to my side before sliding an arm around my waist. "He's fed," she murmured. "We're good for a few hours. Let's go down the medical wing and sit with Ice. He'll want us there when he wakes up."

My neck twisted, and my eyes met her kaleidoscope green and browns. "I thank God every day he gave me you."

"You should," she breathed, fitting her head into the dip in my shoulder. "I'm awesome."

Dad approached, his fingers working as he did grabby hands. "I'll take our boy," he offered. "He doesn't wanna be stuck in a hospital room when Grandpa could take him for a walk down the river to see the boats."

I lowered my mouth to my son's fuzzy head and kissed him, inhaling his sweet baby scent before handing him over to Dad.

Pop let out a little *whoop* and turned to mosey on up the corridor, following the other men as they all headed for reception.

"You think I'm ever gonna get to spend an hour with my boy before that ornery old bastard comes and kidnaps him?" I asked my woman.

"Probably not, but I love that JT has that, so I'm not complaining." Anna's hand slid across my chest, and she stepped in front of me, her hands snaking around my nape. She looked up at me with soft eyes and parted lips, and I knew I'd never seen anything more beautiful, and I never would.

"Love you, Freckles," I murmured.

She went up on the balls of her feet and touched her mouth to mine. "Love you, Jamie."

"Worried about my brother," I rasped. "He's got a gaping fucking hole in his chest and a heart that keeps giving up on him. I've lost men before; lost buddies, brothers, but this one's hitting hard 'cause it's Iceman. He's at the heart of what we do here, baby. He's the one who stood by me through all my bullshit, through Ace's betrayal, through the dark times, and then he helped pull me out of the storm. Where would I be without him? What would I do...?"

"Jamie," she whispered, her nails scratching into the back of my skull. "Iceman's been at death's door for days."

My heart jerked.

Anna smiled. "But he hasn't walked through it. What does that tell you?"

"He's fighting," I rumbled.

"Yeah, he's fighting," she agreed. "But he's also not giving up. There's a difference."

For the first time in days, I felt my shoulders relax slightly. "What if he never wakes up?"

"Really?" my woman drawled. "He's all up in our business any other time. That nosy ass won't want to miss out on much more. He's probably bored out of his mind and itching to cause some trouble."

I reared my head back and chuckled—something else I hadn't done in days—then I pressed my forehead against my ol' lady's and told her, "I love you."

Chapter Twenty-Two

Saint

Bones had started to reduce Jacob's medication the night before. He was still being given some strong pain relief, which I was glad of, seeing as they'd only recently sewn his chest back up, but the meds he was filled with shouldn't have stopped him from opening his eyes.

So, now it was a waiting game.

Hendrix had cleared the waiting area, so the only people around were Kathy and Doug, Hendrix and Anna, Diablo, and, of course, Bones. Freya had a shift at the hospital, so she couldn't be there, and the Wyoming chapter had gone home the day before.

The only time I'd left Jacob's side was to shower, which was awkward because I couldn't get my bandages wet. Plus, it was hard to wash my hair when I couldn't lift one arm, so I needed help.

Cue Talia.

My friend had been amazing throughout the ordeal. She'd dealt with the record label, the press, and even the cops. Sam's dad had threatened legal action against Diablo and was using his connections to put pressure on the local PD to prosecute. It was a joke how he was so concerned about his son now he was dead, but never gave a shit when Sam was alive. We'd talked before about how Sam was paraded as an accessory and then expected to keep his mouth shut and stay out of his dad's way behind the scenes.

Boomer even told us about a conversation he had with Sam the year before.

They were drunk when Sam confessed that he'd been groomed by his dad's second wife. The woman seduced him and took his virginity when he was fourteen years old, and they subsequently carried on an affair. Eventually, Sam's dad found out, but instead of doing the right thing and prosecuting her and getting Sam some counseling, he used it as an excuse to divorce her and blackmail her into relinquishing her rights to alimony.

It worked out perfectly for him because he'd already met wife number three, so it paved the way for him to get rid of the woman he was with, and do it cheaply, too.

It was no wonder Sam lost his mind; he'd been sexually abused and neglected emotionally all his life. He obviously had major hang ups and abandonment issues and lost his shit. Don't get me wrong, it was no excuse for shooting people, but I got how he ended up in that place mentally, even if I didn't agree with his actions.

After an afternoon on the phone and a lot of shouting and foot stomping, Talia triumphantly told D he had nothing to worry about. She'd threatened Sam's dad with going public with all his bullshit and the asshole backed down immediately.

God forbid his adoring fans saw him for who he was.

But still, at least Diablo could rest easy in the knowledge that he wasn't about to get sued by a team of lawyers with unlimited resources and a taste for vengeance, thank God.

The band had decided to take a hiatus before we recorded the second album.

I wanted to be there to help Jacob with his recovery, and I also wanted us to start our lives together.

Almost losing him had taught me what was important, and as much as I loved my band and my music, it didn't mean anything without my big, bad biker by my side. I loved playing, and I loved performing, but I hated the dark side of show business. The paparazzi, the toxic online culture, and constantly having to defend myself against people I didn't even know was exhausting, and I wanted a break from it.

Even if I never released another song, I could still live comfortably off the money I'd already earned and my royalties for the next ten lifetimes. My future kids were set for life, so money wasn't a worry at all. However, I wouldn't stay away for long.

I couldn't.

Music was my first love, the thing that brought me my first taste of freedom when I was a young, repressed girl with dreams of breaking free from her stilted life, so I could never give it up completely.

Bones had removed Jacob's breathing tube that morning. He still had the drain coming from his chest and was hooked up to a heart monitor, but I was relieved to see some color back in his cheeks and even more relieved that he was breathing unaided.

He wasn't out of the woods completely, and Bones had warned us that he may develop complications or an infection, but he was off the critical list for now.

The road ahead wouldn't be easy but I didn't give the first fuck.

As long as I had Jacob with me, I'd find a way to cope. We had the best care and the best people to help him with his recovery. Hendrix had told me about all the rehabilitation facilities the club had access to, so I knew Jacob was in good hands.

I sat on the bed beside Jacob, legs crossed with my back to his feet, staring at his face with our fingers entwined. When he woke up, I was determined to be there for him in case he was confused.

"It could take hours," Kathy murmured from the chair next to the bed.

"It won't," I assured her, my heart beating steadily and my tummy tugging toward my man. "I can feel him."

"Did you feel Jake move?" Doug asked from his place at his wife's side.

"No." I smiled. "I can feel his heart."

And it was strange because I could, and not just then either. I'd felt flashes of him since the night before, when Bones had reduced his medication. Jacob was fighting to come back to me. I could sense his internal struggle, and it was beautiful because it showed me he was still in there and everything would be okay.

My breath whooshed out of me when his finger suddenly twitched.

I smiled and breathed, "Baby. I'm here."

Jacob's eyelids didn't open, but they began to move, like he was suddenly in REM sleep and his mind was coming back to life.

Like *he* was coming back to life.

Keeping my gaze on my man, I murmured, "Doug. Could you get Bones? Tell him it won't be long."

I heard Kathy let out a quiet sob, and then the door clicked as Doug left the room.

Something burned in my chest, but it wasn't unpleasant, more like the hot summer sun burning life into the earth. It felt good and natural and right. Maybe it was my soul waking up because it had its mate back at last.

Jacob's finger twitched again, and I laughed when I saw his eyelids flutter.

"Come on, baby," I whispered. "Open your eyes. Let me see those icy blues. I've missed them so much."

A tiny grunt escaped his throat, and his eyelids fluttered again, but that time they fluttered open, and stayed open, and he stared at the ceiling.

"Welcome home, baby," I murmured.

Jacob's dazed gaze lowered, and our eyes locked.

My heart soared.

"I love you," I told him huskily through the tears burning my throat.

Love you, he mouthed, his lips hardly moving.

Something clicked together inside me, and my world tilted back into place.

My man was even more beautiful than before, but maybe being robbed of him had made me see deeper. Jacob had died for me; how could that not be an extraordinary thing? People claimed that they'd die for the person they loved all the time, but when it came down to it, would they?

Jacob did, and it filled me with awe for him because it was proof—not of his feelings—I never doubted those—but it proved the type of man he was. Being without him felt like I'd been plunged into darkness, but now the long night was over and the first ray of light shone on me. And we all knew that where there was light, there was hope.

Lighter days were coming.

The door clicked open again, but my gaze remained on Jacob's.

"Well, well, well," Bones drawled. "It's about time." I felt his presence beside the bed, and he murmured, "Can you move aside for a minute, Saint. I need to check his vitals."

Jacob's fingers lightly squeezed mine, and his eyes flared slightly.

"No," I said, smiling, "I'm not moving. Check his vitals another way."

Jacob's lips twitched, and his eyes crinkled with a small smile.

Bones chuckled and somehow worked his way around me, taking Jacob's blood pressure and listening to his heart, and all the while, our gazes never left each other.

I had my big, bad biker back.

And I'd never let him go.

Chapter Twenty-Three

Iceman

Once Bones removed the drainage tube from my chest, my recovery was pretty straightforward.

It took time, of course, but he had me on my feet within days and as much as I was in agony and begged him to let me piss in a bottle rather than go to the bathroom, in hindsight, getting moving again helped my muscles to start working as they should.

I think Bones and Saint almost came to blows a few times. Bones was a young doctor and, like Freya, had qualified early because he was some kind of medical prodigy genius whose grandfather invented some heart valve contraption. But along with his confidence, also came a touch of arrogance, and if there was one thing Saint hated, it was an arrogant man. Therefore, she pushed back more often than not. I saw a different side to her because until then, I'd only ever witnessed sweet, so when she turned fiery it shocked me at first, then very quickly turned me the fuck on 'cause she only ever got fiery for me, and what man wouldn't love that down to his dick?

None, that's who.

Except, I couldn't fuck, it hurt too much. Even the pain of getting a half-chub took my breath away, so I had a lot of semis go to waste.

My mom and dad hung around for a week after I woke up. I loved my parents to distraction, but their bickering drove me insane, so by the time they left for the airport, I was ready to see them go. I gave them a promise that we'd visit for Christmas, so Mom seemed happy to leave as long as I promised to FaceTime her every night so she could check on my recovery.

That was also the day I moved out of the medical wing and back into the suite with Saint. I felt bad for my woman because she had to run around after me, but I was okay to move around by then, so I went downstairs to eat and sit in the bar for an hour every night and shoot the shit with the boys.

It was there that I finally got to talk with Diablo.

We got on well, and always had, but we'd never been close. I didn't really get Diablo and his decapitated body parts, chop-a-cock thing, so I tended to keep him at arm's length. The thing was, Saint and D seemed to have become new BFFs, so I had no choice but to spend some time with him, and I was pleasantly surprised when Hendrix told me how D had stuck to Saint like glue while I'd been out for the count and made sure she was safe and protected.

A man like that deserved my respect, frankly, because he'd earned it, and not just by saving my life, but also by caring for Saint the way he did when I couldn't. He saw her heart, the same way I did, so we had that in common at least, and it was something I could work with at long last.

We were sitting at a table because it stung like a motherfucker to get up and down on a bar stool. Diablo had joined us, and Saint had taken Gigi to the ladies' room.

I took in his black eyes, his olive skin, and his dark beard, noting how two men couldn't be more different. Diablo was good-looking but for some reason, he wasn't popular with the ladies or even the club whores. They fucked him and didn't complain about anything but they also didn't flock around him the same way they did with, say Gambit and me (pre Saint, of course).

"I never thanked you," I muttered.

He hitched a thick, black brow. "That's because you don't have to."

"You saved our lives," I went on.

He waved a hand nonchalantly before reaching for his beer with it. "Honest, Iceman. It ain't a thing."

"Never be able to repay ya," I continued, ignoring his protests. "Never be able to make up for what you did."

"You've got nothin' I want," he muttered, his eyes sliding in the same direction Saint had disappeared in not long before.

I took in his wistful gaze and the pink of his cheeks and said, "Yeah, I have. Owe you everything, and you can take anything apart from her. She's the one thing in this world I could never give up."

His eyes slashed toward mine, and he sighed resignedly. "Yeah, brother. I know."

Suddenly, I felt choked up because more than anything, I wished there was a way he could get what he wanted, even though after everything he'd done for me and my girl, I'd kill him if he so much as tried.

"Owe you huge," I repeated. "You've got my marker."

One side of his mouth tipped up. "That's a start."

I grinned.

"Diablo!" a voice bellowed.

We both twisted in our seats to see Veep at the threshold of the bar.

"Is your phone on silent?" he bellowed.

"Yeah," D bellowed back. "I was watching TV with Saint, and I didn't want to be disturbed in case she fell asleep. Guess I forgot to switch the ringer back on."

Blade held a hand up to stop the convo. "Don't need your life story, Princess. Certainly don't need to hear about your day watchin' the fucking *Kardashians* and *The Real Housewives of Bumfuck Nowhere*. Prez wants ya in his office."

"On my way," D said, getting to his feet. He drained his beer and went to amble away.

"D!" I called out.

He stopped and twisted his neck to look at me.

I smiled. "You'll find her one day, brother."

He tilted his head. "Who?"

"Your woman," I explained. "The one you wanna go to bed with every night. The one you wake up next to every mornin'. The one you breathe for. She's out there somewhere."

He stilled for an instant, frozen to the spot. Then, after a minute, he gave me a lopsided grin and a chin lift before turning around and strolling away.

My eyes followed him, and I said under my breath, "You'll meet her, bro. You've got too much heart not too, but in the meantime..."

I twisted again in my seat, ignoring the pain the movement sent searing through my chest, and caught Heather's eye. Shooting her a conspiratorial wink, I jerked my chin, signaling for her to come over.

She beamed, put her drink down, and came waltzing over. "You okay, Iceman?" she asked sweetly. "You need another drink?"

"Where's Arizona?" I asked.

"Showering. Carina made her vacuum the first and second floors today, so she's freshening up before she comes down." Her forehead furrowed questioningly. "You okay?"

"I'm good, sweetheart," I murmured. "But I wondered if you'd do me a favor. You and Arizona. First of all, I need to ask you something, and I need you to be honest. Have you gotta problem with Diablo?"

Her eyes narrowed slightly, but she shook her head. "He's different, and a bit weird, but I haven't got a problem with him. He's quite sweet, really, when you get to know him."

"Good. The thing is, Diablo did me and Saint a solid, and I wanted to do something for him, a bit of a treat. Did you know the dude's never had a threesome? And you know how you're all up in Gambit's dick 'cause you like his cologne? Welllll, D's never had that either."

A light gleamed in Heather's eyes, and she smiled huge. "Really?"

"Yep, really." I waggled my eyebrows. "Do you think you and Arizona would be up for...?"

"I'm up for it if she is." Heather giggled coquettishly. "And you're right, he does deserve a treat." She pulled out her cell phone and clicked on it before holding it against her ear. "I'll ask her now."

I sat back in my chair, suddenly feeling very pleased with myself.

Maybe I couldn't give Diablo what he really wanted, but one thing I could arrange was for him to have the night of his life. One he'd never forget.

The fucker deserved that at least.

"Baby," I breathed, my hips jerking uncontrollably as Saint sucked me deep down her throat. "Fuuuuuck."

Her fingers stroked my balls. I felt her throat close around the tip of my dick good and tight as she swallowed, then she hummed.

"Goddamnit," I yelled. "Fuck yes!" I closed my eyes and clenched my jaw as my cock erupted like a lava-filled volcano.

Saint hummed again, and I almost hit the roof when I was catapulted to the goddamned heavens. The cum spurted from my dick and down my woman's throat with a force that shocked even me. My eyes rolled in the back of my head when I felt her throat work as she swallowed it all down as if it were the best beverage in the world.

"Jesus fuckin' Christ," I panted softly as I drifted back down to Earth. "What the fuck...?" I was so spent that I couldn't form a coherent sentence. My woman sucked me off so good that she made me forget how to goddamned speak.

She slid her hot, tight little mouth up my length and released me with a pop before she moved up the length of my body and burrowed her head into the crook between my neck and shoulder, asking, "Better?"

"Fuck yeah," I scraped out, my chest rising and falling so hard that I thought I was about to bust a fucking stitch. "Never in my life have I come that hard," I panted, my eyes drifting closed. "Jesus fuck, Saint. What magic is it you weave?"

"Throat control," she announced.

I cracked an eye open. "Huh?"

"Singing lessons taught me how to control my voice and do throat exercises. Seems you're getting the benefit of that at the moment, though I guess someone has to because the fans aren't."

A chuckle left my throat.

Fans' loss, my gain.

"Was thinking," I murmured. "Why don't we give it a few weeks so I can heal a little more and get off my pain meds, then we could jump on a flight, go to Vegas, and get married."

Her body stiffened.

I pulled my head free of hers and peered down at her face. "You okay?"

"Yeah," she breathed.

"Yeah, you're okay, or yeah, we'll go to Vegas?" I asked.

She wriggled up the bed so our faces were close and whispered, "Both."

Leaning forward, I kissed her softly. "You wanna call your folks and ask if they wanna come?"

She shook her head, her gorgeous blue eyes clouding over with pain. "No. Unless I marry in a church, it doesn't count in their eyes. According to Dad, Vegas is the Devil's town. He wouldn't step foot within ten miles of the place." She let out a snort. "He won't even come to LA."

"You wanna get married in your dad's church?" I asked. "It's not really us, but I'd do anything to make you happy."

She shook her head. "No, you're right, it's not us. Vegas is perfect. Can we get Elvis to marry us?"

"Fuck yeah," I agreed. "That'll be hilarious. But now I've gotta dilemma. Hendrix is my closest brother, but we owe Diablo everything. Who am I gonna ask to stand up with me?"

"Hendrix," she declared. "I'll take Diablo."

My forehead creased. "Huh?"

Her eyes danced with humor. "D can be my Master of Honor. Get it? Matron of Honor... Master of Honor?"

A laugh escaped my throat, and I watched Saint hold her breath as she took in the expression on my face.

I used my hand to catch her jaw and tip her face so I could touch my mouth to hers. "Love you, Songbird," I croaked.

"Love you, too, Jacob," she whispered, then from nowhere she began to murmur familiar words that burrowed deep down into my soul...

Stage lights, sultry nights, halcyon ice blue.

Her fingertips swept over my eyebrows, and her gaze locked with mine.

Crowd chants, and your face haunts. Empty without you.

Lost pride, lost chance, lost love, lost souls.

Beyond my comprehension. Beyond my control.

Crowd chants, but your face haunts. I'm empty without you...

My eyes closed slowly as the emotions hit me from all sides.

It was mine.

That song.

It was all mine.

"Jesus, Saint," I breathed, the enormity of the moment hitting me deep. "It was for me?"

She smiled. "Everything's been for you since that first night, Jacob. You haunted me as much as you say I haunted you." Her tone hardened slightly along with her eyes. "I just dealt with it in a way that didn't involve club whores and group sex."

I wrapped an arm around her neck, grinning from ear to ear. "Some might say I lived the rock 'n' roll lifestyle, baby."

"You certainly had the groupie part down," she drawled.

I clasped her face in my hand again, pulling it around so I could see her beautiful face. "All in the past. Nothing comes close to you. Had a love once that I lost, and I swore I'd never love like that again, then I met you, a girl who blew that theory out of the water. Gonna get married, have babies, and live happily ever after, You down with that, Saint McClure?"

Her eyes welled with tears, and she beamed me another megawatt smile and said the words that made me feel like I stood ten feet tall.

"I love you, too, Jacob, but then what do you expect? You're my muse."

For some reason, seeing Saint's face put me in mind of a different face. One I hadn't seen for twelve years but loved all the same. I settled back on the bed, clasping my woman to me, and sent up a prayer.

Wherever you are, Allie. I hope you're at peace.

And hand to God, I heard Allie's sweet voice whisper faintly...

I am now, honey. I am now.

Epilogue

Four Years Later

PRESS RELEASE

The hottest gig in town went off without a hitch last night at Radio City Music Hall in New York City.

Saint Irons made her astounding comeback in front of an 'intimate' audience of 5700 superfans who traveled from all over the world to witness the rock princess perform twenty of her most famous tracks along with her band, Saint's Rapture. They were joined by special guests, Noah Hart, front man of the biggest band in the world, Dischordium, and the sensational and talented newcomer Kady Stone.

Four years ago, the band went on hiatus after a scandal involving their bass guitarist, which ended in tragedy. The recording of their second album was put on hold, and Saint moved to Virginia with her new husband, Security Specialist, Jacob Irons, to start a family.

The music world mourned the band's loss until two years ago when Saint's Rapture began to appear in bars throughout Virginia, Maryland, and Wyoming, delighting the patrons by playing impromptu gigs. The band blew up again on social media, along with the hashtag #whereissaintplayingtoday, and their first album, *Empty,* re-entered the charts, hitting the number one spot in eighteen countries. The long-awaited second album, *Molten Ice,* was released one year later and has been another resounding worldwide success, going platinum in twenty-three countries and breaking all previous streaming records.

Tickets for last night's gig raised a total of eleven million dollars for charities that help children of abuse and trafficking, and online bullying and trolling, the most significant sum of three million dollars being donated by action-hero star Hunter Page and his husband, hairstylist to the stars, Tristan Forbes-Page.

Saint's Rapture were also delighted to announce last night that their newly formed record label, BeatsPM, has signed Kady Stone to a five-album deal and is looking forward to creating musical magic with the talented young singer/songwriter.

Saint's Rapture would like to thank everybody for their ongoing support and also announce a special concert in collaboration with Dischordium and other musicians at Madison Square Gardens, with all proceeds going to the aforementioned children's charities.

More details to follow.

Contact: Talia Fields, CEO, BeatsPM
www.beatspmmusic.com

You can find Iceman and Saint's playlist here:
https://open.spotify.com/playlist/2YUqeTpYL9IbAk89ikbC9j

THE END

Thank you for reading.

Acknowledgments

Well, this one was different, wasn't it?

I always thought Iceman would be a twat who needed to give his head a good shake and fight for the girl, but nope! Totes cinnamon roll, the likes of which we haven't seen since Bowie, allll the way back in book one.

I've always said these characters write themselves, and this one proved me right because Jacob was a dream and probably one of my favorite heroes to date (Hello, romantic). Though I have to say, it probably won't last, I'm sure I'll be writing assholes again pretty soon, so hold onto your hats.

I'd like to thank Nicola, Jayne, Mylene, Madz, and Claire, my wonderful alpha readers, and my ARC team, who keep me laughing and entertained.

Nicola, my fab PA, sounding board, and life organizer. What would I do without you, Moo? I guess cry and get drunk a lot?

And of course, thank you, reader. I hope you're enjoying the books as much as I am. I'm blown away daily by all your kind comments, reviews, and support.

Next up is a little writing break while I attend some signings and spend time with my daughter, who's on school break. Then it's onto Donovan O'Shea's book, which I'm really excited for as I loved Callum, and I get to revisit that wonderful Irish humor and go back to Hambleton to see Maureen and the Speed Demons original gang.

Love and Light.

Jules
XOXO

Stalk Jules

Jules loves chatting with readers
Email her
julesfordauthor@gmail.com

Join her Facebook Group
Jules Ford's Tribe | Facebook

Instagram
Jules Ford (@julesfordauthor) • Instagram photos and videos

TikTok
https://www.tiktok.com/@julesfordauthor?lang=en

Printed in Dunstable, United Kingdom